ABRAHAM'S WELL

"Foster is one of the brightest lights in Christian fiction. She takes us to places that our hearts sometimes fear to tread, and she rewards us with wonderfully complex characters who live with us long after the story ends."

—Angela Benson, author of
Telling the Tale: The African-American Writer's Guide

"Sharon Ewell Foster is a beautiful fresh voice in today's world of fiction. Her compelling stories draw us to a place where we somehow feel we belong, a place we want to visit again and again and again."

—Karen Kingsbury, author of *One Tuesday Morning*

"Foster introduces a vibrant new voice to inspirational fiction, offering wisdom and insights that are deep, rich, and honest."

—Liz Curtis Higgs, bestselling author of
Bad Girls of the Bible

"Foster's prose is often evocative and eloquent."

—*Publishers Weekly*

"To read a book by Sharon Ewell Foster is to have had an inside look at the heart and mind of God."

—Regina Gail Malloy, Heaven 600 Radio

"Foster is an author who allows God to use her through her novels. . . . With every page, readers are left feeling inspired and hopeful with the knowledge that through God, all things are possible."

—Lisa R. Hammack, Ebony Eyes Book Club

"Foster's characters are unforgettable; full of life and unhesitatingly charming."

—Kweisi Mfume, former President and CEO, NAACP

ABRAHAM'S WELL

A Novel

SHARON EWELL FOSTER

BETHANY HOUSE PUBLISHERS

Minneapolis, Minnesota

DEDICATION

⋅⋅⋅⋅⋅⋅⋅⋅⋅⋅⋅⋅◆⋅⋅⋅⋅⋅⋅⋅⋅⋅⋅⋅⋅

For the people of New Orleans and the Gulf, for the African and Native peoples of the United States, for the Dalit Christians of India, for the homeless and displaced, and for all of us who have each walked our own trail of tears. May the Breath Giver hear our cries, see our tears, and come to us.

I am black, but comely, O ye daughters of Jerusalem,
as the tents of Kedar, as the curtains of Solomon.
I am the rose of Sharon, and the lily of the valleys.

SONG OF SOLOMON 1:5, 2:1

Books by Sharon Ewell Foster

Abraham's Well

Ain't No Mountain

Ain't No Valley

*Ain't No River**

*Passing by Samaria**

*Riding Through Shadows**

*Passing Into Light**

*Multnomah Publishers

ABOUT THE AUTHOR

SHARON EWELL FOSTER, a crusader for truth, justice, and the American way, has worked for years to share the stories that need to be told. This double–RITA Award finalist and *Daily Guidepost* contributing writer weaves tales that span racial, religous, age, and gender boundaries to share the best of the human heart. A former U.S. Defense Department instructor, writer, and logistician, Foster is the author of the bestselling and Christy-Award winning *Passing by Samaria,* the Golden Pen Award–winning, *Essence* bestselling *Ain't No River,* and *Passing Into Light,* which was recently translated into Russian. She travels all over the U.S. writing, speaking, and sharing goodwill.

ACKNOWLEDGMENTS

Thank you to my children—Lanea and Chase—my first editors. Thank you to my father and brothers, to my Cousins LaJuana and Angela. Thank you to my Aunt Jenelle and my Uncle R. Lovelace, and to my extended family—the Ewells, the Morrises, the Shermans, the Lees—including the Starks family. Thank you to all the Indians in my family for sharing photos and stories. Thank you to my agent, Mark Sweeney; to my editor, Joyce Dinkins; to David Horton and the editorial staff at Bethany House; to the entire marketing and publicity staff—especially Linda White, Brett Benson, and Tim Peterson; and to Carol Johnson.

Great-Aunt Jewell Ewell, Anderson County, Texas
circa 1910. "I am dark but comely."

PART I

"*It should be remembered that hundreds of people of African ancestry also walked the Trail of Tears with the Cherokee during the forced removal of 1838–1839. Although we know about the terrible human suffering of our native people and the members of other tribes during the removal, we rarely hear of those black people who also suffered.*"

WILMA MANKILLER,
former Principal Chief of the Cherokee Nation, *Mankiller: A Chief and Her People*

CHAPTER ONE

In the East, it is the movement of the Atlantic waters that brings land storms. Black, heavy clouds thrown about by the ocean sweep in and overtake the sun, darkening the skies. It is hard to predict the weather, with the ocean running things. But here in the West, you can see storms coming from far off, rolling in gray and angry, fighting with the dust. I sit on my porch, here, and watch them.

There has never been a better brother than Abraham. Even now, all these many years later, I miss him. I try to remember that he had to go ahead of me, but I still miss him.

When I remember how things were long ago—I remember that we were free, at least for a while. Not free like now, but free. There were no fences. And even back then, we had the well.

What I remember most often is the dancing stream waters, clean enough to see the pebbles on the bottom, and fish swimming—darting, nibbling at rocks. I remember three boys wading at the edge of the stream, laughing boys grabbing at fish.

13

There was sunshine and laughter.

There were mountains. Green—grass, trees and such—stretched on forever until it met with the blue of the sky. Gray clouds would blow in with rain and, just as quickly, roll back out again.

I would take everything back if I could. I would make everything be like it was, I would never have touched the honey.

But, wait, before I get ahead of myself, before I tell the story before it's ready to be told.

I'm an old woman and I do that sometimes.

I do not know exactly when I was born. I do know that I am very, very old. I speak the language of the People, *Tsalagi*—even now, though I've spoken English for a long time, my thoughts are still Cherokee. Their ways are my ways.

I was born before cars. I was born before the War Between the States. Long ago, many of the old ones used to live to see more than a hundred summers, and I think I must be like them. I have seen babies born, I have seen death, and I have walked the Trail of Tears—*Nunna daul Isunyi*—The Trail Where We Cried.

I have been a slave and I have been free. This is my story, the story of my family, the good and the bad of it.

I tell my story so that maybe someone else will live.

Some of my ancestors, they tell me, came from over the great waters, taken from their home faraway in Africa. I do not know that language, or the clan. But the people I do know have been here always, like the waters. I am Armentia. I am Cherokee, *Aniyunwiya,* one of The Principal People, and I am Black.

And with all I have to tell, the greatest truth is that there was never a better brother than Abraham. Of course, Abraham was not his real name. A name is a sacred thing, my mother and all the old ones told me. Your name is who you are and your name in the mouth of your enemies can be your undoing. Of course, some people now say that what they told me back then is just superstition, but I still believe. So, a real name is never told among anyone except the real people, the Cherokee people, The Principal People.

But, again, don't let me get ahead. I'm old and sometimes I wander.

Like I said, I was born before cars. Nowadays—it's been nigh almost twenty years since the turn of the twentieth century—we might see a car or two in a week's time. They come and when they go, they shake everything around them—like stones in a pond, or too big fish in a stream. Who knows? A time may come when we might see that many of the machines every day. It's hard to believe, but I have seen many things I would not have believed to see.

We lived, back then, in what is now called North Carolina. Of course, back then Cherokee people were spread all up and down North Carolina, South Carolina, Virginia, Tennessee, Georgia, even Alabama and Kentucky—no boundaries. Our home didn't have the state names back then. The green of the southern Appalachian Mountains was our home.

It was different than it is now. Today it is so loud you cannot think, with the car horns, radios. Even inside the cabin, the house, there is always noise, some humming that won't let you think.

But years ago, before fences and wires, when people lived to be old, it was quiet. It was quiet enough to hear the frogs croaking, to hear a bird's wings flapping and to know what kind it was. It was quiet enough to hear that there was water nearby, quiet enough to hear the wind talk.

The day I want to tell you about first, well, it was in the days when there were no fences, when all the land and all the good of the land belonged to all the people in common, and when there were not as many White people as now. The Principal People didn't pay for land to own, water, or fire back then.

The Great One gave and we received. It was in the days when we lived on the land that the Great One gave to us, when we lived on the land that held the dust and the bones of our fathers.

I think I had seen eight or nine summers then. And I could run then! Oh, I was fast! You might look at my shriveled skin and my knotty knees now and not believe it, but you'd be fooling yourself! I was so fast I could almost outrun the waters.

If you look at my ankle you can still see a star-shaped scar. See, right there. I got that scar running one day. Hit a stick so hard and quick, it made a star. Child, I tell you I was fast!

But I could not run like Abraham, who taught me how to run. He really could outrun the waters! Bless my soul, that boy could outrun anything . . . almost anything.

We were part of the Deer Clan. You know there were seven Cherokee clans back then. There was the Blue Clan that made medicine from a blue plant and the Long Hair Clan that wore their hair in fancy ways. Those Long Hairs could put on a show, even the way they walked was like they were dancing and showing off. Then there was the Bird Clan that hunted birds and flew with messages from place to place, while the Red Clan were healers. There was the Bear Clan and the Wolf Clan—where most war chiefs came from. But we were the Deer Clan—we caught them and we could run like them. But Abraham was fastest.

At the Green Corn Festival there was no one faster than Abraham. People would gather from all over to eat together, tell stories together. It was a big time held when the first green appeared on the corn. Part of the festival was games, and Abraham was always fastest. Folks came from all over to celebrate, and we prayed, we cleansed ourselves from our wrong in the waters. At the seven-sided council house, inside there was a fire, an eternal flame, a sacred fire that was the beginning of all the fires in every village. Though I only saw it once myself, they say that living flame traveled with us on the Trail Where We

Cried. They say that eternal flame still burns today.

I know many of these things because my mother taught me. Among our people, it is women who teach, women who pass on life. It is women who pass on land. At least, that is how it was before things changed, before our lives changed.

But that day I remember, the one I'm trying to tell you about, was a warm day. Not hot, though most of the trees were still green and had their leaves, but not so hot I wanted to sit in the mud.

The three boys left the flat place where we lived, where our log houses were, and they walked between trees, puffing their chests out like men. They were older than me, but they were not men, though they walked proud like they had wives and children. See, they weren't old enough yet that they had to work in the cornfields or the cotton fields. The day was coming soon when they would work long hours, but then they still had some free time. They might tend sheep or watch over the milking cows, but they did not work like men, or like our father who tended the horses.

I had already brought the people working in the fields water from the well—that was my sometimes job. After that, I sat playing with the doll I had. It was a corncob, you know, dressed in scraps of cloth. When I caught sight of the boys, I followed them first with my eyes through the corn rows at the rim of the clearing where we lived with other families. Then when no one was looking, I followed behind the three boys through the corn rows, into the woods, ducking behind trees, standing still and letting the wind talk over my breathing. I didn't want them to hear me and chase me away, chase me back to my dolls and the other younger girls. Abraham always said that, for a girl, I was good at keeping still.

The forest floor was covered with old leaves and pine needles and helped me follow without being heard. The sun was my friend and came down through the leaves and boughs to help me see the way to go.

Soon I knew where they were headed. I could hear the waters dancing and talking ahead. The three boys did the things boys always do, wrestling with each other, laughing and trying to outdo each other, trying to be men.

When they got to the stream, they waded in, not trying to be quiet anymore. But I stayed back at the edge of the woods, using a large rock and the trees to cover me.

The three boys waded at the edge of the stream, grasping at fish, but grabbing more handfuls of water than trout. Soon they were wet well above the knees.

Johnnie Freeman—we always said his whole name—was the first to fall in the water and Golden Bear laughed, pointing at him.

Johnnie Freeman was my brother's best friend. Even when I was a girl, I thought Johnnie Freeman was beautiful, and if things hadn't changed, when I was a woman, I am sure I would have married him. Against the sun, he was black and smooth and his hair was like a sheep's wool. He was skinny like Abraham, but he had broad shoulders. And he had beautiful lips, like berries, stained like he'd been eating purple berries. I'm telling you, I would have married that boy.

Golden Bear's missionary name was Timothy, but everyone still called him Golden Bear. No one kept his name a secret. He was too funny for anyone to want to curse. His skin was like copper, but it always looked like the sun lay on his head and shoulders like a blanket. That was the golden part. He was golden, but he also had a little round belly, like a cub that had eaten too many berries. His whole family had that same look—except for his mother who was lean and quiet. And sometimes when he played in the games—the games the men and boys played on special days—he looked just like his name, a round Golden Bear.

Johnnie Freeman and Golden Bear were doing more splashing than fish catching. Abraham was doing what he usually did when he was with his friends, pointing and laughing as though he had never seen a better show.

Sometimes when I saw him that way, laughing with his friends without me, though I liked them all, something inside me got mad. Maybe there was some sickness on my name, but Abraham was my brother. I was jealous. He belonged to me.

Abraham shook his head at his friends, laughing like he was an uncle, like he was one of their teachers. "Left up to you two, we would be going back empty-handed!" He puffed out his skinny chest while he pointed to the three fish he had already managed to catch. "Good thing there is a man along!" The three pretended they were men, though they were no more than three summers older than me.

Johnnie Freeman was wet up to his navel. "You wouldn't have those fish if we didn't scare them your way."

"And you wouldn't know how to catch fish if I hadn't taught you how!" Water trickled down Golden Bear's straight black hair to his shoulders, down his chest, then curved around his belly. "Don't lose your head, little man!"

Then they were all in the water. Sometimes they couldn't be seen over the rock that hid me, then I would see them rising from the water like three strange, great, laughing fish.

Abraham was so beautiful that day. He was the color of leaves in the fall—brown, gold, and red. His hair was black, like Golden Bear's and Johnnie Freeman's, but when it was wet, it was shiny and curly, like our mother's.

They rolled in the water, splashing and warning away any fish or birds that they might have caught.

I had been hiding so well, but jealousy routed me out. *"U-s-di!"* I stood up. "Hey, little babies!" I knew it would get them mad, especially since I was younger. "You can catch each other, but even the dumb fish are too wise to be caught by you!"

Johnnie Freeman, Golden Bear, and Abraham froze, caught, their eyes on me. Which was, of course, what I wanted. "You were so loud even a girl, a little girl, could follow you," I taunted them.

Abraham was smiling now, kind of like he was proud of me. Even Johnnie Freeman grinned, all his white teeth showing. But Golden Bear tried to act like a man. He puffed out his chest and pointed at me. "Armentia, you should not be here!" He looked at Johnnie Freeman and Abraham to back him up. "You should be with the other little girls, playing with dolls, learning to cook and weave." He threw his hands in the air. "Learning women's ways."

I shook my skinny little girl's hips, mocking him. "Learning women's ways!" I wiggled my stomach, poking it out like I had eaten too many berries. "You are no man to teach me, to tell me what to do. Instead of playing with boys, you should be playing with bears!" I lifted my hands like claws, hunched my back, wiggled my belly again, then wiggled my pretend tail while I took lumbering steps on top of the rock. "You should be playing and learning the ways of your people, the bears!"

Golden Bear acted like an insulted cub and gave chase. He charged out of the waters after me. Scampering up the banks like a mad little bear, he ran toward me. But as I've said, I could run.

See, Abraham, my guard taught me. My brother's real name was The One Who Guards His Family. My mother said the Creator sent him ahead of me to watch over me. "Some girls don't have brothers before them," she said. "But you have a brother to go ahead of you, to protect you, to shine the light ahead."

So, Abraham taught me to run.

Now, Golden Bear was fast, even with his belly. He was a

proud member of the Deer Clan. But even though I was a little girl, because of Abraham, I was faster.

I could hear Golden Bear's footsteps pounding behind me. He whooped, like he was chasing his enemy, to frighten me. "I'm going to catch you, little fox, and make soup from you!"

I knew Golden Bear was only teasing. He wouldn't hurt me any more than Abraham would. He was only chasing me because his pride was wounded. But my legs didn't know the difference, so I ran so fast my little feet almost liked to set the grass on fire!

I could hear Johnnie Freeman behind us laughing. "Whoo hoo! Look at that girl run!" If things hadn't changed, I tell you, I would have married him!

But the voice I could hear most clearly was Abraham's. "Run, Armentia! Don't look back! Run!"

I picked them up and put them down as fast as I could, hearing my heart keeping time! I knew if I could reach the clearing, I would be safe. Golden Bear would not touch me, not even to tickle me, in front of the people. I headed for the cornfield, pushing my way through the rows, the hard green stalks fighting against me. I could hear Golden Bear's feet so close behind me. I could feel his hands reaching out to grab me.

Abraham's voice was not far behind him. "Keep running, Armentia!"

I dodged in and out amongst the stalks, some of them slapping me in the face. Why hadn't I just stayed quiet behind the rock? I kept running, thinking of the clearing ahead—if I could make it there I would be safe—with Abraham's voice in my ears. But I knew Golden Bear, even with his jiggling belly, was not far behind.

When I was six steps from the clearing, I felt his fingers, like bear claws, on my shoulders!

"Duck, Armentia!"

I ducked like Abraham told me and burst into the clearing,

running straight to where my mother was grinding corn. "Need—some—help, Mother?" I panted out the words and plopped down on the ground beside her, my chest heaving. I grabbed an ear of corn from the stack in front of her, looked over my shoulder, sticking out my tongue at Golden Bear.

Of course, my mother was wiser than I wanted her to be at that moment. "Girl, where have you been?" She brushed her curly black hair away from her forehead and out of her eyes with the back of her hand. "Who are you running from? Are you bothering the boys?" She wore two heavy braids that hung down her back to her waist. Her hair was so thick, sometimes in summer it gave her headaches. She looked at me and sniffed. "You have been running with the boys and you smell like a little goat! What have you been up to?"

"Mother, see the fish!" Before my mother could grind the truth out of me, Abraham, my protector, was at my shoulder, dangling his new caught fish. He leaned down from where he stood and briefly touched his forehead to my mother's. It was his special greeting for her. "See the fish?" he repeated while straightening himself. "Armentia caught one of them." He showed her the smallest of the three.

My mother looked at him, at me, then back to him. "Oh, get away, One Who Guards His Family!" She smiled at him. "You will say anything to protect this one." She pointed with her grinding stone. "You don't fool me."

"No, really," Abraham lied for me. "I am teaching her to catch fish. Maybe I will teach her to hunt. Who knows what the winters ahead will bring? She is a girl, but she will have to be ready."

My mother smiled, her head down, still grinding corn. "You don't fool me, Abraham. Things are the way they have always been. We are the people and this is the land the Great One has made for us to share. There is growing time and harvest time and the time when the snow falls. It is as it has always been, nothing will change. The sky is blue, the birds sing, and the land will always belong to all the people," she nodded. "The well will always be deep, and you will always protect her. The One Who Guards His Family will always go ahead of his sister."

In the middle of the clearing where we lived, there was a well. It was the well that I drew water from for the workers. The well provided water for our family and all the families nearby, so that we did not always have to go to the stream for water. It was a deep, deep hole. There were large gray stones piled around it. If you peeked over the side, there was nothing to see but deep, deep black. It looked like hopeless nothing, like an empty heart, except that if you dropped a wooden bucket tied with a rope to the bottom of the well and pulled that bucket back to the top, that bucket would be filled with water like crystal, cold and clear. It was almost sweet.

"Even that well is not as deep as Abraham's love for his sister." My mother smiled at me. "So deep he tells tales for her. Things will always be the same." She set the ground corn aside. She would make corn cakes, wrap them in lettuce and cook them in ashes from the fire. "It was the same with my brothers, with your uncles."

Abraham touched a free hand to my shoulder and then joined me, sitting at our mother's feet.

"You see, this is Armentia's fish," he still insisted. "The little one. The other two are mine."

My mother began scraping corn kernels from some of the cobs. She dropped them in the pot of water boiling over the outside fire. It was still too warm to cook inside, so the flame made the air shimmy like waves in the stream. She shook her head at Abraham. "You do not fool me."

"And coming back, we practiced our running."

My mother began to hum. She added ground hickory nuts to the boiling corn. Abraham and I nodded to each other. She was making hickory nut grot. We would be eating good tonight, our bellies full like Golden Bear's.

Of course, we always ate real good. There was always fish, or deer, or wild pig, or rabbit, and corn bread cooked over the fire, or in it, like tonight. There were wild greens that the women plucked from the ground, and the three sisters—the beans, corn, and squash. There was plenty to eat. She cooked enough for our family—my father, my mother, my brother, and me—and she also cooked enough for Mama Emma and Papa. They lived in the bigger house, the main house next to ours.

Mama Emma and Papa were mixed blood, half White. My Mama Emma's name was Emma Sanders and my Papa's was John. I don't believe they had real names, Cherokee names, but I called them Mama Emma and Papa. Mama Emma wanted it that way. She didn't have any children, and sometimes she pretended I was her little girl and let me sleep in the main house with her and Papa instead of sleeping in my family's smaller family house. She held my face in her hands and rocked me in her arms. She combed my hair, pulling her fingers through my curls.

She bought me fancy dresses, and she taught me the Cherokee alphabet. She even promised that, when I was older, she would teach me to read. When she let me sleep in the larger house—it had two big rooms—I slept in my own little bed. She hugged me, kissed me, and tucked me in.

"Armentia must be able to run." Abraham was still talking, twisted in his own story, like he was telling a dream he could see ahead. "Who can tell what things will come?"

My mother laughed and waved Abraham away. "You were born an old man, Abraham. An old spirit speaks through your mouth. Go find your father. He is tending horses. We will be eating soon."

At dinnertime, I ate fish and too much hickory nut grot until my stomach was like Golden Bear's. My father laughed at me, blowing out his cheeks to make his face round.

That night, I slept at the bigger house, at the main house with Mama Emma. Her and Papa's house had a large stone fireplace, freestanding beds, and a table with chairs—one chair that I usually sat in.

Tucked in my bed, a bed with nice sheets, I looked out the window at the sky. It was black with many, many stars like shining pebbles in the stream. I fell asleep watching while Mama Emma pulled and carded thread from sheep's wool. For a while, by lamplight, my own mother sat with her, weaving the thread into cloth. While they worked together, for as long as I was able to keep my eyes open, I counted shelves of golden jars of honey stacked against the wall.

We were a beloved family. We were all Kituwah's children.

CHAPTER TWO

$\mathcal{M}$Y HONEYED DREAMS WERE GOLDEN, STICKY, AND sweet.

I awoke the next morning, my mother shaking me. "You must go into the water before we eat," she told me. She frowned like she smelled a goat. "You must wash and say your prayers."

Lots of things had changed already in those days. Sometimes for festivals and such we dressed up in fine skins and beads and feathers. But, the rest of the time now, we wore clothes like the White man, maybe hoping the outsiders would think their clothes made us as good as them. Only the old people still wore the clothes of our people.

"Who says their clothes are better?" the old ones would ask. And it is not what a man wears that makes him wise and true, they said. It is what is in the man's heart. "Don't think less of yourself; don't dishonor yourself, to be accepted by others. They will never fully accept you. You will be something they don't like dressed in their clothes."

There had also been a time when we all stood in the morning waters together and said the seven prayers, purifying ourselves and washing our wrongs away. But our ways were changing. We no longer all gathered to pray.

I grabbed my doll with one hand, wiping sleep from my eyes with the other. There was still just one thing on my mind. I turned at the door, looking between squinted eyes at Mama Emma, who was smiling at me. I pointed with the hand holding my doll at the shelves and shelves of honey. The daylight shining through the doorway made the jars glow, like the color that blanketed Golden Bear—like the gold that some whispered that White men had found in the hills around us. I didn't open my mouth, but kept wiping my eyes, letting my pointing finger do the talking. My mother shushed me. "You know that honey is to sell."

It was more precious than skins. My Mama Emma gathered honey the way her Cherokee mother had taught her, she said. When the men took bear and beaver skins to sell at the trading post miles away, Mama Emma took along her honey. She said it was the Cherokee in her that made her able to get the honey, to talk to the bees, but it was the White in her that made her love it so. "The White people come for it, buzzing to buy it like bees, like it came from their hive. If we cannot sell skins, we know we always have honey. And they will buy it," she said. We did not eat it often ourselves. It was a sometimes treat. Mostly we set it aside to rely on; we could sell it if times were lean.

"Don't beg for honey." My mother shushed me again.

I kept rubbing and pointing, hoping my Mama Emma would override my mother's words.

"If you eat all your seeds, you will have nothing left to grow." My mother's hand steered me closer to the door.

I still pointed, my corncob dolly dangling, hoping my Mama Emma would give me what my mother would not.

My Mama Emma, her hair in a long, straight braid twisted at the back of her neck, her long dark blue skirt dusting the hard-packed dirt floor, walked to me and patted the top of my head.

Standing so near my mother, they looked alike. Both had dark eyes, high cheekbones, and noses like small buttons. They were about the same age, but my Mama Emma was lighter, her skin almost white. Her black hair was straight, while my mother's heavy, thick curls were the color of coal. And my mother's soft skin was copper brown.

I could tell that my mother was losing patience. "Armentia, stop begging." She pointed outside. "To the water."

But my Mama Emma did what I hoped she would do. "Oh, I think I can spare a little honey for my beautiful, sweet baby." She came close, and I leaned my head against her waist, while batting my eyes like a doe at my own mother. My Mama Emma smiled at my mother, and then patted my head. "But first you must do as Sara says. First you must take to the water." Mama Emma was the only one who called my mother Sara. "Your honey will be waiting for you. I promise."

Running to catch up with the others, I dropped my doll at the door of my house, and then followed the other girls and young women to the stream.

The water was cold from the night. It made my fingers wrinkle and it opened my eyes.

When I returned, my hair wet and springing on my head, there was a strange wagon and horses tied in front of my Mama Emma's front door.

At first, I thought the wagon must belong to a missionary. They came to visit us many times. They taught us words and to pray like the White man. But soon, I saw this was something different.

CHAPTER THREE

$\mathcal{G}$OLDEN BEAR, JOHNNIE FREEMAN, AND ABRAHAM crowded around the wagon. They were so wrapped up in what they were doing, they didn't hear me coming. When I got closer, I saw the subject of the commotion.

A Black boy watered the two horses. He looked to be about their age. Dust covered his feet, almost like socks.

We had seen Black people before. Johnnie Freeman and his family were Black and there were others with us. My family was Black, Cherokee and Black. But this boy was something different.

"What is your name?" Golden Bear, Johnnie Freeman, and Abraham kept asking the boy.

He didn't answer. He shrugged, his head down, and kept watering the horses.

I pushed in between Abraham and Golden Bear so that I could get a closer look. The boy was dark, not as dark as Johnnie Freeman and his lips did not look like they had been kissed by purple berries, but he was darker than Golden Bear. Maybe my color. His clothes were torn, he was dusty, and mostly he looked at the ground.

"Do you know him?" I asked Johnnie Freeman.

"No." Johnnie Freeman pointed at his torn clothes. "I think he is a slave."

"A slave?" I could not take my eyes off the boy.

"Someone owns him, like Mama Emma and Papa own you," Johnnie Freeman said to me. "Only he's a White people's slave. I think that's why he can't talk."

"Own him?" I looked at Abraham.

"Yes, Armentia. Not family like us. He works for his people."

It was silly. I knew Abraham didn't know what he was talking about. "But we work. Everybody works." People worked in the fields, my mother cooked and wove cloth, my father tended horses, and I carried water from the well.

"But they own him, Armentia." Abraham sounded like he didn't want to explain to me; he was more fascinated with the boy. "They can sell him if they want to."

Mama Emma would never sell us. Abraham was telling tall tales again.

He talked to me but his eyes stayed on the boy. "They can take him from his mother and sell him away. He's probably already been sold." Abraham looked at me briefly. "He can't go and come when he wants to. They lock him away, tie him. They can even beat him if they want to. Under that shirt he probably has scars, they beat him so bad."

I looked at my brother, wondering how he could know such things. Maybe he had learned these things from my father, or when he went away to train with the men, with the uncles. Maybe he was just showing off—still pretending to be a man! Nobody we knew had been beaten. It was shameful to be beaten. No one was beaten, except for stealing, and no one we knew was trifling enough to steal and shame themselves and their families. It was not the Cherokee way. Mama Emma would never beat us.

And everybody was free to come and go, even animals were free to come and go. "Abraham, I'm going to tell our mother if you don't stop making up tall tales!"

Abraham kept talking. "And see how skinny he is? They probably don't feed him but like a person feeds a dog."

"Abraham, I'm going to tell Mother." I kept hoping the wind would blow so Abraham's words would carry and my mother would hear his foolish talk. I kept hoping the wind would blow and make the boy's shirt flap so I could see the scars. What must he have done to be beaten so badly? "How come? How come they treat him that way?"

" 'Cause he's Black."

Nobody was blacker than Johnnie Freeman. I looked at his beautiful skin and berry lips, thinking again that someday I would marry him. "But Johnnie Freeman is Black."

"Yeah, but I'm free. My people are free."

"I'm Black. My father is Black. Abraham is Black." I looked at Johnnie Freeman for a second. "Not as Black as Johnnie Freeman." No one was as black and pretty as Johnnie Freeman. "But we're still Black. "

Suddenly, that thing about the scars got the best of me. I stepped closer to the boy. He was taller than me, like Abraham, Golden Bear, and Johnnie Freeman.

"What's your name, boy?" I spoke loudly in case he was almost deaf. "Lift up your shirt!" I demanded. I was going to prove once and for all that this was just another one of Abraham's tall tales. "I said, boy, what is your name?"

Our father, who was walking toward our house, going to meet our mother, heard and called to us. "You will scare him to his death. He doesn't know the words of The People." My father laughed at us as he joined our mother. "He only knows the tongue of the White man. He only knows the United States words." He laughed again, he and my mother, heading toward the house.

My father's truth only made the boy more fascinating. Mama Emma and Papa spoke some of the White man's words, but not with us, not at home. I had heard them with the missionaries, or when one of their White relatives came through. But the words were not their true words. Even I knew a few United States words, but it was not the language of my people. It was not Cherokee.

"But he isn't White. How can he not know the language?" I asked Abraham. "We know the language; Johnnie Freeman knows the language."

"No," Golden Bear answered. "He is White."

Johnnie Freeman laughed at Golden Bear. "He doesn't look White to me."

Golden Bear tried to explain what I don't think he understood any better than me. "His people are White. The people who own him, so he's White."

I stepped closer to him. United States? I tried to remember the words the missionaries had taught me. I pointed at him. "Boy?" I said.

He stopped rubbing the horses, looked at me, and then at the others. He nodded.

"Girl," I said, pointing to myself. "Armentia."

He pointed to himself. "Ephraim."

I looked over my shoulder at Abraham, Golden Bear, and Johnnie Freeman. They were boys, puffing out their chests like men. But it was me that had gotten Ephraim to talk. In my excitement and pride, I forgot that he didn't know the language. "You got scars under that shirt? Where you from?"

Ephraim looked confused and frightened again. To calm him, I tried to think of other words the missionaries had taught us. I scratched my head. "Jesus," I said.

"Jesus," he responded, brightening.

I tried hard to think of something else. Finally, I remembered another word. "Amen!" I bowed my head.

Ephraim smiled and bowed his head too. "Amen!" he said.

Once we'd gotten him started, once he opened his mouth,
we didn't let up. One minute he was holding on to the horses'
reins for dear life. The next, we had Father speaking to him.
My father took the horses, and we took Ephraim down to the
stream.

Every step he took across the grounds and through the
cornfield, he looked back over his shoulder at the horses and
the main house, like he was expecting someone to call him
back. Like he was doing something wrong. He took halting
steps like he had to think about each one, like he was just learning to walk. Sometimes he looked up, like there was a cloud
over his head and he was expecting it to burst wide open at any
minute.

When we got to the stream, Ephraim stood still like a tree.
For a minute, then he got to shaking.

Golden Bear gave a whoop and jumped in! "Come on in,
Ephraim!"

Abraham touched Ephraim on the shoulder and then hurled
himself into the water.

Poor Ephraim stood there shaking like a chill had caught
him, swaying side to side like a hard breeze was blowing him.
He looked at me, pointing at Abraham and Golden Bear. He
was jabbering something awful.

But the worst of it was when Johnnie Freeman, grinning
and showing all his teeth, gave a yell and jumped into the water.

Ephraim put his hand to his mouth, pointing, jumping up
and down, looking back over his shoulder! Never seen anything
like it.

He pointed at Johnnie Freeman, ran close to the water's
edge, then came running back to me. He grabbed my hand like
as to drag me down there. Then he hollered something, waving

Johnnie Freeman out of the stream.

Johnnie Freeman threw his head back and laughed. He waved back at Ephraim, only he was waving the boy toward the water.

It was the craziest thing I'd seen. "What's wrong with him, Johnnie Freeman?"

"He's scared!"

"Scared of what?"

Johnnie Freeman walked to the edge of the stream and began to scramble up the bank. "He's scared of the water. Slaves ain't supposed to swim. My daddy told me they tell them if they go in the water, they'll drown."

"What?"

"It's supposed to keep them from running away, from getting in the water and swimming away."

While all this was going on—Ephraim jabbering and pointing, Johnnie Freeman grinning, and me trying to figure it all out—Abraham and Golden Bear were laughing, wrestling, and waving at Ephraim to dive in.

Johnnie Freeman grabbed one of Ephraim's arms. "Help me talk him in. He trusts you more than any of us."

Someday I planned to marry Johnnie Freeman and I couldn't resist after he showed so much good sense. So, I grabbed Ephraim's other arm and started trying to coax him forward, like I'd seen my father do with scared, wild horses. "Come on, now, Ephraim. You ain't gonna drown." Of course, he didn't understand a word I said. I'm pretty sure the horses didn't understand my father either. But I hoped something in the sound of my voice, in the look in my eyes, would let him know everything was all right. That's what I was hoping, because I sure didn't want that boy to buck and take to running. And at that moment, it looked like things could go either way. Especially with Johnnie Freeman laughing his head off.

"Stop it now, Johnnie Freeman! You gonna scare him

crazy!" I hated to speak to Johnnie Freeman that way, but we had what could be trouble on our hands. Once I got Johnnie Freeman to back down to just a big old grin, I started speaking more softly to Ephraim. "Come on, now, Ephraim. It won't hurt you."

Sometimes he'd look at me, just his eyes in my eyes, and he'd take a step or two. Then a bird would squawk, or Golden Bear and Abraham would start up a racket, and Ephraim would stop still like a scared deer.

"Come on, now, Ephraim. It'll be good for you." A few minutes of coaxing and a thought came to me. "Jesus," I said, pointing at the water.

The look on Ephraim's face said he didn't have no idea what I was talking about, but he was trying. "Jesus?" he said back to me.

I nodded. "Jesus." He knew I was trying to tell him something, that everything was okay. So, he'd look at me, then at Johnnie Freeman, and between the two of us he kind of stumbled his way the fifteen steps to the stream. When we got to the edge, Johnnie Freeman grinned, let go of his arm, and dived in, splashing like he hadn't seen water in a whole lot of moons.

"Come on in, Ephraim. Come on in and take a wash! You ain't gonna drown!"

Ephraim looked at me and I nodded him forward. He was still shakin', but he took a big swallow and edged his toes into the water. He just inched them in, jerking them back like he thought he was going to get burned. His feet were so dusty, when he drew his foot back out, half of it was covered with thick dust, the other part was dark and muddy where the water had soaked through.

Johnnie Freeman got up from where he was thrashing around in the water like a crazy person and took Ephraim's hand. "Come on, now."

I nodded at him. "Go on, it's all right."

Ephraim started in slow, but all of a sudden he closed his eyes and jumped! It was the prettiest thing I saw up to that point. Not as pretty as Johnnie Freeman. It was different, but it was still pretty. That jump, it was all full of courage. He did it like he was willing to die trying, like he was getting himself free! He hit that water like Golden Bear going after food! When he stood up, patting himself down, and saw that he was all there, that boy gave a yell! I don't know what he said, but he was grinning! Then he started dancing around, his britches and shirt soaking wet.

Pretty soon, it seemed like that boy forgot he was a slave and that he was supposed to drown. He was laughing and jabbering, only this time you could tell he wasn't scared no more. He was splashing and dancing, grabbing with his hands in the water at fish. It was a sight to see! Pretty soon, all that dust was mud, then it was gone, and you could see the real color of his shirt and pants, his skin, his hair. Pretty soon, he was just one of us, and that cloud over his head was gone. He kicked and flopped in the stream, but his shirt stayed in his pants and I never did get to see those scars.

We stayed out there awhile, and Ephraim didn't look over his shoulder anymore. The boys lay out across a big rock, letting the sun dry them out. We probably could have stayed out there forever, enjoying the water, the sun, and Ephraim getting free, except we could hear mother calling us.

Ephraim stayed free most of the way back, but somewhere 'bout the center of the cornfield, the cloud came back, his head went back down. When we broke into the clearing, he broke for the horses and wagon, kicking up dust as he went. Once he got there, he stood there, holding tight to the reins, dust covering his feet again.

Later, when it was suppertime, my father took Ephraim's arm, led him to our cabin, and sat him down to eat with the rest of us. He smiled, gobbling down the food, but the way he was free before, at the stream, didn't never come back.

Mama Emma didn't come to get the portion of food for her and Papa. Instead, Mother was to take it to the main house for her, and since there was so much to carry—they had a guest, my mother said—she would let me go with her to help carry.

All our attention had been on Ephraim, his tattered clothes, and the supposed scars. So, I had not even given attention to my Mama Emma and Papa having company in the great house. If I had not been so fixated on Ephraim, I might have noticed that my father carried extra meat to my mother and that my mother's cook pot was boiling earlier than usual. Ephraim was so exciting that it wasn't until suppertime that I paid any attention to the cooking smells.

I helped my mother dig the yams from the fire ashes where they had cooked. My father, Abraham, and Ephraim ate while we gathered things to take to the main house. I carried the bread cakes and the baked yams. I smelled the hot yams as I walked, my stomach grumbling. Watching Ephraim, I had missed everything. But when I got to Mama Emma's house, plates of hot food and steaming corn cakes in hand, I didn't miss the White man sitting in my chair or the jar of honey sitting on the table in front of him.

CHAPTER FOUR

*T*HAT NIGHT, IN MY OWN BED—NOT THE NICE FREE-standing one like the beds in the main house, not the one with nice sheets, but the one with only two legs that was propped against the wall, tied there by ropes—I could not sleep. The stranger, the White man, was sleeping in my bed.

I could not get the vision out of my head of the man sitting in my chair, a jar of honey—the honey I had been promised—sitting in front of him.

I didn't know his name, but I had already decided I didn't like the man without speaking a word to him. When I'd returned from delivering the yams and corn bread, I had tried to enlist Abraham in my dislike, but he'd been more interested in the food and Ephraim, who ate like he hadn't eaten in years. Ephraim slept across the room from me now, in a corner, balled up in a quilt. If I was him, I would leave the White man.

But the strange United States–speaking boy had lost his glow once I'd seen the stranger with my honey. Mama Emma

38

had hovered over him, fussing with his plate, as though he were a chief.

"Who is he?" I'd asked my mother. She told me that he was some of Mama Emma's White family here to bring news, then she would say no more.

Lying in the dark, watching Ephraim and listening to Abraham snoring lightly from his bed, I strained to hear the words of the adults who still sat outside our door in the blue-black of the night. I could make out my mother and father's voices and the voices of others who were part of our clan, including Golden Bear and Johnnie Freeman's folks. Their voices were low, so I could not make out the words. But I could hear trouble. There was no celebration in their voices.

Since I could not understand their words, my mind wandered back to the honey. How could Mama Emma give honey to the man? She had not even given me the honey she'd promised me. She had not only forgotten the honey, she had ignored me, focusing all her attention on the White man.

When I became a woman, I would have shelves and shelves of honey, I told myself. And I would not share it, except with my children, not even for money. When I fell asleep that night, I dreamed that I was wading in the stream at the edge of a forest, a golden, sweet stream.

No one shook me awake the next morning. Everything was quiet when I finally woke. Ephraim, the strange man, and the wagon were gone. There was no sign that they'd been there except a kind of worried quiet.

I stumbled from my bed and found my mother weaving like she did almost every day. Pulling carded threads, she wove material used for socks—made from the coarsest, thickest wool—for denim, and the finest cotton fibers that were used for Mama Emma's dresses and sheets. Usually, my mother smiled and sang work songs, or bragged with the other women about how fine her work was, about how beautiful the colorful designs were that she wove in blankets. But she was quiet that day, her mind in another place.

Even when she combed my hair after I came back from bathing in the stream, she did not fuss over it as she usually did, making sure every curl and kink was in place. Normally, she made two thick braids, then twisted and pinned them above my ears. That morning, she braided my hair, but let the plaits fall as though she didn't have time for details.

When I went to find Abraham, he was not himself either. "Go away, Armentia. Not today. Play with your dolls." He waved me away. He sat in a circle with Golden Bear, Johnnie Freeman, and a few other boys. I kicked dust at him, thinking, or hoping, he would chase me. But he did not even frown. Instead, he turned back to his conversation.

I ran away from them. "You sit with your chests all puffed out! You are not men!"

Alone, I sat drawing pictures in the dirt—faces, horses. When I tired of that, I played with my doll, talking to it loudly. Bored, I was about to throw it into the high grass when I heard horses.

It was the missionaries.

I knew because Missionary Wilters had a saddle that jingled, little shiny bell things that hung from his horse's reins. The other children heard too. All the girls and the smaller boys ran to meet them when they entered the clearing.

Though Missionary Wilters was a White man, he spoke the language of the people. Usually, he came alone, but this time there was another missionary, one with hair the color of orange yams.

"Jesus! Jesus!" We waved our hands in the air, running toward them before they could dismount, waiting for them to give us treats. "Jesus! Jesus!" Simply saying the word usually brought us candy or something else sweet.

Jumping down from his horse, Missionary Wilters patted us

on our heads, handing each of us a sweet goody. *"Tsa-du-li-has? Do you want it?"* He laughed while we swarmed around him. His heart was good, the old people said.

The new missionary walked beside him, looking, but he did not touch us or give us anything sweet to eat. When we crowded around him, he shrank back from us. We followed them to the circle where they always met with the adults.

I sat behind my mother and listened. When the circle formed, my mother began to sing in United States words, words the missionaries sometimes called *English*.

In dat great gittin' up mornin'
Fare you well, fare you well
In dat great gittin' up mornin'
Fare you well, fare you well

It was her favorite song. I did not know the meaning of the words, but I knew my mother's heart.

De Lord spoke to Gabriel
Fare you well, fare you well
Go, look behin' de altar
Take down de silvah trumpet—

Soon others joined in with her.

Blow yo' trumpet, Gabriel
Lord, how loud shall I blow it
Blow it right, calm an' easy
Do not alarm my people
Tell 'em to come to judgment

I sang the parts I knew, making up words to fit.

Gabriel, blow yo' trumpet
Lord, how loud shall I blow it
Loud as seven peals of thunder

41

Wake de livin' nations
Place one foot upon de dry land
Place de ther on de sea

I watched my mother's face. Her eyes closed, her brow was smooth, and her face relaxed.

Den you'll see de coffin bustin'
See de dry bones come a-creepin'
In dat great gittin' up mornin'
In dat great gittin' up mornin'

There were a few more songs, songs I didn't understand any more than the other one my mother sang, and then Missionary Wilters read from the great book he carried. He tilted his head to the sky, closed his eyes, and began to pray in English. The yam-haired missionary, eyes closed, stood beside him. Missionary Wilters's voice got louder and louder. The birds seemed to quiet, to listen.

I did not know the words, but I had learned his ways. So, when he took a deep breath and lowered his head, I knew that he was finished.

"Amen!" we all said together.

The circle broke and the women went to their cabins, returning with food we all shared. Missionary Wilters, speaking the language of The Principal People, sat cross-legged, a tin plate balanced on his knee. "Have you thought about what I said, before?" He picked at his food. "You know, what I been saying to you?" He spoke the language of the People in a funny way, a broken way, like a man finding his way in the dark with no moon. "You want to move, don't you? West of the Mississippi there will be all kinds of opportunity for you. The land is wide open, no White men to get in your way." He smiled.

One of the elders, dressed in skins, smiled in return. "We thank you, but we choose to stay here, here with the bones of our fathers. There is no reason for us to leave. We are happy here. The opportunity you offer, new places, maybe you should take it for yourselves."

Several of the men, including my father, laughed.

Missionary Wilters kept trying. "Some people say, if you would just take this new start, instead of being stubborn and staying here, that you'd be civilized in no time! You could build schools and churches. It could change all your lives." He took a big bite and swallowed.

Golden Bear's father, his belly hanging over his britches, frowned. "What is civilized? To do it the way of the White man, is that civilized? If we eat what the Great One grows for us, that is wild? To only eat what we can do for ourselves, what we plant, and reject what the Great One gives, that is civilized? Only your way is right?" His wife touched his arm and pointed, directing his attention back to his plate.

"The Lord loves us all, but you have to admit you've learned a thing, or two." Missionary Wilters looked around the circle smiling. "You've learned about the Good Book and salvation. You got to be mighty glad for that."

Golden Bear's father ignored his food. "You speak truth. Though we prayed and asked forgiveness before the White man came, you have taught us of the One who says all men are the same, and that all men must worship in spirit and in truth. You also show us men who say they are truth, but lie and keep other men in chains."

Missionary Wilters turned his back on Golden Bear's father and tried to reason with the others. "Well, if you can't leave, if you won't go, at least think about dividing up the land. Get deeds, parcel it out. Let each man stake his claim. That way, you've got your piece and what's not being used, other men can settle."

My father, who was usually silent, grunted. But Johnnie Freeman's father spoke up. "How can you divide up what belongs to all of us together? Can you divide up the sky? Can you say this bird or that tree belongs to me and not my brother?" He laughed. "Soon you will say that water belongs to one man and not another, and you will try to sell water and land to those that do not have."

The other men joined him laughing and shaking their heads.

"Soon you will tell us that the day will come when some own land and others will have no food and no place to lay their heads."

Some of the people laughed. It was impossible to believe.

"I'm just trying to protect you. Why can't you people be reasonable?"

"You mean, why don't we do it your way?" Golden Bear's father was growling.

One of the elders interrupted. "Enough. We are all brothers here. We are all related. We are the Beloved Community. We will not argue. Let's see the children dance and sing!"

CHAPTER FIVE

After the missionaries' visit, Golden Bear's father talked of the forts; the ones he had heard would be used when we were driven from the land. He said that we should prepare to fight, that the White men, not even the holy men, could be trusted.

"They will not take the land. They will not force us out. There are treaties," the men said to Golden Bear's father.

"Those treaties mean nothing, they have been broken. Now the New Echota Treaty signs our lands away."

"No one will pay attention to New Echota. It was not signed by our leaders. Major Ridge signed, but he is not a leader. Boudinot runs the Phoenix paper, the Cherokee newspaper, but he is not our leader. No one will honor such a treaty," the men told Golden Bear's father.

"The White man will honor New Echota because it gives him what he wants—our lands, and maybe gold in the hills. Then he will put us in stockades. He will starve us. At the end of bayonets, he will kill us!" His eyes were full of fire, but

Golden Bear's mother sat with the women. She was quiet, her eyes to the ground.

"You talk too hot," the other men told him. "When clouds come, you expect fire instead of rain."

One of the elders interrupted. "We must not fight amongst ourselves. Our strength is in the one—one mind, one heart. Together we are strong. We must not let fear or desperation divide us." He pointed around the circle at all the faces. "We are one."

Soon all the troubled talk was forgotten and things went back to normal. I gathered water from the well, Father tended horses, Mother wove cloth, and Abraham, Golden Bear, and Johnnie Freeman walked around as though they were men.

Everyone was settled except for me, still bothered about my honey. Everyone was happy, except for Mama Emma, who smiled less than before.

It was during those days that I learned that the strange White man, the one who had eaten my honey, the one who came with Ephraim, was one of Papa's relatives. The stranger had come to convince Papa to leave the land before bad days came.

It only made me dislike him more. How could people think of taking our home? How could we leave the trees we knew and the stars in the sky? How would the land and the water live without us? Even the fish would cry. How could we leave the well?

The White man was a bad man. I was sure of it. Each day, still remembering him sitting in my chair and eating my honey, I hated Ephraim's White man more, the White man who made scars on Ephraim's back.

And I was mad at Mama Emma. If honey was so precious, why did she give it to a man who wanted to take her house, to take our lives, to take my Mama Emma's smile away from her?

That night, when the grown-ups gathered at the fire to talk about things to come, while the children sat not far away, I stole away after the one thing I thought would make me feel better.

CHAPTER SIX

*E*VEN IN THE DARKNESS, THE HONEY JARS CAUGHT THE moonlight. I stooped, reaching for the lowest shelf. I took one jar and clutched it to my chest. It would be enough, and no one would notice it missing.

I looked at the other jars lined up on the shelves.

Once I started eating, one jar might not be enough. How could I tell just sitting there in the dark on the cool dirt floor? There were lots and lots of them, and two wouldn't be missed any more than one. I had never had my fill of honey. And who knew if I would ever get the chance again? That is, until I was grown and had my own shelves and shelves of honey. Most likely, one would not be enough. So, I took two jars.

Who knew when I would get another chance? I took another . . . and another.

Quietly, I grabbed six jars and set them gently on the dirt floor. I wouldn't be greedy. I would only take what wouldn't be missed, and what I could carry without clanking so loud that I gave myself away.

I carefully moved the remaining jars around on the shelf so no one would notice anything missing. When I was satisfied, I gathered the jars in my skirt and in my arms. Sneaking out of the house, I saw Abraham, Golden Bear, and Johnnie Freeman, sitting near the men. They were not men, and I was sure they did not see me.

Hunched over to cradle the jars, and moving quietly like Abraham taught me, I inched my way through the corn rows and then into the forest. The jars were heavy, but it was worth it. Peeking over my shoulder to be sure I wasn't being followed, I stayed close to the edge so the moon could help me see my way. I made it to the stream safely, and only broke one jar climbing along the edge of the stream to find a place to sit. I rested my back against a tree near where the honey spilled.

In the moonlight, the honey lost its golden color, but looked like thick, glimmering crystal water seeping into the ground. I touched it, careful not to cut my hand on the broken glass, then touched my finger to my tongue.

It was sweet and good, like when you've had a taste for something, get it, and it's just right. It was the sweetness I had been hungering for. I wanted more. I opened the first jar. Looking around, before I put my hand in it, I thought maybe I would hide the other jars away. When I came down to bathe, on some other night, I could come back and eat more.

I stuck two fingers in the jar, and though it was cool outside, the honey was thick but slightly warm to my fingers. When I lifted them from the jar, they trailed a shining, silvery, wet ribbon. I lifted it to my mouth. Sweetness hit my tongue, and I closed my eyes. The honey covered my lips and dripped down my chin onto my neck.

When I came to the end, I tilted the jar to my mouth so I wouldn't waste any. When I was satisfied nothing was left, I opened another jar.

After that, I guess I went crazy.

I had my own celebration out there by the stream! Opening jar after jar, nobody to stop me! When I got choked up a couple of times, I just stopped until everything cleared, and then started digging in again! The only thing that could have made it better was firelight, drums and dancing.

I was drunk with honey, with the moon and the water, so the hand on my shoulder caused me to about jump out of my skin.

CHAPTER SEVEN

RMENTIA!" IT WAS ABRAHAM. "WHAT ARE YOU doing?" He looked at the empty jars and groaned my name again. "Armentia." His fingers touched my sticky face. "Look at you!"

He took me to the stream and washed my hands, face, and chin. "We have to get back before anyone notices you missing." He used his feet to shove the empty jars into some nearby bushes. "Why would you do this? What if Mama Emma finds out?" He asked me the questions as if he didn't expect an answer.

He held my hand on the way back, as though I was a little girl, as though he was afraid for me.

"What if I had not come for you, Armentia? What if I was not here? Why would you go ahead of me? I go ahead of you."

He did not give me a chance to answer. We walked by the edge of the woods, finding our way by the night light. "What if a bear found you? What if the clouds came and hid the light?

What if there was no moon for you to follow? How would you find your way home?"

We stopped suddenly. "Close your eyes, Armentia." He held my hand still. "Feel the ground beneath your feet. Breathe in the smell of the trees."

In the dark, with my eyes closed, I could feel the softness of the grass, the tender prick of the pine needles. I smelled the sharp, sweet scent. I could smell honeysuckle nearby.

"Reach out your hands."

The dark coolness touched my arms, my fingertips, the wet places on my dress. The back of my hands brushed against the rough bark of the trees.

We walked that way through the forest and into the cornfields. The ground was drier there. The cornstalks slapped my hands.

"Remember, Armentia," Abraham said. "None of us know how things will change."

In the shadows, I opened my eyes and we skirted the edge of the clearing where the adults sat around the fire and well.

"Go to bed," he whispered to me at the doorway to our log cabin. "Leave your dress near the door."

In the darkness, I watched him walk back to join the other boys. As soon as I undressed, I fell into a deep sleep, but it was a sleep that did not last long. While it was still dark and I could hear the sleeping sounds of my family, my stomach woke me. It sounded like a bear was in my belly. It called me outside and I found my way to private bushes by the moonlight and stars. The wind seemed to laugh at me. Seven times my stomach called me outside. By morning I felt like a dress scrubbed too long on a hard rock. I tried to be quiet, but I could not stop groaning and woke my family.

My mother pressed her cool hand to my forehead. "Armentia, what is wrong with you?"

I groaned again, but before I could speak, Abraham

answered for me. "She probably ate too much *pashofa* last night. I saw her sneaking some extra." He leaned over to touch his head to my mother's forehead. "Don't worry. Her stomach is just angry with her, that's all."

Pashofa was my favorite food—beaten corn boiled with fresh pork—but now I didn't want to hear of pashofa, honey, or food of any kind.

Abraham laughed. "She ate like Golden Bear last night."

My father, pulling on his shirt, looked at me and then at Abraham, shook his head and left to tend Papa's horses.

"You stay in bed," my mother said. "I will make you some healing tea."

Abraham walked with my mother out the door. They brushed past my hanging dress. Some time in the night, in between the seven times I was called to the bushes, Abraham must have cleaned the honey stains from my dress. All the signs of my mischief were gone.

Three days passed. Most of them I spent sipping tea, asleep, or out in the bushes. But the third night, when I was feeling better, Mama Emma appeared at the door.

"Who took them?" she demanded. Her eyes were red, her hair hung loose and wild around her shoulders. A black leather belt dangled in one hand. In the other, which she held in front of her, were broken pieces of a honey jar. "Who stole them?" Her look burned my skin. "Did you think I wouldn't miss them, you stupid child? Did you think I wouldn't know?"

The woman in front of me pretended to be my Mama Emma, the one who said I was her pretty daughter, the one who kept me at her house. But I knew it was an evil spirit, one of the little people from the forest, from the hills, wearing her clothes. Mama Emma had been acting strange since the White man's visit, since the news that we would have to move. I knew it was not really her.

"I should throw you in the well! You are good for nothing!"

My stomach that had been growling for three days, suddenly dropped like an empty bucket down the well.

"Six jars are missing! I counted them! Six jars!"

My mother stood between Mama Emma and me. "Why are you yelling? She has been sick. Why are you yelling?"

Mama Emma shoved her aside, sent her tumbling backwards until Abraham caught her. "She belongs to me! You all belong to me and I'll talk to her any way I please! Don't forget your place, don't forget who you are! She's a thief and I will treat her as a thief!" My mother staggered aside. Abraham braced her in his arms.

"Who else would steal the honey? Who else begs for honey?" Mama Emma shook the glass pieces at me and stepped closer to my bed.

My mother, still looking stunned and speaking in a soothing voice, tried again to defend me. "But she's been in bed for three days."

"Of course, she has. She's been sick from eating the honey. She ate six jars!" She sneered at me. "I found the empty jars, five of them besides this one," she threw the glass pieces on the dirt floor, "hidden in bushes by the stream!" Mama Emma lifted the black leather strap that was in her other hand. "If you steal, you pay!" It was not Mama Emma who yelled at me; she never yelled at me. It was the sickness that had changed her.

The One Who Guards His Family quickly stepped between Mama Emma and me. "It was me," he said. His back to me, he covered me with his body. "I stole the honey!"

Mama Emma kept her eyes on me. "Don't lie, Abraham."

"It was me!" my brother covered for me. "You gave the White man honey. You have so much. I wanted it." His chest was heaving. Behind his back, I held his hand.

I wanted to speak, to tell the truth. But I was afraid, and Abraham made it easy for me, he squeezed my fingers, telling me I should not speak.

"You want to stand for her? You want to lie for this thief?" Mama Emma smiled, not like herself, but like a jackal stalking a rabbit. "So be it. She steals, you will pay!" She stormed out of our cabin, her skirts leaving a trail of dust behind her. We watched her from our doorway. She stopped just before entering her own. "We have treated you too well. Now our goodness is ruining our lives. Count on it." She lifted the belt. "This is not over!"

Papa made my father tie Abraham to a tree.

It was not true, what I was seeing. I could not believe it was my Papa. My Papa was kind. Some kind of sickness must have gotten hold of him too. He would change his mind. He had never beaten one of us. He loved us. We were like his own children, all of us family. He would not beat my brother now.

While my father tied Abraham, I could not hear the words, but I saw my father's lips moving. I saw tears coming down his face. Maybe my father was reminding my brother that he was in training to be a man, that he must be brave, and that he must not cry. Papa tore Abraham's shirt from his back. I thought of the boy Ephraim and I looked away. I looked around the circle at all the people. Papa made all of us come to watch.

Inside me, I could hear Abraham crying even before Papa hit him. I could feel how shamed he was, how people would point at him and wonder. Inside me, I felt sick. I wasn't big enough to stop it. I wanted to leave, to run away and hide, but I could not leave him. If I could not save him, at least I would be there.

"The White man says we treat you too good, we treat you too much like family." Papa held the handle of the horsewhip, making circles on the ground while he talked. "But you need to know who you are. You are slaves. You have to stay in your place."

It felt like Papa, before raising the whip, was beating all of us.

Mama Emma stood in front of the main house. She still did not look like herself, her hair loose and wild.

My mother held me tight at her side. I could feel her trembling. My father came and stood beside her. He put one arm around her waist and wiped the tears from his face with his free hand.

When Papa raised the whip, I tried to be brave, but I closed my eyes. It cracked and then there was a ripping sound, not like a shirt, but like when a raw chicken leg is ripped from the body. I opened my eyes and saw blood on my brother's back. I made myself watch the next lash; it was my punishment. The whip dangled in Papa's hand, then came alive when it cut through the air. When the tip of the whip hit The One Who Guards His Family, his skin opened like a seam, pink and red and white showing. Or like a too ripe melon splitting open to the heart. My mother dropped to her knees and rubbed dust in her hair. My father stood straight like a tree, silent except for the tears on his face. I tried not to cry, to be brave for my brother, but those tears just came on out anyway and I cried out loud like any little old baby.

Papa hit Abraham like he was a stranger. Like he was hitting a stubborn mule; no, worse than that. He hit my brother like he didn't matter. I kept hoping Abraham would yell out that I did it, that he would tell on me. It would have felt better, I think, to be hit than to think he was tied there being hit and bleeding for me.

But Abraham never said a word. He moaned, he whimpered, but he did not speak. By the third lash, he had fainted.

Papa hit him six times, one for each jar. "It's not finished!" Mama Emma yelled from her front yard. "He ought to be thrown down the well!" She shook her fingers at Abraham and I knew for certain it was not my Mama Emma; it was an evil spirit. "You can believe it's not finished!"

Then Papa hit him one more time, so Abraham and all of us would never forget.

It's been more years than I can count, but I still remember. Just like Papa intended, I won't ever forget. And I hate honey right up to this very day.

CHAPTER EIGHT

After the beating, my father's hair turned gray. I don't know how—one day it was black and the next day it was white. He'd always been quiet, but he stopped smiling.

After the beating, he untied the ropes and carried Abraham into the house. He wouldn't let my mother wash Abraham's wounds; my father did it himself. The other men would come and sit with the two of them. They talked so quietly, the only one whose words I could make out was Golden Bear's father. "No man should make a slave of another one. It is against the way of our people. Look at this boy. Look at this fine boy." Then he would shake his head. The songs they sang were crying songs.

Because the men were around him, I could only sit with Abraham when the men were away in the fields. I brought him water from the well, though he hardly ever drank any. He kept his eyes closed and when I came near him, he winced like just being steps away from him made him hurt.

"Abraham, I'm sorry. I'm so sorry," I whispered when no one was around. Sometimes his eyes fluttered like he heard me.

My mother cooked, but Abraham couldn't hold much more than a little soup. I didn't do much better. How could I eat with my brother that way? I brought him shiny pebbles from the stream and wildflowers, but when I saw him there on the bed they did not seem good enough and I left them outside the door.

The moon rose many days before Abraham walked with us again. I wish I could tell you that when his scars healed everything went back to normal.

How could it?

Abraham went sometimes with the boys to the stream, but he did not take off his shirt and his chest did not puff out like a man's. None of their chests puffed out. At the games, at the time of the next green corn, Abraham sat aside. Though everyone expected him to run, though everyone came by to show respect, he didn't run. He stayed to the side, all my family did, and we left early.

We became friends again, Abraham and I. Not that we ever stopped loving each other, but I didn't know what to say. What could I say that was big enough to make up for what had happened? Finally, I settled on saying nothing.

While he sat on the dirt floor one evening, I sat next to him. We sat that way, the dark taking over the light. Finally, when missing him got the very best of me, I laid my head on his shoulder. Abraham put his arm around me. That's how we made up.

Mama Emma did not look at us the same after the beating. She stayed further away from us. Or, maybe, it was me that did not look at her the same. She had hurt my brother, and it did not help that—because of my silence—I had helped her. It wasn't just Abraham in pain.

Like I said, I wish I could tell you everything went back to being the same. But that beating opened our eyes and made us see some things we didn't want to see. Wasn't much difference, after that, between us and Ephraim. A slave is a slave is a slave, and a slave master is a slave master is a slave master.

And wrong is wrong. You see, I got to confess something. It's hard to tell, but sometimes we called people like Ephraim *niggers*.

I didn't tell you before, tried to cover it up in the story, because I was ashamed. But what I'm telling you now is the truth. We weren't the only ones saying it and we didn't start it, but them is just excuses. You can't get free of something shameful keeping it a secret. It's an ugly word, I know that now, but we said it. I said it, and I got to tell the truth.

We said it. You know, like because our people were Cherokee we were better. I guess that's just human, everybody needs to feel better than somebody. But that ain't no excuse; wrong is wrong.

In my mind, I thought my people—the people that owned me—were better because they were Indians, because we were all Indians and family. But somebody that will use somebody's life up just to make their own lives better—well, there ain't no excuse for that whether they're Red, White, or even Black. It don't make them right or glorious whether they wear gray or whether they wear feathers. It's a shameful thing, and I've had to take that to the altar.

When Ephraim was with us, we called him nigger like there was some difference between him and us. And we said it without thought or shame, like calling a bird a bird. But that lashing taught us that we were just fooling ourselves.

That beating said there was no difference between Ephraim's people and my people. And there was no difference between us and Ephraim. That probably hurt us all more than the lashes. We were all slaves. There wasn't no difference at all.

One evening, not long after the green corn, a storm blew through. The sky was gray, almost black, except you could see the clouds moving by in shifting layers—some going this way and others going that way. The smell of rain was heavy in the air. You could hear the horses whinnying and the lambs bleating like they knew something was coming.

There wasn't any thunder yet, so I kept to what I was doing. I drew pictures in the dirt with my toes while I lowered the bucket into the well for water. In the midst of my drawing, sometimes I peeked over to check on the bucket's progress.

People were making their way in from the fields. Not running, but looking over their shoulders like they were expecting white fire from the sky, and like if they kept their eyes on it they could do something about it.

Rain started beating down then, just all of a sudden. It didn't tiptoe in, starting gentle; it came in like a raid. Bucket now in my hands, I stood at the edge of the well looking at the sky, watching the people come in from the fields, and feeling scared.

The rain was coming down even harder, and when I looked up, people were running.

Lightning crashed right beside me!

Well, it was about fifty or so paces away, but that is still fifty paces too close!

It was like everything stopped and got quiet, except for the bucket in my hands. That old wooden thing slipped through my fingers like a greased pig and shot on down the well, rope flying behind it like a rat's tail. I watched it flipping and flapping, flying down that dark hole, and at the same time I could still feel that fire in the air and it seemed like the smart thing for me to do was to head for my home.

I was picking my feet up and putting them down. If lightning struck again and hit me, it wasn't going to be because I was standing still. I could see my mother's door, but because I was scared it seemed so much further away. But I kept my eye on it. I didn't see anything but that door.

It got dark early and stayed that way. The way I remember it, the sun didn't shine too much after that.

CHAPTER NINE

$\mathcal{B}$UT ONE FINE MORNING—IT WAS THE BRIGHTEST morning I'd seen in a while—I heard Missionary Wilters's jingling horse coming up the path. I'd sworn off of honey, but other sweets still tempted me. Like always, I ran out to meet him, laughing with the other running children. When their horses came trotting in, his and the yam-haired missionary's, I held out my hands. I smiled and yelled with the other children, waiting for him to give us something good.

Instead, Missionary Wilters, who always took the most time with the children, brushed past us after quickly tying his horse. He headed for the adults who had begun to gather in the center of the clearing near the well, the other missionary following behind him. I tugged at the younger missionary's coat. He frowned at me, jerking himself away.

There was no singing, no praying, no reading from the Good Book. When all the people had gathered, Missionary Wilters just started talking. "You're going to have to give up your land! There's no arguing about it. It's coming, the government's said so. And the best thing to do is to not fight it. You'll have to go in peace. West of the Mississippi. It's good land." Missionary Wilters wiped his forehead with a blue-and-white handkerchief. "You're going to have to go peaceful. Think of the women and children." He looked around the circle.

Papa, frozen except for the muscles that worked in his jaws, stared at the missionary. "This is our land!" He took a deep breath and froze again. "This is our land! The government is saying we don't own the land because of our skin? It is the place of our fathers' bones and dust!" He jutted his hand forward, shoving it in the missionary's direction. "And I am half White; does that part of me get to keep the land? Greedy men use color, use the government, and even use God to get what they want!"

Mama Emma stood by Papa, crying and frowning, her eyebrows knit together. She looked at Missionary Wilters and then around at the rest of us.

The missionary swallowed. "I'm not against you, you know that. I've been talking and talking. But there's no more time. This country's busting at the seams. And I don't know . . ." He looked down at his hands, then back at us ". . . maybe it is our right. Maybe it is our responsibility. Maybe even our manifest destiny, as they say."

Golden Bear's father frowned and shook his head. "There has been much talk, talk to try to make us believe what we don't believe. There is talk, but we see and hear of the forts that the White man is building . . . forts to carry us away." He looked around the circle. "I told you so."

"Why, that's just plain foolishness. Don't believe idle gossip. I told you that before. What we want is what's best for you. Your people will progress better west of the Mississippi. There's open land there. You'll be free of the interference of White men who mean you no good."

My father, who had stood silently during most of the talk,

stepped forward. "You mean, move there because the White man does not want that land *now*. And when the White man wants more, he will say it is best for us if we move again. If a man wants my wife and family and he says to me it is best for me to move on and give them up, can I go? No, I am married to them as I am married to the land."

In a way that wasn't common for him, Missionary Wilters raised his voice. "There is no more talk now! You've got to get ready. We don't know the date, but the move is coming." The missionary wiped his face. "Maybe if you'd been willing to divide up the land . . . every man stake a claim to his portion. Maybe if you'd gone ahead west like the Old Settlers. But it's too late now. President Andrew Jackson has given the order." He spoke like a father speaking to unruly children. "Talking is over."

Golden Bear's father, his belly hanging over his breeches, raised an eyebrow. "The Great One gave us this land for all to share alike; land for all, water for all. The Great One gave this land for all so that all can eat, so that each one would have a place to lay his head. It is the way of The Principal People. It is not our way, it is not the Great One's way, to own things that cannot be owned: the sky, the land, or even men. Are White men greater than the Creator?"

Missionary Wilters looked at the younger missionary, the one with yam-colored hair, like I sometimes looked at Abraham when I got myself into a mess too big for me to handle alone. He cleared his throat. "The government of the United States is sovereign. You mustn't just think of yourselves, you must think of the whole nation. This is for the good of the whole nation."

Johnnie Freeman's father looked up from where he was whittling on a piece of wood. "We are thinking of the good of our nation . . . the Cherokee Nation." He carved carefully on the soft wood. "How is moving all of us, stealing our land, taking our homes, all that we've worked for, supposed to be good for us?"

The missionary with yam-colored hair jumped to his feet, his face red. "Nobody's stealing. You got that all wrong. You—the free Blacks and Whites that live here," he pointed at a few people around the circle, "the order won't apply to you. You're not compelled to go to Indian Territory. You're free to make your own way. You're free to make your own choice."

Johnnie Freeman's father stopped whittling and stared at the man. "Stay here alone, just me and my family? How long you think we'll be free? How long before we'll be grabbed up by slave hunters and sold as slaves?" He shook his head. "Leave my people?" He touched his forearm to Golden Bear's father's arm; black against copper. "Nothing between us different that matters." He raised an eyebrow. "Hear these words I'm speaking? I speak Tsalgi. See my family, my friends? These are my people." He pointed around the circle, then pounded his chest with his fist. "These are my people! Where they go, I go!"

Papa sat down on the log beside him; it was the closest Papa had sat to any of us since Abraham's beating. Golden Bear's father nodded.

Mama Emma stayed to herself, looking around the circle like all of us had done something wrong to her. Mama Emma's mouth made a thin line, a line with the corners turned down. When her eyes lit on Abraham, who sat with the other boys, they narrowed to slits—like she'd found the thing that had been stinking in her house. Her expression said the stinking thing was my brother. She was not the Mama Emma I had known. She was not the Mama Emma who had held me in her arms, the one whose neck Abraham and I had hugged all our lives. Something had to have poisoned her.

Johnnie Freeman's father was still talking. "Stay here or give up everything I've worked for? Give up the land God gave to all the people to some greedy—why, they're not even fit to be called men. I don't call that much of a choice."

The younger missionary reddened. "Well, you can belly-ache all you want, but it's coming!" He spoke with fire, like someone who believes he is right. "We didn't come here to argue—"

Missionary Wilters held up his hand to silence the younger one. There were no tears on his face, but his words were weeping. "We come in peace. You know I've been coming amongst you for years, preaching the Good News." He looked at the elders and then around the circle. "You know that. I've never lied, never cheated. I've tried to do right. I've tried! I've tried!" He ran his hands through his brown hair. "I don't like this any more than you do. If I thought fighting would do any good, I'd take off this collar and stand with you. Don't think I ain't prayed about it."

I could see tears in his eyes now. He was wringing his hands.

"I don't know what you want me to do. I've tried! And I don't want to see any of you get killed over something like this. Land ain't worth dying over. There's more land out west. And these men mean business!" He wiped his forehead again. "What do you want from me?" He shifted from foot to foot. "We're taking a chance even coming here." He pointed at himself and the younger missionary. "I'm just here to warn you. Talk is heatin' up. It'll probably be next spring. Only a heartless man would force you to make your flight in winter. But be ready! That's all. Just be ready!"

CHAPTER TEN

THE MOON CAME AND WENT MANY TIMES, OLD AND NEW, and people talked, waiting for something to happen. Some of the leaves began to turn the color of fire early. Some cool days came and most of the old people said it was a bad sign.

Men would gather around the fire and, instead of laughing, their voices would eventually rise in anger. Some of them prepared to fight. They rode away on horseback, staying for days, and returned with guns. Women stopped gathering to show off their weaving. They were too busy trying to make quilts, coats, and warm socks in case the bad news was true.

My mother sang sad songs while she worked, rarely teasing with Abraham and me. But the biggest change was in Mama Emma. She no longer smiled. She kept her head bowed and would not look at us. Mama Emma did not want anyone near, like she was in pain—and we were the cause of it—and the pain made her angry. She spent most of her time in the main house and never invited me to sleep there again. I hardly ever saw her and only heard her when she was yelling at my mother for some weaving error, or some other mistake she was supposed to have made. When Mama Emma saw Abraham, she shook her head and spoke curses at him, like he was the cause.

Confusion wound itself around the people like a silent, sticky vine. They were too busy trying to prepare for something they could not believe and hoped would not happen. And because they did not want to go, the people argued even more than they prepared their stuff to leave.

When many days had passed and no one had come to force us off the land—when the days got shorter, the leaves began to fall, and it was too cool to move—some of the people began to talk. The White men who pretended to be our friends were like foxes, they said. Papa's relative and the missionaries were liars; men who tried to trick us, to frighten us, so they could take our land without trade or war.

A wise woman, one of the bravest and most honored elders in the village, spoke to the people. "We did not heed the warnings of our Beloved Woman. Nan'yehi was strong in battle. We know her legacy. She warned us not to give our lands to the White man. She told us he would never be satisfied. But we did not listen to the voice of our Beloved Woman." She shook her head. "Now, the young spirit, the greedy spirit resides among us.

"We must remember that we are the teachers. We must trust that the Great Spirit has brought them to us because we are old and wise. They are children and we must teach.

"The young spirit has many toys—big guns, fancy clothes—things that moth and rust destroy. He has many shiny beads, but he does not know the value of things that last—truth, love, honor, friendship, and respect for all men. It is our job to teach."

"If we are quiet, if we don't cause trouble, we will stay alive," someone answered her.

"Don't be foolish. Trouble will always find you." She pointed around. "Trouble has already found us! Are we going to lie down?

We must not surrender, not even to save our very lives."

The wise woman stood to her feet. "The student is greedy and unruly. But isn't that the way with our own children? Still, we must lead, we must not take on his ways. We must teach the student to share. We must teach the student to love, to respect all men and women. The student is difficult, demanding, and frustrating, but we must not give up. We must teach the student the ways of The Principal People. We must not let ourselves be distracted by his things.

"Even if it is hard, we must not run from our burden. If we fail to teach him, to give him our best gift, the gift of honor and brotherhood, we will be sorry."

Another voice accused her. "You speak trouble to us. Too many have already died."

She pointed to the ground. "When a man walks someplace, we see the footprint of who he is. We see the influence of who he is—both good and bad. If he is whole, he makes a complete print. If he is broken, we see that too.

"We can see who he is by the way he changes the place. We can see who he is by the children he leaves behind."

She pushed her foot down on the ground, leaving behind a trace. "We see the print of the man who walks among us. Mostly, he does not see—rare is the man, the great man, who will look behind to see what he has done. Only a great man will look to see what his influence has taught others to be.

"So this man we see, he is a young man, a man who could be great. He has taught us about writing and reading written words. He has taught us about organization. Some of us—like Reverend Bushyhead, Stand Watie, John Ross, and Major Ridge, and Nan'yehi—the one White men call Nancy Ward— have walked the halls of his Congress in Washington, D.C. He has taught us about building tall buildings and shown us fancy clothes. We look at the good of this man's footprint and say, 'Here is a great man!'

"So, we have learned from him. We have adopted many things. Because we are older, we can love ourselves and still appreciate what he brings. So, we have adopted the good things. Sequoyah has made us an alphabet. The great ones among us have made us a government, a supreme court.

"But, the young spirit is not yet truly great. We also see that this man is broken. We see his footprint on the road. This man walks in fear—I do not know what happened to him—but he is afraid to live side by side with others, with others who are different. He must conquer and be superior because he has not learned to live side by side. He fights, he kills those he fears, or does not understand. He thinks that having many things will keep others from seeing who he really is. He does not see that others can teach him, can help him be whole, and that there is still much for him to learn. He resents those who offer him wisdom. He does not see that the Breath Giver has also given us great things, that we are a great people and that we have much to share. He cannot see that we can help him. He cannot recognize the gifts of others, so he walks away from us still stumbling and broken.

"We have tried to love him, to share with him what we have. But love is not enough. If he is not willing to see, if he is not willing to feel the hurt that comes with learning and change, that comes with seeing the truth of one's own footprint, then he will not learn. Then he will not be healed and that broken footprint will follow him around.

"We must take the good he offers, but we must choose to leave the bad.

"There are also among us those who are young, those who do not want to see. There are also those among us who enslave others, who steal from others, who fight with others—and if we call the White man wrong, we cannot call them right. Though they are our brother, it may be better to cast them out—to go forward missing one sick hand rather than let it infect the whole body."

It got dark early that day, like it seemed to so many days since Abraham's beating. Gray, fat clouds rolled in; you could smell heavy rain in the air. All of the women and children moved quietly in their cabins, while the wind swirled up dust outside. I could hear the animals making a racket and hoped that my father would be home soon.

Mama Emma suddenly appeared at our cabin door, her arms behind her. Her hair hung about her shoulders. Her eyes looked like fever. "Abraham!" She called my brother outside. "Go to the stream for fish."

My mother came near the doorway. "But a storm is coming. We have plenty of meat for tonight."

"I said I want fish!"

"It is too dark for him, fire is coming from the sky."

"I said I want fish!"

My mother grabbed her shawl. "Then I will go."

"No!" Mama Emma pulled a black strap from behind her back. "I said Abraham, and I mean Abraham!" She shook the strap at him. "Now, go!"

Abraham nodded to my mother. "Don't worry. I will get fish and be home soon."

"See that you do!" Mama Emma spun, her skirts flapping, and turning against the wind made her way home to the main house.

I grabbed his fishing string and handed it to him. He shook his head and grabbed his fishing net. By the time Abraham got to the cornfield, it was dark as any night. His shirt was blowing and he ducked his head against the blowing leaves and dust, against the hard raindrops that began to fall. He turned and waved to me. I stood at the door watching until he disappeared.

My mother tried to act like she wasn't worried, but I saw her wringing her hands. She busied herself stirring the boiling pot of corn. With the wind blowing and the cool, she now cooked inside. She prepared corn cakes and greens. But by the time my father arrived, Abraham was still not home.

"She sent him for fish! In all this weather, she sent him for fish! Who knows what could happen to him!"

My father turned back toward the door. "I will find him." I watched him leave now, smelling the rain and the crackling light in the black sky.

The storm came and went, but there was no Abraham. When my father returned, his shirt and pants soaked, his hair drenched, he stepped inside the door, and then he cried. "He is gone! I hunted up and down the bank, I waded through the water. There was nothing." He held up Abraham's fishing net. "Nothing but this."

"My son! The One Who Guards His Family, where is he?" my mother wailed. She looked up at my father. "What has she done to him?"

When Mama Emma came for her portion of food, she was smiling. Not the smile from before she was poisoned—not like warm, sweet apples plucked from a tree—this smile was hard like ice. She looked in the pot. "No fish?"

My mother was shaking. "What have you done with him? Where is my son?" She stood, the large wooden spoon she used to stir the pot still in her hand. Her face was flushed, the closest I had come to seeing my gentle mother angry.

"Your son? He belongs to me!" Mama Emma's smile widened. "All of you belong to me, and I do with you what I please!" More hard, cruel ice. "Now, give me my food!"

No one slept that night. It was dark, the candles out, but there was no sleep-breathing. I kept looking out the window at the well. The moon was now shining right over it. *"I should throw him down the well!"* I had heard her say it! If my mother and father had slept, I would have run to the well and called his name. *Abraham! Abraham! Are you there?*

But with them awake, I could not go.

When I could sleep, I dreamed of my brother crying for me.

Armentia! Armentia! It was too terrible, so I woke myself and waited until morning.

Before the light could break the night, when the earliest birds called to me, I ran to the well, calling his name! I whispered loudly, "Abraham! Abraham!" I dropped the bucket down the well, but all I heard was a splash.

My father heard and came for me. "Armentia, you must come inside."

How could I go inside with Abraham gone? How could I leave with my brother down the well? "She threw him down the well! I know it! She said she would!" My father carried me inside.

My mother cried while my father dressed to go searching again. He nodded toward the main house. "I must go tell him that I have to search for Abraham." My father left, heading for the main house.

When he returned, his head down, Mama Emma and Papa walked ahead of him.

Mama Emma was smiling again, but not cold like before. "Everything is going to be fine now." She spoke as though she had done something for all our good. She stooped down to pat my head and smiled at me. "Why, he's not down the well. I sold him," she said. I pulled away from her touch. She said it like it was nothing, like saying good morning on an ordinary day. "I sold him to a man that promised to protect us, to protect our land so we don't have to leave."

"S-sold him!" My mother fell backwards into a chair. "You said you were never going to sell us. We are family."

The ice flashed. "Don't be surprised. I told you it wasn't over. He's a thief and he gets a thief's reward."

My father's head was bowed. He looked crumpled, like all the life was out of him. I couldn't say or think a word.

Mama Emma softened again. "I did it for all of us. The price he brought will keep us all here, safe. They told me they would catch him at the stream and take him away. It was for all of us. It's all over now." She explained as though she did not see why we could not understand her reasoning.

I tried to imagine men at the stream catching Abraham. If they were on foot, they could never catch him. No one could outrun him. Not even the deer could keep pace with him. I saw him running through the woods, finding his way even in the dark. He would know the feel of the leaves and the pine needles under his feet, the feel of the trees against his hands. He would know the smell of the cornfield. Abraham would know how to be silent so that the wind would cover him. They would never catch him. I closed my eyes. When I opened them, he would be standing in the doorway, grinning, a bunch of fish in his hand.

But I knew that they would not try to catch him on foot. They would use horses. They would throw ropes to catch him, and use rags to cover his mouth. They would throw him over the saddle like a pelt and carry The One Who Guards His Family away.

All that day, the next day, and for moons to come, I waited for him. I watched the cornfield at the edge of the circle. I looked down the path that led to our village. When no one was looking, I would go to the forest and call his name. When I drew water, I would look down the well into the dark for him.

"Abraham! Abraham!" I whispered his name.

I looked for my brother. I watched for him. But he did not come home.

I only saw him again in my dreams. "I go ahead of you," he told me.

I prayed that he got away, that he was running, and that someday he would come home.

I cried the day he left and kept on crying for many days to come.

CHAPTER ELEVEN

ABRAHAM CARRIED HIS NET TO THE EDGE OF THE STREAM and knelt there. Though it was not usually done alone, though it was not usually done in the face of a storm, it was not unusual to fish at night.

But this was not night; it was a different kind of darkness. It was wet. The wind was blowing, stirring the trees.

He would have to be patient, to watch where the fish swam. Though it was early, the sun was covered. There was no sun or moon, just heavy, shifting clouds. He looked around him at the trees and high grasses blowing in the wind, at the large stones and the pebbled ground. Abraham had found his way by memory and feel. He looked back at raindrops hitting against the stream, only an occasional shimmer.

By day, it was all colors—green, brown, blue, and yellow. But in the darkness, it was all black, white, and shades of gray.

Snap!

He turned when he heard the sound—not the lumbering crash of a rushing bear, or the whoosh of a stalking panther—it was more like the gentle step of a deer, or maybe the waddle of a raccoon.

He relaxed his back, turning toward his net. He lowered his shoulders. He would get the fish and then get home to his family. His mother was stirring the pot now. His father was probably home from a day's work. Armentia would be waiting for him. He smiled. It was probably all his parents could do to keep her from bolting out the door on her way to the stream to find him.

The One Who Guards His Family felt them before he heard them come upon him. Their hands, grabbing him like claws, were on him before he saw them.

One man clamped his hand over Abraham's mouth, wrapping his large hand in a lock that crushed Abraham's breath.

The One Who Guards His Family bucked, jerking his body, while another man grabbed and bound his feet. The two that held him, they were brothers, both Principal People. He had heard that some of his people had become like them—slave catchers, bounty hunters. But, until now, he did not believe. "Quiet, boy!" they hissed at him. "Stop fighting so it will go well with you!"

Abraham flailed with his arms, but the White man that was with the two kicked him in his side. The blow took the breath from him. First stars, and then there was blackness.

When he could see again, his hands were tied behind him, the rope from his hands leading to his bound feet. A rag was stuffed in his mouth and tied around his head.

"Hurry up! We don't have all night to do this!" the White man said. "Take him. Load him into the wagon!"

The other men, the two betraying brothers, lifted him and began to walk. As they walked, the White man slipped a burlap bag over Abraham's head so that he could not see.

Soon, the sound of their footfalls almost unheard, they stopped, and Abraham could hear the nervous hooves of a tethered horse.

He heard the White man's voice again. "Get him into the wagon! But be careful this time. This one will bring us good money!"

· The two men lifted him—their hands gripping him as if he was not one of them, gripping him as though they had forgotten he was their brother and that he could feel.

The bed of the wagon was rough and wooden. Though he could smell hay, there were just a few blades here and there.

His mouth was gagged, he could not yell. He was a man—he would not moan and beg. He scooted himself, splinters sticking him, into a corner, into as dignified a position as he could manage.

At least his family was safe. At least he was alone.

Inside, he cried. The Great One would watch over his family now. The Great One would watch over him.

Under the hood, rain still pelting him, he closed his eyes. He would not beg.

Abraham knew he would never see his family again.

CHAPTER TWELVE

AFTER ABRAHAM WAS STOLEN, THE DAYS TURNED COLD. I thought it was because of sadness and I did not expect it to warm again.

Without Abraham, I thought there would be no spring. But, it did warm. The grass came again and the stream thawed.

Men went back to the fields to plant corn, women folded the heavy quilts away. Mama Emma smiled again and walked among the people—though she did not come to our house. "See, I was right. I had to do it to keep us all safe." When she spoke now, there was no coldness; I knew she honestly believed what she said to us. "Besides, Abraham was a wicked boy. You remember that he stole, don't you?" She said it as though she was certain she would convince us. "You remember that he had to be beaten? He was a thief! You remember the scars?" Mama Emma seemed surprised that our family could not wipe the hurt and anger off of our faces.

Mama Emma went to other women's cabins for her portion of food. My mother avoided Mama Emma and did her spinning in our cabin. My father continued to tend the horses, but walked with his head down. And I dipped water from the well, still calling down now and then for Abraham, still looking for him in the woods.

And the missionaries still came.

One bright day, after the corn began to green, the yam-haired missionary came alone to see us. He brought sweets, he prayed and sang. He stayed that day with us, and that night he led the men down to the stream. They would go down to the water to ask forgiveness, he said. They would go to ask the Great One what He wanted them to do.

I followed from a distance, watching and listening.

When they got to the clearing where the boys would go to fish, where I ate the honey, the missionary told them to build a fire. All of the men gathered wood, and when the fire was lit, they sat around it in a circle.

The missionary looked toward the sky and began to speak some words loudly in United States. Papa jumped to his feet, yelling, and then they—other men with guns—were upon them.

Men with guns, White men, came out of the woods, some on horseback and some on foot, but all with ropes, bayonets, and guns. They herded our men into a circle, like I'd seen my father herd horses, and those that ran or fought, they roped or hit with the butts of their rifles. One man was shot. Weapons were taken from the few of our men that had brought them.

I jumped to my feet! I would fight them! I would save the men! But in my head, I heard Abraham's voice and hid again.

I stood among the trees, quiet like Abraham had taught me. Men were shouting—men I had known all my life. Terror was on the men's faces. Some were angry, like Golden Bear's father. Papa was arguing and was knocked to the ground. When I saw the men rope my father, I backed further into the woods. While the sun watched, they dragged him, like an animal. The men surrounding them pointed guns and bayonets.

Then Abraham's voice came to me. "Run, Armentia! Run!"

Stumbling over nothing but fear, I kept falling as I ran through the woods. Running, I found my way by touch through the trees and then the cornfield. When I burst through into the clearing, more strange men were there. They held my mother, other women and children, and Mama Emma outside in the clearing. The women, old people, and children had blankets and a few goods with them. Mama Emma wore her best clothes; there were jewels in her ears.

Some of the men pointed rifles at them, while other men dragged more women and children screaming from their cabins. The men yelled at them, shouting United States words. "Get a move on! We don't have all day! Move it!"

I stood at the edge of the clearing, afraid not to join my mother, but afraid to give up my hiding place. So, I froze until my mother saw me. She yelled my name; then a soldier said something to her that I could not hear. I ran to her and threw my arms around her waist.

"You are here, my daughter! You are alive!"

We both cried. "Your father will come," she whispered to me.

I began to tell her what I had seen at the stream, about my father and Papa and the other men, but one of the men pointed a gun at me to quiet me. "Stop all that gibberish!" My mother put her hand over my mouth.

While they lined us up, soldiers entered the cabins, dragging tables, chairs, bedding, all that we had outside into a pile. They confiscated any rifles, any guns, anything that could be used for hunting. When they entered the main house, some of them came out with armloads of honey. They threw the jars at the pile, laughing.

When they had gathered all of us, the men pointed us

toward the path that led from our village. Their faces were mean and I was glad that I did not understand all the words they said. They pointed guns at us. They prodded us to move along faster, some of us falling over each other.

We walked along behind them, surrounded by them. Behind us, our homes went up in flames. Red, orange, angry flames, and we could feel the heat behind us as we walked. Afraid to talk, some women and children cried, some fell on the ground begging until we saw one of them whipped for it.

We cried. The bones and dust of our fathers cried with us.

Chapter Thirteen

*I*t was a terrible, hard time and it is a hard story to tell.

We walked until we came upon a wire pen, like something for enclosing animals. At bayonet point, we were shoved inside, people on top of people, crying and wailing. The sound was like cattle bawling, like crying sheep. Soldiers threw us inside. They called the elders foul names, knocking some of them to the dust.

It was more terrible than you could imagine.

Before long, you couldn't tell one of us from another. The soldiers and the men didn't care. Mama Emma was wrong about selling Abraham; the evil came anyway. And when it came, it swept over her just the same as it swept over us.

And the worst was at night. People whispered, choked with weeping. Thinking that they had been planning it all along—people thinking about, making plans to hurt other people—it made the pain worse. They had imagined in their minds gathering us up, burning our homes, putting us in pens. And it seemed like a good idea to them, so they planned it and they did it. And while they were doing it, they still didn't feel any shame.

People cried because they were separated from their loved ones. You could hear them crying, calling out names.

"John, are you here?"

"Mary, my child, where are you?"

"Grandmother! Grandmother! Come to us!"

My mother called for my father, afraid for us to move from the spot where we sat. I thought of the men by the stream, the angry men, and feared that my father was dead. And what of Papa? Maybe he was dead too. Hardest of all was thinking of Abraham, thinking that if Abraham found his way back, he would not be able to find me. Our cabin was gone, the cornfield gone; all that remained was the well. How would The One Who Guards His Family find us?

When dark came, our sleep was fitful. We sat upright, our heads nodding; we jumped at any sound. Like lambs or cows before slaughter, we were anxious, moaning. We were afraid to close our eyes.

Before morning, groups of our men were thrown inside with us. They were bloodied and frightened by the betrayal. They had all been stripped of anything they might have used to defend us, to free us. They were angry at being powerless and angry at being afraid.

But what I saw most was hurt, and shame that they had allowed themselves to be betrayed. Shame that they had trusted, had let themselves be kind to people they shouldn't have trusted.

And that's what you need to remember while I'm telling you this story, many times hurt and shame sound and look just like anger.

There were so many bloody men, it was hard to see or recognize our own. We worried, my mother and I, that my father was not among them, that we would not find him.

Soldiers guarded outside of the fence. They laughed at us, they mocked us. They laughed at the tears we cried. They sat around their fires eating and drinking. They were mean to us—except for one soldier I remember. Out of the eyesight of the others, he passed pieces of bread to us. He whispered to us. I do not know what he said, but there was a sadness in his eyes.

In the pen, I saw others from far away, others of my people who had gathered with us for large celebrations, members of other clans.

Throughout the night, my mother called out to my father. *"Husband! Husband, are you here?"*

Many people never found their loved ones; but late in the night, before daybreak, my father found us. We looked away from the bruises and lumps on his face. We gathered with others we knew, like Johnnie Freeman and his family, and Golden Bear's family.

Most of us, other than crying, were silent. But Golden Bear's father spoke angry words. "They will kill us. We have been betrayed!" The pain had silenced some men, like my father. But it was anger that spoke through Golden Bear's father; it was also that hurt and shame I told you about before.

We shared amongst us the little that we had—pieces of corn bread, some cold biscuits from the kind soldier.

When morning came, the soldiers led us further down the road.

My father and Johnnie Freeman's father were silent, their heads hanging down. Some of the men cried. But Golden Bear's father growled from his belly. "They are taking us to the forts."

By the time we reached Fort Butler, our numbers had swelled as others joined us.

CHAPTER FOURTEEN

THEY REMOVED US. THAT'S WHAT THEY CALLED IT. BUT it was not removal; we were married to the land. They dragged us kicking and screaming at gunpoint from the arms of the land, from the arms of the one we loved. It was all planned; it was all as sure as the rising of the sun. We were stripped from the arms of our beloved, yet they wanted us to sing instead of cry.

It was not just the grown-ups who cried. Where my heart had been was pain. My stomach ached. And like Golden Bear's father, my pain spoke as anger.

I ran at one of the men on horseback, a man who reached with his hand to push the head of one of the elders. "Leave him alone!" Standing in front of the elder, to protect him, I balled my fists at the man on horseback.

I was snatched off my feet!

My father's voice, his arms around me, his face close to me, whispered in my ear. "You must not fight, Armentia! You must be quiet so that we can stay alive!"

My mother and father loved me. How could I question

their wisdom? And so, to stay alive, many of us lost our voices.

One morning they removed us from the pen and we began to walk again. We traveled in a line of sorts, but some traveled close to the front while most clustered somewhere in the middle. The old ones, the feeble, the babies, rode in wagons piled around the supplies and cook pots. But there wasn't room for all the weak ones and some of them fell behind.

As we walked, I noticed the bump of a baby that Johnnie Freeman's mother carried in her belly. His father stayed close to her; he gave her most of his food. It was not long before his ribs were showing. All of us found our ribs, but his showed sooner.

The soldiers would not touch us. They would not handle us with their hands, as though something unclean would rub off on them.

Papa walked with most of us, but Mama Emma often straggled behind. By then, she had lost the jewelry in her ears, her best clothes were muddy and torn. She reminded me of Ephraim, a gray rain cloud over her head.

We settled into a sameness—not enough food, no place to lay our heads except on each other. It was not a sameness of comfort; it was the same because we had no choice. We prayed for rain to wash us and then for sun to dry the ground. And the guards used us for sport. "Sing us one of your songs! Dance for us!"

CHAPTER FIFTEEN

$\mathcal{I}$T WAS A LONG WALK; MANY, MANY DAYS. THE LINE OF people stretched so far I could not see the end. When we stopped at night to make camp, those that arrived first were already making fire before those at the end of the line arrived.

The soldiers, carrying guns, herded us along. They told us we were going to Fort Butler. A place for us to rest, to get refreshed before the move west, they said. It was all good for us, it was all best for us, they said. It was about making our lives better—they had to move us to make our lives better, they said.

Our hearts knew better, but our heads needed to believe what they told us.

There would be food there and warm clothes and wagons for us to ride in, they said. So, the people were glad—or, as glad as you can be about a bad thing. I guess when you're in terrible bad, not so bad seems pretty good.

My father was silent, but not Golden Bear's father. He told us we were fools to believe the lies. We were being blind, he said. He shook with anger. "They are taking us to the fort places I told you of, and many of us will die. It is better to die here, our blood poured out on the land that belongs to us."

Not once on the walk could he find peace. It might have been the Wolf Clan, the warrior in him that could not lie down. I was quiet because my mother and father had warned me. But my heart was with him; my heart wanted to fight.

We were far enough from our homes that the land, though Cherokee land, seemed strange to us. We walked by day and camped by night, the soldiers guarding us to keep us from escaping. As we walked, some of the ones who walked with the soldiers—Red men in uniforms—would go ahead of us to hunt. They brought back birds, sometimes deer or a wild pig, but it was never enough for us to be full to smile. When it was time to camp, the men would cut down a tree to make a fire. My mother and some of the other women would cook. But it was not enough to bring a smile.

A few moons after we started, the sun was on our heads, and I heard a familiar jingling. I looked behind me, but could only see more of my people walking. I turned back to watch the way ahead of me. Then, some of the people behind me began to stir. There was some shouting. When I turned back to see, there was a man on horseback. I squinted my eyes to see.

It was Missionary Wilters. He rode near us, tossing blankets to some of the people. He smiled but I did not see many smile back. I could feel some brief hope among the people, but there were few smiles.

He got down off his horse and walked with us that day, and that night he stayed at camp. He hugged those of us he knew. Some people cried. Some children begged him to help us. He lifted them in his arms and shushed them. He'd brought beans and some measure of corn. So the cooking that night smelled of home. When I closed my eyes, I was almost there; but my heart could not be fooled by my nose.

"I didn't betray you," Missionary Wilters said later as we sat around the fire. "I know you don't believe me."

Golden Bear's father shook his head. "A lie told to the face, even with gifts," he pointed at the food, "is still a lie."

Missionary Wilters's face reddened. "They didn't tell me they were coming. I thought there was still time. They sent me away. I was fooled too. You might not believe me, but God is my judge." Missionary Wilters hung his head. A tear slid down his cheek. "The government is mad with me, too, you know? I don't know what I could have done. I tried. I tried." He wiped his arm across his face. He touched his forehead to the cheek of the child he held. He pointed at the soldiers. "They say it's my fault, that people like me have kept you from going.

"But it's the honest truth. I didn't know." He looked around the fire at all of us. "I want you to stay alive. Go peaceful. We have to believe it will get better."

When we woke at morning, Missionary Wilters was gone. So, we walked alone the rest of the way to Fort Butler, where they promised food, where they promised us the good days would begin.

The corn and beans he brought lasted a few days. While it lasted, we children walked by each other, sometimes chasing each other, sometimes even smiling. It was not like before, but we still worked up a smile from time to time. But not the old ones; their faces were frozen in frowns, in sadness, like the stream frozen in winter.

And Golden Bear's father still walked in anger. He yelled. His feet could find no peace on the road. "They will kill us," he said. "They are murderers! They smell like men who kill for no reason."

He paced back and forth that night.

In the morning, Golden Bear's father was gone. As though he was covered by a cloud, or an eagle's wings, he had gotten past the guards. His spirit had transformed and as a wolf he had sneaked by the soldiers, some of the old ones said. He had escaped into the hills, the people said. And the old ones told stories of other Cherokee people who had hidden away in the mountains, who had escaped the removal, others who would not give up their lands. "He will join them," some of the people said.

For the next days, even after the food was gone, we walked as though we were satisfied. The escape filled our hearts.

The soldiers made us walk faster. They prodded some of the elders with guns. But, still, there were smiles. *Golden Bear's father got away!* The word passed up and down the line. *He is in the mountains now!* The old men walked like young boys. *He will find others and they will come for us.*

The soldiers searched for Golden Bear's father but could not find him, the people whispered. Others talked of slipping away to join him.

The days of Golden Bear's father were good days on the Trail. We laughed and talked by the campfire like people with hope, like people with a home. People patted on Golden Bear and his family, treating them like honored people. "Your father is a great man!" the people said. "The Great Spirit has freed him to rescue us!" they said. Even Golden Bear's mother, always quiet, managed a smile.

Golden Bear, Johnnie Freeman, and I had not talked much since Abraham was taken from us. It had not seemed right to go to the stream, to try to laugh there without him. It was not right for us to make new memories there that might cloud the old ones that included my brother. When we were apart, it was easier not to think about him laughing and running, about the wind, about how beautiful Johnnie Freeman was, and about the water-speckled sunlight on Golden Bear's belly. Those nice thoughts always led us back to the nightmare of his leaving, of his removal.

But at the hope of Golden Bear's father's escape, though the three of us could not stand much to walk together, when no one else was looking, we nodded at each other.

At night, I dreamed that his father had found Abraham and that the two of them ran together. I dreamed that they met by the well, then had gone to the stream to cleanse and pray, and were now on their way back—cleansed and full of power—to rescue us.

One day, when the sun was still high, two of the soldiers who had gone searching rode up at a full gallop. They dragged a cloud of dust behind them.

It was Golden Bear's father.

CHAPTER SIXTEEN

 $\mathcal{T}$ HE HORSEMEN WHO DRAGGED GOLDEN BEAR'S FATHER
pulled even with the line of people and told us to stop. It was
hard to recognize him—what was left of him. He was beaten
and used up. The soldiers forced him to his knees while others
gathered around. Two of them held out his arms like eagle's
wings. While they held him, Golden Bear's father lifted his
hanging head and, though it was hard to understand him, began
to sing one of the old songs, the songs of our people, a song of
victory. He sang like when we lived in our village. He sang like
when we were still held and kissed by the land we loved, except
now the sounds were garbled because of his wounds. The old
women began to sing with him, but it was not the song the
soldiers wanted to hear.

My parents held me close, almost hidden away between
them. I fought to see. I opened my mouth. I wanted to sing. I
wanted to fight.

Right there, in front of us, the soldiers shot Golden Bear's
father.

Three times.

Every time they shot, it was like a punch to my stomach. I opened my mouth to scream, to stop them. But after they shot him, they shot one of the old women who would not stop singing, and held guns to the heads of those who tried to come to her aid. Fear choked me.

I closed my mouth. I buried my face in my mother's skirts. That was the day I learned what happened to people who fought, to people who spoke or sang too loudly. That was the day I lost the courage to be angry.

It was a brave death for his father, but Golden Bear's eyes turned old that day. He never walked with the children again. He stayed close to his mother.

We traveled many more days before we saw the wooden gates of the fort, Fort Butler.

"Inside are good things," they told us as the wooden gates swung open. They promised us food, baths, and shelter. But it was as Golden Bear's father had warned us; it was death.

We were all together in the place. There was no stream, no high bushes, no separate places for men and women. We were all together.

We loved, we ate, we slept, we cried in the smell of it. The blankets they gave, they threw even them into the smell of it.

As the leaves turned colors and fell from the trees, we were still in the smell of it. It was too long in the fort of death.

The babies cried at first. Then many of them died until it was rare to hear a cry, or they gave up—just went to staring at the dark wooden walls.

Many old people died too. It was too hard for them. Their memories called to them and they did not have the courage or strength left to stay with us.

Mama Emma, or what was left of the woman I had called Mama Emma, stayed to herself. She gathered what was left of her best clothes around her and made herself a separate small space on the foul-smelling mud floor. Behind the wooden walls that held us, she made a place that she seemed to imagine was the main house. She would not even let Papa live there, so he stayed with the rest of us.

One night, some soldiers, drunk and holding everyone back with guns, dragged Mama Emma away.

I thought they would kill her. In the distance, I heard her screaming while the soldiers laughed.

Mama Emma came back in the morning, her face bruised, her lips bleeding. She staggered, grabbing her torn skirts around her. She stumbled to her spot, her muddy main house, and collapsed.

Papa went to her and then carried her to lie with the rest of us.

The soldiers came again on other nights, not for Mama Emma, but for other women, and even girls, who sat alone.

They were not real men, these White soldiers. The Red soldiers were not real either. They were evil spirits, poisoned by the little people who lived in the hills, the ones who did bad things. That's what I told myself. That is what I wanted to believe. It made it easier, thinking they were not real.

But as I watched them, I knew it was not true. When they talked to each other, they smiled like real men. They talked like real men. They must be evil men, then, I told myself. But they did not walk like evil men. They walked, talked, and smiled like men who thought they were doing good, like men who thought they were doing right.

It was only when they looked and spoke to us that their faces soured. They frowned like they thought that it was us, my people, that were the evil ones. We were the ones who were not real to them.

My father, Johnnie Freeman's father, and Papa kept all of us close after that. Golden Bear and his family huddled with us and the soldiers stayed away. Together, as a family, was the only way we were safe.

Many of the faces held fear. Others were waiting for death to come. When he was sleeping, I watched Johnnie Freeman's face and tried to remember, to remember the stream, and when things were good. In all the ugly around me, he was still beautiful. He would nod to me, like he remembered too.

Someday, I would marry him.

While we were inside, Johnnie Freeman's mother had the baby. Not in her cabin, or outside in the presence of the Great Spirit with other women attending. She had the baby in the mud and the swill. The women tried to protect and cover her, but with the soldiers looking at us, the mud around and in us, it was hard not to believe that we were the dogs, the animals that they said we were.

She nursed the baby one time, but the baby had come too soon. The baby did not like the fort place and left us. There was no burial ground for the baby or for any of those who died. There was no way to join their bones with those of our fathers.

How could they not care, those who kept us? How could they not weep for us? It must have been because they told themselves we were not like them, we were uncivilized, we were savages. Even in death they owed us no kindness.

So, we used our hands to dig through the dirt, the mud, the human sludge to make a place for Johnnie Freeman's baby brother. We gathered stones to lay, to cover him.

The old women sang a mourning song. Even the littlest children cried.

Some of the women prayed and, at first, my mother would join them, singing. But as more days passed, as the fort began to stink more and more like uncivilized death, my mother no longer joined them. And inside of me I wondered how they could keep praying to one who did not love us, who loved the White man more. He took our land away and gave it to them.

He took our joy, the land of our fathers' bones, and gave it to them. He took Golden Bear's father. He took Abraham, The One Who Guards His Family. If He took so much of us, how could The Principal People believe He loved us?

I only thought the words, but my mother gave them voice. "He has forgotten us," she would whisper some days. "He loves the White man and He has forgotten we are His children," she said. "I will know when I leave here," my mother said. "Either I will die here like a pig in this filth, while other men laugh, and I will know He does not care. Or, He will take me from here, and when I leave, He will show me a sign."

After that she was silent.

I watched her day and night, hardly sleeping. I prayed that if God still heard, He would not take her from me. I was afraid that if I closed my eyes, when I awoke, like Abraham she would be gone.

When the women asked her to sing, she would not speak, only opening her mouth to say what was necessary. It was that way for a long time—my mother without a song, and the woman I had called Mama Emma—the one who owned me—without a smile.

Death walked among us and many of us did not leave that place. Those that we could, we buried there. Each day, two or three died. We held our breath hoping there would be a day without one dying, hoping it would not be us. Sometimes, a day or two would go by with no death. But, then, a day would come when we would have to pay back what we owed—five, six, or seven.

It was every day, but there was no way for our hearts to accept it. We cried as hard for the first as for the last.

I cannot tell you exactly how long we were inside the walls of death, but when they opened the gates for us to leave, the days were shorter and the birds were already gone. It was cold.

The smell of the place, of waste and death, was on us. It was on our clothes and in our hair. We were outside the wooden gates and walls where the air was clean, but we carried the death smell on us.

Every day, I learned more United States words. The soldiers laughed at how we smelled. "Stinking injuns!" they called us, as though we had not wallowed in the mud and sadness they gave us. Some of us, like me, like Johnnie Freeman, they pointed to, laughing, and called us "Niggers! Nigger injuns!" as though it were something even worse. It was a sad way to learn the words of the United States.

New soldiers in clean new uniforms guarded us now. A young lieutenant, McHugh, now led the way.

It was good to leave Fort Butler behind, to know that no more of us would live or die there. None of us would have to wallow there. But, when we had gone a ways and looked back, we saw a long line of people, our people, people like us, walking in the gates we had just left behind.

I held my mother's hand, still afraid she would disappear, afraid that though she had lived through the captivity, she would still sit down now and die. "See, my Mother, we are leaving."

She walked silently.

"See, we are alive." I tried to sing her song for her, the one she loved.

In dat great gittin' up mornin'
Fare you well, fare you well
In dat great gittin' up mornin'
Fare you well, fare you well

But she would not smile.

When we had gone not many steps, my mother stopped. She stared up into a tree and, then, she smiled.

Perched on a branch with no leaves was a spring bird. A red

bird. And it looked at my mother and sang. It sang truth to her.

My mother began to sing in response.

The red bird singing truth was my mother's sign. But, soon, she was given an even greater sign.

Chapter Seventeen

$\mathcal{T}$HE LIEUTENANT LED US TO WATER. IT WAS NOT OUR stream and the weather was cold, but when the lieutenant signaled, we waded in. We rubbed, scrubbing Fort Butler from our hair, from our skin, from what was left of our clothes. He let us stay there until we were clean, those of us still alive.

When we came out of the water, we saw the strangest sight lumbering on the shore—a Red man weighed down with new blankets and the Good Book calling to us.

We had never seen anything like it, my family and me, though some of the people seemed to know Reverend Peter Oganaya, a Cherokee preacher, very well.

As we walked, the preacher moved to the back of the line, bringing the stragglers forward. "Sheep, stay close to the shepherd," we could hear him calling. "Don't get far behind. The wolves grow fat on the ones who fall behind."

"What wolves?" a woman asked. "There are only people here."

"Sometimes men are wolves, sometimes they do not even

know they are. They don't even recognize themselves." The Red missionary nudged her and some others closer to the group.

When he spoke, his voice carrying on the cold wind, my mother smiled. She said God had heard her and that the red bird was a sign of the Red preacher who came to walk with us.

I was happy to see my mother smile; it was like a feast, like new rain. So I did not disagree with her about the missionary. But I believed that Abraham, wherever he was, whispered to that bird to find us, to guard our family, to go ahead of me.

The red bird, the preacher, was the whisper of my brother come home. So I began, secretly, to call the preacher Red Bird.

We were so glad to be in the fresh air that for the first few days, we ignored the cold settling around us. We were willing to suffer the chill in trade for sunshine and sweet air. But pretty soon, we could not ignore the cold's cruel face.

Like when we started out for Fort Butler, we only had so many wagons. They were filled with supplies and some goods of people like Mama Emma and Papa. What room was left was for the old people, the babies and little children, and for the sick to ride. It was hard walking. The ground was cold and hard, it did not give to our feet, and it was rocky. And though the Red Bird had brought blankets, there were not enough and the cold began to set in old and new bones. We thought we had left death behind in the fort, but he followed us, claiming someone every day—there was no time to stop crying.

But I was a child then, and like children, I couldn't stand to be always sad. There was no difference then, just like today children hunger to laugh. So, a bird flying overhead, a crooked stick on the ground, a squirrel running up a tree—they were all excuses for us children not to cry. They were all excuses for us to laugh, or play, or imagine that we were somewhere else.

We played for ourselves, but mostly we played for our mothers.

I tell you there's nothing sadder than seeing your mother cry. When my mother cried, I wondered if things were ever going to be all right again. It was like her heart and the hurt in her heart crawled up right inside of my chest until I couldn't breathe anymore. So, when I was hungry or sad, I tried not to show it. I tried to make her laugh instead. So, I guess, just naturally I sang and skipped when I could find any excuse.

Nothing sadder than the tears of a mother, except for the tears of our fathers, the wetness rolling down their faces. And, no doubt, our mothers and fathers were holding back their own tears from us for as long as they could for the same reason. But the old ones didn't have the strength to pretend, their mouths down, their eyes turned down with pain.

What their faces said was what was true in my heart.

At night when the sky was dark, the moon covered with clouds, I looked at the stars and tried to imagine myself back at home. Most times it was hard and I only ended up crying. Other times, I was there by the crystal stream, standing in the musky forest with my eyes closed, or running through the corn, the stalks brushing my outstretched hands. My feet thudded on the ground as I ran for the well, Abraham's well. Only he wasn't there. When I got to the well and he wasn't there, I cried. It was too much for me and I would be back on the cold ground on the Trail Where We Cried.

It's something I don't wish on anyone, to be put out of your home. You might think the hard thing is leaving stuff behind—the dresses, the baskets, the shoes. You might think that having your guns taken, so that you cannot hunt for food, was the worst. But that is not the worst; it's that sometimes in your sleep you go back there, the place whose rhythm is yours—you breathe like that place, you smell that place, you flow in that place. You go back there and you are whole and at peace again. But then when you wake up, you don't know where you are. Each morning you are taken away again; each morning you must leave the place you love. No matter where you go, you are never home again. The tall grasses are gone, the water, the well. Again your feet leave the places you know. It is new heartbreak every morning.

My feet knew their way there, the place where we lived. They will never know their way again.

Shoes wore out, blankets matted with mud and snow. Mama Emma, the woman who had been my Mama Emma, kept herself away from us, as she had in the fort. She stayed away, like if she touched us she would get something on her.

"She's gone crazy trying to save herself," my mother said. "If she walks away from us, she thinks they will treat her differently. She won't stink like one of us. She thinks she will survive." Instead, she looked lost and alone.

In those days, walking the Trail, we passed over much ground. Sometimes, we passed by the farms of people, Cherokee people—mixed bloods pale like White men, and even some who were brown like us. They talked to the White man in his language. They pretended they did not know us, that they had not eaten and danced with us, that we did not know the same mountains. "We are Black Irish," some of them told the soldiers. "We are Black Dutch." They grinned and pointed at us like we were strangers. They were trying to save themselves, even through lying and shame, and to hold to the land of our fathers. It made our spirits low, but we said nothing. Who can hate his brother for trying to live?

The Red Bird, the missionary, herded us together. "Stay together, my little flock. The wolf will eat the ones who stray, the ones who stand apart." He smiled at us, snow frosting his broad-brimmed black hat and shoulders. "Stay close, stay warm, and live!"

He nodded at me and my mother as he passed us by. "He who has an ear, let him hear!"

One day, in the cold, the woman who had been my Mama

Emma stumbled. Papa went to her, lifting her, but she fell again—her face flushed, her eyelids fluttering to show the whites.

The Red Bird, his feet pounding through the cold, white powder, ran to reach her and to lift her onto one of the supply wagons, now almost empty of supplies. There were only empty pots and some other of Mama Emma's things. Younger children, wrapped in blankets, teeth chattering, noses making yellow water, crowded together on the wagon. "Make room for her," Red Bird told the children. Wiping their noses, they scampered to the back.

Red Bird touched her face, brushed her hair from where it clung to her wet forehead. He peeled the muddy wet blanket off of her and motioned to the children. "Come. You cover her." Like pieces of human fabric, the children gathered around her, lifting their blankets to include her, pressing and draping their bodies over hers. "Be her blanket," Red Bird said.

Mama Emma and the children rode and slept that way for many, many days.

Things never got better on the Trail. It might make the story easier for some folks to hear, but it wouldn't be the truth, and only the truth will make us free.

When the old ones died along the way—the ones who remembered who we used to be before we changed our clothes and our lives to be accepted by others—we tried to bury them in the old way. Then as more died, we carried them along with us—sometimes twelve, fourteen, sixteen frozen and piled on a wagon—and buried them when we could find a place. Then, as it got worse, they forced us to bury them in mass graves. But the further we traveled, most times the ground was too cold to bury them and there was no time to say the special prayers or sing the special songs. Because of the cold, the graves got shallower and shallower, then we gathered stones to cover them. As more died and the days grew colder, the soldiers complained about the time we were taking to bury our dead.

We could not give them burials that honored them. As we walked away, leaving them behind, some of the women would sing.

Ooh nay thla nah, hee oo way gee'.
E gah gwoo yah hay ee.
Naw gwoo joe sah, we you low say,
E gah gwo yah ho nah.

It was all that we could do for them. We sang the song to soothe us as we continued up the road.

More White missionaries came to walk with us for a time, here and there, even when the cold was most bitter. They would bring things to us, some food, a few articles of dry clothing—some even stopped to look into our eyes and cry with us—but they did not stay long.

Reverend Jesse Bushyhead, another Cherokee preacher, passed by us one day. Wearing a turban on his head, he led a group of people. He stopped, he and the Red Bird embracing, and prayed with us and then continued on his way.

But our missionary, our Red Bird, Reverend Oganaya walked all the way with us. When snow came and cold made wetness run from our eyes and thick water from our noses, it came from his eyes and nose too. When winter made our feet bleed, his feet bled too. When some of us straggled behind, he came for us. "Come on, little sheep," he called in the frozen air. "Stay close," he reminded us. "The wolves are near and they are hungry." He waved the stragglers forward.

"Why are you with us?" some would ask.

"The good shepherd lays down his life for his sheep. He who has an ear, let him hear!"

He sang with us at night when we made camp and he told us stories as he passed among us serving us food and bandaging our wounds. "The one who does not serve, he is not a shepherd. The one who takes and does not give, he is a wolf. Be gentle lambs, but be wise and discerning so that you will know the true shepherd's voice. He who has an ear, let him hear!"

CHAPTER EIGHTEEN

WHEN THE MOUNTAINS WE KNEW AND THE TREES WE knew faded into the road behind us, when we camped beside foreign waters, he was still there. Though my mother was stooped against the cold, because of the Red Bird she walked straighter. "The Great One is with us. He walks this trail with us," he said.

Golden Bear, who growled more since the murder of his father, answered him. "How can the White god be with us and not with them?"

The Red Bird smiled at him. "He is with all of us. He walks with all of us. When we are first, He walks with us. But He holds the hands of the poor and the last. He sings songs to the brokenhearted." He touched the top of Golden Bear's head. "And He is not the White god. He is the Great Spirit. You know that."

"But they say He is their god. They say He gives them the land of our fathers." Golden Bear spoke the doubts that were hidden in my heart.

"He does not give; men steal. Men have stolen long before we were born. Those that steal make up excuses to steal; color, language, dress are just excuses."

"But they say He is theirs," Golden Bear persisted. "They show us pictures of Him that look like them."

The Red Bird laughed again. "The wise—no matter their color or language—know better. The wise know that God is the Great Spirit and they know that the Son of God is like the beryl stone—He reflects the beauty of those who come to Him. So He is all colors. Those who steal will steal anything—those who need to steal to make themselves whole—they will even try to steal Christ. Still, it is not so. No man can steal what cannot be stolen, what belongs to everyone."

As he spoke, I thought about the soldiers who laughed at us. "Vermin! Lice!" they called us. They called us, the children, nits. "Nits make lice," they joked.

"But they laugh at us. They call us names. They want us to sing to them!" The words raced up from my heart, from my belly, and poured from my mouth. "They want us to sing to them!" The taste was bitter on my tongue.

They wanted us to smile with them while they lied to us. They wanted us to be happy that we were being carried away. They wanted us to forget our home. We walked away from the waters we knew, bound for Indian Territory, bound for the west side of the Mississippi River, for strange waters. We soaked the path we walked with our tears.

Yes, we wept over the death, the cold, the hunger. But what made us cry most, what made Golden Bear's father willing to lose his life, was about secrets.

When a man or a woman steals your cow, somehow it helps the pain to be able to say, "I was done wrong." You still got a loss, but it makes it better when the people around you nod and say, "Yes, you've been done wrong." You been hurt, you got a wound, but somehow being able to cry about it and having people say, "Yes, it happened," . . . in some kind of way it helps the sting of the thing go away.

But when you get injured and folks want to pretend it didn't happen, want to bury it and hush it up—well, now, that just makes the thing worse. When you see them steal the cow right in front of your face and then they say they didn't do it, or it's for your own good that they stole the cow—well, I tell you, that's some bitter medicine that won't make you well. It's even worse when they want you to pretend it didn't happen, so they won't feel bad about stealing your cow from you, when they don't want you to cry so they won't feel guilty, so they can hide it from the Lord.

Now, that's just crazy, and crazy will make you cry. It's like the soul on the inside of you, the spirit on the inside of you be crying out to the Great Spirit. You can't even help yourself. So, those tears just keep falling, falling, falling down.

"When one, two, or many hurt you," Red Bird said, "it is hard to be strong and remember that it is not all of them who hurt you."

I remember so clearly, Red Bird told us to dry our eyes.

When we came to the Mississippi River, it was not our water. It was black and wide. They told us we would have to cross on ferries, a few at a time. So, we camped in the cold, in the snow and the ice, at the frozen water's edge. Many died there—some from sickness, some fell into the frozen waters. We cried, thinking we would all die there, thinking we would never be home again.

"The Great Spirit knew you would walk this trail, He knew you would cry many tears, just like those who walked trails before you." Red Bird walked among us, some of us huddled together waiting to cross. Some lay on the cold, wet ground. Waiting. Many wished to die, thinking that would be better. Red Bird told us we had to survive. "The Breath Giver and the ones who walked before you, whose bones have been left on trails away from the places they loved, who have cried until the road ran with tears—they know. They cry an ancient song with you, and God hears." Then he sang words to us.

> By the rivers of Babylon, there we sat down,
> yea, we wept, when we remembered Zion.
> We hanged our harps upon the willows in the midst thereof.
> For there they that carried us away captive required of us a song;
> and they that wasted us, that plundered us, required of us mirth,
>   saying,
> Sing us one of the songs of Zion.

He sang the song to us for many days, for it took a long time for us to cross over. Many died waiting on both sides of the Mississippi. But Red Bird kept telling us, "He who has an ear, let him hear!"

Red Bird kept singing even when the river was far behind us.

Back then, I heard the words, but I did not understand. Many years passed before I did.

Way back then the Lord brought them back, those other people that were carried away, who were taken from the land they knew. He gave them a new song.

> When the LORD turned again the captivity of Zion, we were like
>   them that dream.
> Then was our mouth filled with laughter,
> and our tongue with singing: then said they among the heathen, The
>   LORD hath done great things for them.
> The LORD hath done great things for us; whereof we are glad.
> Turn again our captivity, O LORD, as the streams in the south.
> They that sow in tears shall reap in joy.
> He that goeth forth and weepeth, bearing precious seed, shall doubt-
>   less come again with rejoicing, bringing his sheaves with him.

The Breath Giver brought those people back singing a new song. He brought them back reaping and rejoicing. Truth be told, I'm an old woman, but I'm still believing that day is going to come.

CHAPTER NINETEEN

It was the way of our people to honor the dead, to bury them in caves, in mounds, or piling on rocks. But I told you that was not always the way on the Trail. The snow came down hard; sometimes the ground was frozen so it wouldn't even yield to a pickax. There weren't always rocks. The days were short. Hands froze in the cold. The lieutenant hung his head at first, then his face turned like stone. There was no time, he said. The soldiers took our loved ones and dragged them away. It is a shame to tell, but we left some of them there along the Trail—their frozen bodies at the edge of the woods, snow catching in the corners of their mouths.

This is shameful to tell, but it's true. I've been trying not to tell you. No one wants to tell.

We lost too many people.

We lost too many people to count. We even lost Johnnie Freeman.

It is hard to tell this part of the story. So, I beg your pardon for taking so long, for crying. It's been a whole lot of years, but it's still just the same for me.

I would tell the story without it, but it wouldn't be the truth without it. Even the most painful parts must be told.

You see, the shoes my sweet Johnnie Freeman wore weren't meant for walking long trails, for walking so far. They wore out somewhere along the way. All of our shoes, those that had them, wore out. But it didn't fare well for him.

My sweetheart cut his foot. Just a little old cut. Because of the cold, we all had stinging toes and fingers. Then burning feet, then numb feet. We all had cuts. We all had bleeding feet. We all had bruises. His was so tiny, just a prick.

They tried to take care of it as much as they could, I reckon. When people are working so hard to live, a little cut doesn't seem like much. But soon his foot, then his leg swole up and turned dark and rough like a tree, not his beautiful black color.

By then, my sweet Johnnie Freeman was riding on one of the wagons like the old people and the littlest children. When I could, I walked alongside him and talked to him. Talked to him like it was before.

When no one was looking, I stole a kiss from his berry-colored lips.

I even whispered to Johnnie Freeman that I loved him and that when he got well I was going to marry him, hoping that would make him want to stay. But I think by then, he was already gone—he'd gone back to the stream we knew, back to the well.

He couldn't keep his eyes open and when they did fly open, wasn't nothing there but white. My poor Johnnie Freeman had to fight so hard to breathe, his chest heaving and making rattling sounds. My mother and father pulled me away from the wagon then. Just his father and mother—her arms empty from the too-soon baby she had already lost—continued to walk there.

Then sweet, beautiful, black Johnnie Freeman was gone.

Johnnie Freeman was one of the ones it was too cold to bury. It wasn't something his mother or father or anyone should have to see. I shouldn't have had to see it.

Such a beautiful boy covered by the snow, my first promise buried in white before his time. That death did something to me. Yes, it did; even to this very day.

I cried when they took Abraham until I thought I would never cry again. When Golden Bear's father died, most of the people wept hot tears. Out of respect, I wailed, but I had no real tears. My well was dry. But I cried again when the baby died in the fort until my tears were gone again. But seeing my Johnnie Freeman there, frozen, not my husband-to-be, but some left-behind thing, it surprised me when the tears came again. No sound, but like water twisted from inside me. After that, there really was no more. Not even for my father.

"Little lamb gone to see Jesus," Red Bird sang as we walked away from sweet Johnnie Freeman.

I watched him, lying there as we walked away, for as long as I could.

"Jesus, make a soft white blanket for a sweet Black boy," the missionary sang.

I don't know if it was the cold or what I had seen, but I was numb until we stepped into Indian Territory. I just held my mother's hand and let her lead me the rest of the way.

PART II

"*Cherokee men, women, and children, including one thousand six hundred Black Cherokees, were prodded westward by Federal bayonets. About ten thousand survived, but President Van Buren assured Congress that their expulsion 'had the happiest effects. . . . The Cherokees have emigrated without apparent reluctance.'*"

—WILLIAM LOREN KATZ,
historian, *Black Indians: a Hidden Heritage*

CHAPTER TWENTY

$\mathcal{W}$E WALKED ONE THOUSAND MILES. MAYBE ONE OUT OF every four of us died. It was hard to find a family that didn't lose at least one. It is a miracle that most of us made it. Though some families were separated and never found their missing loved ones, lost children. Walking, in the dead of winter, from what's now North Carolina, through Tennessee, up through parts of Kentucky, then through southern Illinois into Missouri, down through Arkansas and on into Oklahoma. It takes your breath away just trying to say all that, let alone walk it.

Some people got cars today and still can't go that far. But there we all were: farmers, teachers, preachers, lawyers, children, hunters, elders—all covered with blood, mud, and sorrow.

Because they saw us all the same, they gathered us together in that one place: Cherokee, Comanche, Blackfoot, Shawnee, and many others—some of us who had been enemies except for space—and could not understand that, like White men, we did not all get along, did not all have the same ways. So, pressed together, far from our homes, there was a lot of fighting among us. There was not room to hunt, to gather, so there was fighting and many people died. But that is not my story. That is a tale— the story of us fighting one another—for someone else to tell.

The soldiers laughed and yelled when we reached Indian Territory. How they knew it was the place, I don't know. There was no line across the road. Nothing said it was a better land for us than the land we left—no houses there, no place that was our own. Except, there were some of our people already there, the Old Settlers. They came west before the New Echota Treaty, hoping to flee the White man.

And the ones who made the agreement with President Jackson also came before us. They came when the order first came for us to leave our home, my father said. They betrayed our people at New Echota, Golden Bear's father had said. Twenty men, men who were not our leaders, had signed away our lands. Others said the twenty men, the Treaty men, had no choice, that they and the others who followed them had done what they thought best.

We had nothing, those of us who had held out in the East, but some of them had already built houses. They had fancy wood houses and much land. Some of them even had brick houses with fires burning inside. It was hard, with our stomachs hungry, not to be angry, not to be jealous, not to hate them when they smiled at us with their faces fat and clean, as though their agreement had not ruined our lives. It was hard not to hate the ones—even though we had the same blood, the same ances- tors, even though we were all Aniyunwiya—who came before us. It was hard not to blame them for my Abraham.

The truth is, the Trail didn't just separate us from the land we loved; it split us apart from one another.

Though we were all together in that place, the Trail Where

We Cried was like a line, some kind of fence between us that separated our people.

It didn't matter what was said, not even that some believed that moving west was best for us. People had too much heartache, loss, and tears. It does not seem right, but maybe sorrow and anger was all we had left of where we had been, souvenirs of our life before. It was hard to let it go.

When we stepped into Indian Territory, Mama Emma and Papa looked just like the rest of us—their best blankets dragged through the mud, the designs gone. They were thin, hair matted, clothes torn.

When we got there, Mama Emma struggled out of the wagon. Leaving the babies that had saved her, she collapsed into the arms of her relatives that had come ahead. She and Papa stepped onto the red Indian Territory clay looking like us. But, it wasn't long before they separated themselves from us, though that was just the beginning of the separating. Safe now, they found others like themselves and put on new clothes.

They took hot baths in a fancy house in town, in Tahlequah, changed their clothes, and combed their hair.

She looked like the Mama Emma I knew before trouble came, even better in a gown made with shiny material. Someone said it came from a place faraway called New York.

Mama Emma made certain that water was heated for us to wash ourselves. She made certain that we had hot food to eat, she made certain we had shelter in a cabin, but she did not invite us inside the fancy house.

In the days that followed, the Red Bird left us. *"Yigaquu osaniyu adanvto adadoligi nigohilvi nasquv utloyasdi nihi!* May the Great Spirit's Blessings always be with you," he said. He had to leave to show others the way, he said. "The Lord walks with me," he said. *"Wakan Tankan Nici Un!* May the Great Spirit Walk with you!" he said as he left us.

It was not our land. The trees were not ours. But when the snow was gone and the green came again, we began to build again—to build a small wooden cabin for us, to build a larger house of wood and bricks for Mama Emma and Papa.

Summers came and went. The wound of our removal covered over with a thin, weak scab. The sun was still with us, the moon, and the stars. Along with Mama Emma and Papa, and others they owned, we had settled into a valley that was a day's walk from Tahlequah.

At the edge of the new valley, along the path to town, was a well. It was not like our old well, but it was deep—though the water was not as clear. And, though it was not mine, when I took my wooden bucket to draw there, I called it Abraham's Well.

My mother continued weaving and cooking, though she was not allowed in the big house. My father tended the horses, but the balance of the sunlight he spent in the fields. There were fences now, and more and more I heard Mama Emma and Papa calling us "field hands" and "slaves." Less and less of the land was owned in common, less and less was shared. Now we grew many cotton plants along with the corn, bent backs and scarred hands. The cotton, picked by bleeding fingers, was carded with the wool. The best cotton made fancy dresses and suits for those who had the most. Wool and cotton were blended for jeans. The coarsest cloth was for those who worked hardest.

Mama Emma and Papa dressed fancy. They went to church at the new brick building. They lived in a brick house and, though it was not the largest, they had plans to make it bigger. They socialized with mixed breeds and pure bloods, but kept their distance from us, from the dark part of their family. It was not just Mama Emma and Papa. There were others who pulled away.

"If they step apart, they think they will live. No one will know who they are," my mother said. She told me not to be angry, not to be hurt. "They still try to save themselves."

I had lost my voice on the Trail, but I was still angry. I was still hurt and shamed. Mama Emma was further away than when she even first began to get sick. Though it was bad to lose our home, it was worse to lose our home in our family's heart.

In our cabin, by the firelight, my father painted all his hopes on me.

"Watch your mother," he would tell me. "She is a good wife, a beautiful wife."

My mother would smile at him as she worked.

"One day you will marry a man, a man with a brick house," my father told me. He would look around. "Not like this one. And you will have a big wedding, with many blankets, with big food, and relatives from all over. You will be a beautiful maiden." He pointed at my bucket. "We will own land of our own. You will not carry the water. You will own the well."

My mother would sit quietly, mending our socks, while my father, who never spoke, poured his heart out to me.

"You will own land that you will pass down to your children, in the old way. We are building schools here, and you will learn to read. There will be more churches. Maybe I will help build the one in which you will marry." Indian Territory was not the place of our fathers' bones. We had lost Abraham, and all that we knew. But my father was determined that we would have good lives. Our new beginning would start with me.

So, he helped—somehow finding time to make the walk and work there—to build the new city. My mother went with him sometimes and cooked for the workers while my father set posts, painted, and did all he could to invest in the new life, in my family's future.

Indian Territory was to be our new home, the place where we could live free as we wanted.

But it was not. The United States, the White men who wanted no one to hinder their freedom, stayed among us. They counted us, put our names on rolls; and they began even to lick their lips at the new land.

Many said they could see it coming, a day when men would even take Indian Territory, but my father was a man of peace. He did not want to hear the words. He chose not to see things in front of him. He drowned his heartaches in hope for me.

CHAPTER TWENTY-ONE

I TOLD YOU THAT THE STORY ABOUT FIGHTING AMONG our people was someone else's story to tell.

But, no, that's not right, is it? I promised *I* would tell the *whole* truth, even if it hurt. The truth is that there was fighting and anger among us.

You see, the land that we were promised belonged to another people; it was not the property of the United States to give. The land the White man promised us already belonged to the plains Indians, like the Ute, Comanche, Apache, and Kiowa. Those great people had their own customs and beliefs and had lived there for generations. It was the place of their fathers' bones. It was the place where they had hunted bison, chasing the great creatures over rolling, open hills of green, mixed grasses. They knew the land. The red earth was theirs.

But it was traded to us against their will.

It's just pure crazy to me. Imagine someone forcing you from your home, the place you've lived and raised your children, where you've planted corn and picked wild blue flowers. After that someone you don't know forces you from your home to a place you don't know, they move strangers into your place—strangers that don't know how the water flows, how the seasons change, who don't have your history, who don't speak to your home or land as you did. The someone, the crazy strangers, do all this because they want land that is not theirs. Sounds like craziness, doesn't it?

Oh, it was a messy, messy business; all of us caught in the middle of it. As you can imagine, the plains people didn't sit horses with any of us over the whole matter. All sides hurt, angry, and betrayed, we took our anger out on one another. It was easier, I guess, to fight one another than to fight the one that was controlling us.

Truth was, it wasn't just hurt feelings—not just someone troubled by a pinched toe—there was blood drawn and lives lost. And blood betrayal demands a sacrifice, a price. Many times that price was paid by innocent blood—some Cherokee farmer, some Ute hunter, trying to feed their families, or some woman and child that wandered into a place of anger.

United States soldiers had to try to keep all that anger bottled up so it didn't spill over the border. They called us savages, in part, I guess, because of the fighting. We were angry and uncivilized, they said.

There was much blood spilt on ground that was already red.

But the fight was not just one group against another—plains Indians against those of us from the East; we also fought each other.

The bad feelings between the Old Settlers and the Treaty men, against the full bloods, only got worse and worse. The Old Settlers were those of our people that came in the early 1830s, giving up on trying to keep our land. The Treaty men were the ones who signed the New Echota Treaty in 1835 in favor of our removal. Instead of choosing each other, people chose sides, and we—those of us who were slaves—just seemed caught in the middle. It was vicious business. Like I said, it was blood business.

Not long after we arrived, amidst the building and planning, the Treaty Party leaders paid a price. Elias Boudinot, the editor of the *Cherokee Phoenix* newspaper, was killed by a group of full bloods. That same day, or thereabouts, Major Ridge and his son John Ridge, two other Treaty Party leaders, were killed. Some said it happened in front of their families—stabbings and shootings. Some said they were stomped to death. It was the price they had to pay for betrayal, some people said. The only major Treaty leader to survive was Stand Watie. The Treaty men blamed Chief John Ross and the men of the Eastern Band for the murders.

Like I said, people chose sides, and Mama Emma and Papa, who were mixed breeds, chose sides with the Treaty Party. The full bloods and mixed breeds fought against each other, attacking each other. They burned houses, freed animals from pens or killed them, and it wasn't much better for us.

In all the confusion, the ones that were against removal, who believed in the old ways, who were against slavery, sometimes attacked us to hurt those who owned us.

There were many stories about beatings, about killings. Swollen bodies found along the roadside.

At the same time, we were helpless against Treaty Party men who threatened us for thoughts we might have about freedom.

It was a dangerous place. It was a messy, messy business.

But, my father drowned his heartache in hope.

CHAPTER TWENTY-TWO

ᴀɴᴅ ʏᴇᴛ ᴍʏ ꜰᴀᴛʜᴇʀ, ꜱᴛɪʟʟ ɢʀᴀʏ-ʜᴀɪʀᴇᴅ ꜱɪɴᴄᴇ Aʙʀᴀ-
ham's beating, worked and built and worked and built, and
talked to me by candlelight. "You will own land," he told me.
"You will own the well," he said.

"Look at how this place is coming along!" Papa, holding a
lantern above his head, stepped into our cabin doorway one
night. Papa never came inside to see us anymore. My mother
stopped spinning to turn and look at him. My father stopped
talking to me to look at him. Papa nodded to my father and
mother, but did not look at me. He spoke to my father. "You
have done well, here. All the men talk of it, how you sacrifice
your time and all that you have to build the new town here." .
It was strange to see him there, especially at night. "No one
would think you are a slave."

Slave? The word hurt, the word humiliated.

"You work like you are one of The People."

"I am one of The People." My father's face was still, but I

124

felt his hurt and saw the pain in his eyes. "I hope for good here," my father answered.

My mother said nothing, her lips pressed tight together.

Papa looked around our cabin again. "Good roof, good walls." He touched the rough wooden boards. "I hope to get the main house finished soon as well. To finish the expansion."

My father nodded. "When there is more brick."

"I think that will be soon." Papa nodded good night. "Keep up the good work. You and your wife work hard. Everyone sees that you are good." He left as quickly as he'd come.

All night, in the darkness, I tried to remember each word that Papa had said. I heard them over and over in my mind, I saw him standing in our cabin. Though there didn't seem to be anything special about what he had said, I was troubled. His visit had meant something, his words had meant something, but try as hard as I could, I could not figure it out.

Early the next morning, Papa called us outside. The sun was just waking, so we had on our sleep clothes. My doll dangled from my hand.

There was a wagon in front of our door. A man in fancy clothes, like Papa, stood beside him. A slave held the reins of the horse.

Papa pointed at me. "There she is." He looked at the man in fancy clothes. "Her name is Armentia." He nodded to me. "Come here so that he can see you."

I did not want to move, but I walked toward Papa and the man, sneaking quick glances back at my mother and my father. What choice did I have? Four men had come from behind our cabin, and they now stood near my parents. The four men looked as though they might hurt my parents.

My father clenched and unclenched his fists, like the muscles in his jaw. When he took one step toward me, the four men stepped closer to him. My father began to pant, looking between me and Papa, but his feet stopped moving as though they were in chains. He breathed hard, his eyes squinted and then grew large like a bear about to protect its cub, as though he did not want me to go near Papa and the man in fancy clothes. But what choice did he have? What choice did my family have? Our lives were not our own.

The man in fancy clothes walked around me in a circle.

"I told you she was pretty. Sturdy too."

"But will she be able to bear children?"

Bearing children? Children were for marriage, for after the ceremony. Marriage was for women; I was still a girl. I looked back at my mother and father. Not sure of what was happening, I wanted to run. But to protect my family, I forced my feet to be still. It got harder and harder to breathe while the men spoke.

"Her mother bore two."

"But is she old enough?"

"She's old enough."

My father didn't speak then. But he ran for me. Two of the four men grabbed at his arms.

It was like a dream, like swimming in the honey, only I knew it wasn't good.

My mother began to wail. "Not my baby! You took Abraham! You already took Abraham!" She fought her way loose from the two men that grabbed her. "She's not old enough! She's not a woman!" The men grabbed her again.

My father began to scream, not words, but sounds, like some animals when they are threatened. His eyes were wild. He jerked free, took two steps, reaching for me, then the men were on him again.

"I don't want trouble," the man in fancy clothes said, looking at my father.

"There won't be any." Papa nodded at one of the men who held my father. The man drew a gun from out of his belt.

I looked into my father's eyes, heard him still screaming.

When the gunman hit my father with the butt of the pistol, I saw his eyes close as he fell.

My mother still howled. She turned between the two of us, my father and me, as though she did not know who to save. But she kept screaming, "You already took Abraham. Leave my baby! She's just a baby!"

I dropped my doll as the man scooped me up and put me in the back of his wagon. He sat high on the seat in front of me. They did not tie me, but my hands and feet were bound by the things I had seen on the Trail. My mouth was silenced by the death of Golden Bear's father. So, I was quiet and I did not run as we bumped along down the road that led past the new well that I called Abraham's. When we were out of sight, I could still hear my mother's call.

Though I would have liked to say good-bye, I am glad my father slept and could not see me. I was glad his closed eyes could not see his hope ride off in shame.

As we bumped along, when we were near Abraham's Well, I thought again of running. I remembered Abraham calling to me. "Run, Armentia! Run!" But the cruel walk, the strangeness of the new land, would not let me move.

The man looked back at me, smiling. "Now, don't you jump off this wagon, girl. You got work to do. I just paid a whole lot of money for you." The man touched the rifle on the seat next to him. "And it would be a shame to pay so much and then see you get shot."

So, I sat there and stared at the ground all the way to the man's farm.

Yes, I was glad my father didn't see all his dreams riding in an old wagon, all covered in red dust that flew everywhere.

As I rode, I thought again about the slave Ephraim, about beatings and chains.

127

I found out later that the man that bought me, Master Will Cauley, was Papa's distant cousin. My sale brought Mama Emma and Papa just enough money for bricks to finish their house.

CHAPTER TWENTY-THREE

THE MAN WHO BOUGHT ME, MASTER CAULEY, HAD A BIG-
ger farm than Papa's, a plantation. It was bigger than anything I
had ever seen fenced in by White men. When I arrived there,
some slave women—women who reminded me of Ephraim—
settled me in a tiny shack of my own, not much more than a
dusty room.

"Look at this one," one of the women said. She pinched my
side. "How is she supposed to have children? Ain't much more
than a baby herself."

The other woman shook her head. "Probably not much
more than ten or eleven."

"What you know, gal?" The first woman looked at me.

"Nothing," the second woman answered. She touched my
hair and smiled at me. "Sure is pretty, though."

The second woman was right. I didn't know anything, just
that I was away from my father and mother, and that, again, I
had lost my home. And I knew that they were right; babies
were for grown married women.

"Well, you just close your eyes and think about something else. Don't frown, don't make no noise." The first woman put her hands on my shoulders and looked in my eyes.

The second woman sighed. "I don't 'spect you old enough to have no baby. Your time ain't come." She pinched me as the first woman had. "If you do, you and the baby will probably die," she said matter-of-factly. "Either way, you probably ain't got long to be here."

Babies? Close my eyes? What was this new place, even stranger than the last?

Since Master Cauley told me he would shoot me if I jumped from the wagon, I had expected chains. I expected to hear the sound of a whip, to feel it on my back. The beating I expected did not come. Truth is, there weren't any beatings at all while I was there.

But he was stern about everyone working. Everybody, even the littlest children, was up at dawn planting and picking, and working until sunset. Even the little children dragged gunny sacks through the fields picking whatever was in season.

He was a hard worker too, always in the fields. His hobby, they said, was tending bees. Well, not really tending them, but charming them out of their honey. Folks said he could see a hive anywhere and walk away with just about all the honey the bees had to give.

They told me there was a queen bee in every hive, just there to lay eggs, to make more bees. That honey was the sweetness in the worker bees' lives, they said.

But Master Cauley could get it away from them with due ease. He took their honey and the bees wouldn't even buzz, wouldn't say a word. Nobody ever saw him do it, but he came back with the proof—lots of honey. And he was generous with it, even bringing a jar to be shared amongst the slaves.

But that was no benefit to me because, as you know, me

and honey didn't sit horses by then.

There were lots of slaves at the plantation. Most of them, I would find out, had come from or were the children of those who had come from Africa. The United States words they taught me were flavored by their home across the big waters.

As I had been fascinated with Ephraim, they were just as fascinated with me. Some of the children would gather around; they would touch my hair. "Why you talk so funny? Where you from?"

"She is a Indian," one would say.

"No she not. She black as us."

"She black as some of us, but she shore ain't black as your people," another would mock, laughing.

"If you Indian, say something."

When I spoke, they laughed and pointed, not bad, but like I was a strange sight—like a red bird on a winter's day.

Some of the people, looking around to make certain no one overheard, whispered words from their native land. It was forbidden to speak the language of their fathers; they could be beaten or hanged. So, they whispered the words, trying hard not to forget. They had been taken away from their homes too, they told me. Their parents had been taken away, and they wondered, like me, if their mothers and grandmothers were crying for them.

"Pretty hair," they would say, touching me.

"Her hair is like Miss Lula and Miss Bertha Bell's children," they said, referring to the women who had settled me in when I first arrived. "She got hair like their children, though she ain't so light-skinned as them."

"Hush, now," one of the grown-ups would interrupt. "Don't let your mouth get you in trouble."

I was a curiosity. "You 'most black as me," someone might say to me. "Ain't much difference but your hair. How you know that Indian talk, again?"

"I told you that I'm Cherokee."

Usually, the person laughed. "You just a nigger, like me." The person would hug me and then go back to shelling peas, snapping beans, or whatever she was doing.

They treated me as a welcomed stranger.

There was always food to eat. There was even no work, just church, on Sundays.

Not far before the entrance to the plantation, there was a white wooden building with a steeple. On Sundays, the White people dressed up to go inside. There was singing, reading, and preaching like it was with the missionaries during the days before we were removed.

Each Sunday, though we could not go inside, we were allowed to stand outside, or sit on the grass, and listen. And when the folks inside objected, sometime later, saying we shouldn't be there, Master Cauley, who hardly ever went to church himself, told us he would make us a place of our own.

He kept his word too. He set aside a place for us down in a hollow where there was a grove of trees. He told some of the men to cut down some trees for logs and make them with flat bottoms—pews he called them—that we could sit on. Another one of the trees, he himself cut halfway. "There's your preachin' stand," he said. So, there was a stand but no Bible, because none of us could read—or no one could admit that he or she could read. Preaching John did the best he could, preaching parts he remembered from hearing others and preaching parts from songs.

Though Master Cauley stayed at a distance, on Sundays he was more likely to walk or ride by where we were churching than to go to the fancy white wooden church.

So, every Sunday we went down to the grove. I didn't say much, just sometimes clapped my hands. But it was good to be there; something about meeting that way reminded me of home. It was good to have a day to try to sing and pray our way out of the sad.

Preaching John was one of the older slaves. Though he was older and black, with gray hair, his stomach reminded me of Golden Bear's. "Why don't you come and join us? You welcome," Preaching John would yell at Master Cauley as he rode by on his black mare.

"No. No, I don't believe much in church. At least not much in a god that would have somebody like me." He would laugh, looking down at Preaching John. "But for certain, what you're doing down here is much more entertaining than what's happening up there!" He pointed toward the church outside his gate.

Master Cauley laughed like he thought it was all so silly. But what was more silly to me was why he kept riding past over and over, like he wanted to join us, but never stopping.

"One day, the Lord going to grab ahold of that man!" Preaching John said it over and over again. "One day, the Spirit is going to get him in His grip!"

It took a while, but, sure enough, it looked like "one day" came!

CHAPTER TWENTY-FOUR

𝒯HE SINGING WAS SO FINE THAT SUNDAY. IT WAS MIGHTY good! Lord, I tell you!

Preaching John was at his finest! He looked at us gathered there, a kind of smiling frown on his face. The smile, I guess, was to show us how much joy he had. The frown was to let us know that he was serious, that Jesus was serious business. He stood behind the stand, one hand smoothing his gunnysack shirt down over his belly.

"On Christ the solid Rock I stand. All other ground is sinking sand! All other ground is sinking sand!" He belted the words out. "What else do we have to lean on but the solid Rock? Who else can we trust?" The more excited he got, the faster he rubbed his belly. "We can't trust Mother; we don't know if she'll be here tomorrow. We can't trust Father; we don't know if he'll be around. But we know that Christ—ah, Christ is the solid Rock on which we stand!" I couldn't help but think of my own family—my family so far away.

Preaching John was rubbing and rubbing. The more he

134

rubbed, the more he yelled, and the more excited we all got! "My hope is built on nothing less than Jesus' blood and righteousness." He delivered the words in a rhyming kind of way, his voice rising like a mountain, then crashing to the valley below. "I dare not trust the sweetest frame, but wholly trust in Jesus' name!"

People were standing to their feet! We understood that feeling—having nothing to trust, not knowing where you will be from moment to moment. Our lives, our destinies weren't in our own hands.

Our futures were in the hands of people whose desires and fancies turned on a dime. Likewise, so did our fates. Maybe their families were something they could count on, maybe they could count on money, or maybe they could count on the future. Nothing was secure for us. The only thing we could count on was the belief that there was something greater than the situation we lived in, and that something greater loved us and cared for us! We stood up because we knew—even though everything was against us—in the pits of our bellies, we knew Preaching John was right! We knew there was a Rock, somewhere, that we could lean on.

I stood up because, even though sometimes I still fumbled a little with the United States words, I knew down inside me what Preaching John was saying. What I didn't understand in my head, I could feel in my heart. I'd lost everything—relationships coming and going, home gone, future gone. I had to believe in something, just to keep getting up each morning. There had been better days before; I had to believe they would come again. I stood up remembering my mother. I stood up remembering the red bird that came to us on the Trail. I stood up because it was a miracle that any of us had survived.

And maybe some people would have said we were making too much noise, but I kind of think we needed all that just to keep ourselves alive, just to keep our hope alive.

"You ask me how I make it?" Preaching John was rubbing his shirt down over his belly like he was about to rub a hole in both of them—him and the shirt! "You ask me how I keep going on?"

"Tell us, Preaching John!" one of the old men yelled, one of the old men so worn out from working that he could hardly stand—one of the old men who had been beaten so many times by another owner, the scar tissue on his back wouldn't let him stand up straight.

"Well, you know! On Christ the solid Rock, I stand. All other ground is sinking sand!" Preaching John looked at us, half smiling, half scowling! "All other ground is sinking sand!"

The sky was so blue; the grass was so green. Preaching John spoke the word so powerful that I should have seen it coming.

Oh, it was a high time, I tell you! Lord! Lord! Lord! I'd found my way back to my seat, but it was so good, I even stood up again to sing.

In dat great gittin' up mornin'
Fare you well, fare you well
In dat great gittin' up mornin'
Fare you well, fare you well

It just seemed like the perfect morning for it. My lungs puffed up like the blacksmith's bellows and I sang it for my mother.

In dat great gittin' up mornin'
Fare you well, fare you well
In dat great gittin' up mornin'
Fare you well, fare you well

I sang it out as loud as I could, like if I sang it loud enough, my mother and father could hear me back where they were.

But, instead of singing with me, instead of following along

like people did when my mother sang, everything got still and quiet for a moment.

"Child, where you learn that song?" Preaching John stepped close to me, holding his hand still on his belly.

I looked around, trying to figure out what I had done wrong. "From my mother. It was her favorite song." I waited for him to tell me to sit down. I should have stayed quiet. Why couldn't I ever get anything right anymore?

"Well, Lord, have mercy!" Preaching John shouted. "It sure is a great gittin' up day!"

People got to jumping in the air! Women were clapping their hands, like it was a miracle!

They were all excited because we all came from different places, from different languages, but somehow we all knew the same songs.

"Keep on singing, child!" Preaching John resumed rubbing his belly.

> In dat great gittin' up mornin'
> Fare you well, fare you well

I sang it for my mother. I sang it for myself.

> In dat great gittin' up mornin'
> Fare you well, fare you well

I sang it for Johnnie Freeman. I sang it for Abraham.

Something happened in that hollow in that grove. We were all slaves—at least that's what some folks said—but right then we got free! It was just like Ephraim, when he jumped in that crystal stream! Each one of us, through that music, found our way to better times!

Then all of a sudden, the master came down the hill, on foot, running toward the hollow! He was way far away, but he would run a few steps and buck. Kicking his legs and waving his arms, he hollered words we couldn't understand. I had never seen a song move someone so!

Preaching John jumped to his feet again. "Here is that great day!" He started leaping like Master Cauley. "Look at that White man jump! The Lord done got ahold of him!"

Master Cauley was still coming down the hill just shouting, flailing, and kicking. He came on down the hill, and ran on past us down to the stream like he was going to baptize himself!

Men and women were dancing, singing, some of them even crying. All of us followed behind Master Cauley and Preaching John.

And I was still singing! Lord! Lord! Lord!

In dat great gittin' up mornin'
Fare you well, fare you well

Even all the children were grinning and clapping—not so much out of joy over Master Cauley's salvation, but out of hope that something sweet, some molasses cake or something, was going to come to us after all of this good time!

I sang, running after them.

In dat great gittin' up mornin'
Fare you well, fare you well

Master Cauley thrashed and splashed his way into the water, Preaching John still hollering behind him and closing in. Master was yet jumping and speaking gibberish when Preaching John laid hands on him.

I splashed in after them, throwing myself into the cold water.

It wasn't until I came up out of the water, until all the rest of us caught up to the two of them, that we realized what was really going on. Master Cauley was red-spotted all over. That's when we realized that when the Spirit touched Master Cauley, it was in the form of a swarm of bees!

It seems that those buzzing bees, on that particular Sunday morning, had had their fill of Master putting his hand where it didn't belong. On that bright blue and cloudless day, just as I was bursting into song, those bees came busting out after the master. While we were praising the Lord, shouting our way to glory, he was hollering and running from the honeybees' retribution.

Over time, Master Cauley recovered, but Preaching John remained pretty disappointed that the Master's salvation was bogus and an accidental show. But when it was hard to find something to laugh about, that story was a repeated source of sweet joy.

CHAPTER TWENTY-FIVE

ON THE PLANTATION, MASTER CAULEY ALSO HAD A WIFE and a daughter, whose name was Miss Lillian. She was their only child and did pretty much what she pleased. She wore pretty dresses—pink, yellow, and blue, like flowers. She seemed to have a new one covered with lace for each day. Master looked at his Miss Lillian like he didn't want a fly to land on her. He brought her gifts—new pretty ribbons and new fabric—all the time. With blond hair and blue eyes, there was no sign that she and I shared any common blood.

One day, soon after I came to the plantation, when I was drawing water, she marched right up to me.

"What's your name," Miss Lillian said to me.

"Armentia."

"Well, Armentia, I want you to come and comb my hair." She grabbed the bucket from my hand and let it drop to the ground. She flounced away with me behind her. She reminded me of myself a little, before I walked the one thousand miles, before I lost Abraham, when we all were one.

We were about the same size, about the same age. Just little girls, still baby-doll-playing age. She had long, straight hair, and she talked while I combed it with a beautiful blue comb painted with flowers. Her mother looked on from where she sat on the porch.

"There aren't any children here at the house, Armentia. You're going to have to be my playfriend," Miss Lillian said.

After that, anytime she felt good and ready, she came for me. "Comb my hair" or "Listen to me read," she would say. I remember her reading me a story about a princess and a frog. I still don't know why a girl would kiss an ugly thing like that. But I liked the attention she gave me.

One day, she touched my hair. "Your hair is pretty too. It's prettier than the others'." I felt a funny kind of feeling when she said it, like I was special, but at the same time it didn't feel good. "It must be the Indian in you." As she spoke, I felt so far from my home.

She took the comb and began to unwind my braids. "I wish I had curls like yours." No one, except my mother, had ever combed my hair.

"Lillian!" her mother called to her from the porch.

Miss Lillian didn't answer. Instead, she sat down again. "Here." She handed the comb back to me. "Comb my hair." She had a smile on her face and she sounded happy, but not quite as much as before. "Combing yours wasn't as nice or as much fun as I thought."

It's hard on a person, being better, I guess.

Other times we just played like two girls, chasing butterflies and lightning bugs, smiling at rainbows, and picking flowers. We played together for months.

One day, she came to the cabin where I lived alone, to fetch me. I was sitting on my cot. Using scraps of material from burlap sacks and such, I was trying to make a blanket. I didn't have any carded wool or cotton, or any way to weave, so I did the best I could. Using a needle and thread, I sewed the bits together. Most pieces were squares, but I'd tried to make flower shapes too. I tried to make pictures out of those old pieces. When I sewed, in my mind, I spoke the language of my people so that I would not forget. Every stitch I sewed was a memory. It helped me remember what my father had told me about my wedding, about the land, and a well of our own. I hadn't shown my blanket to anyone. I worked on it mostly at night by candlelight.

"Oh, so pretty!" Miss Lillian clapped her hands. "Show me how," she said. She wanted to make one of her own. After that day, every time we were together, we spent at least part of the time working on our blankets.

Mine had three flowers in the center. "One for each member of my family," I told her when she asked. "It helps me to remember them."

She said she hadn't thought about me having a family. "Did you love them?"

"Yes. Most surely, I do." I told her the story of Abraham and how he'd taught me to run. "See my ankle?" I showed her my star-shaped scar. Then I told her about our village, our well, and I even told her about sweet Johnnie Freeman. "I was going to marry him," I confided to her.

"Then you must make a flower for him," she said. "And the other flowers need to be brighter."

I told her about losing Abraham, and about losing the land. "But someday we are going to own some land again. We are going to have a home that no one can take from us." I tried to fight it, but a tear squeezed from my eyes.

Miss Lillian touched the wetness as it traveled down my cheek. She looked at me as though I was her little baby. "Now, Armentia, stop your crying. You know niggers aren't supposed to own land. God doesn't want that. You shouldn't worry your head about that." She kissed me again, trying to console me.

"You are just fretting yourself for nothing."

Laying her blanket aside, she pulled my head to her shoulder as though she was my mother. "God made it so White people would own the land. But don't you worry, we are here to take care of you." She patted my head. "I'm going to take care of you myself. So you will always have a place with me. Just don't worry your head dreaming of foolish dreams. You'll worry yourself up a headache." Still patting my head, "You just rest easy."

A good part of me was quieted then. It felt safe and easy laying my father's dream down. Somebody to watch over me, if I just let go of my father's hope for me, that's what Miss Lillian promised.

I let my head lie on her shoulder, listening to her breathe.

Maybe she was right, maybe it was God's plan. It looked that way. All that I had loved had been taken from me—stolen away while I watched, while God watched. There were no beatings on Master Cauley's plantation. There was Sunday and Preaching John. Sometimes there were sweets. But it did not make up for all that had been taken, for all that we had suffered.

I had seen what happened to people that kept fighting, they ended up like Golden Bear's father, dead by the side of the road—his dreams dead with him. They ended up like the old woman who would not stop singing.

It was easier to let it go, right then, to not hope, to satisfy myself with just the little that she hoped for me. So, I rested.

But the resting wasn't easy. Something nagged at me.

When my tears dried, she smiled at me. "All better now?"

I lifted my head, nodding at her.

She lifted her blanket to begin sewing again. "Yours is so beautiful," she told me.

"Yours too, Miss Lillian. You keep on working; it will keep getting better."

CHAPTER TWENTY-SIX

THE NEXT TIME MISS LILLIAN CAME, SHE BROUGHT MORE bright-colored material, scraps from dresses her mother had made for her. Each one of those pieces of fabric lightened my heart.

She kept working on her own blanket, me showing her how. But when the shapes she tried to cut and sew were not perfect, she would get frustrated, rip hers apart, and then sit and watch me make mine. "Look at how pretty yours looks, Armentia," she told me as I added red, yellow, and blue pieces of fabric to my flowers and blanket.

We worked together on them for weeks. Sometimes, like before, she would bring books to read to me when we had finished working on the blankets.

"Teach me." Looking at the storybook pictures, I whispered the words, afraid to speak them out loud. Afraid I would be beaten, afraid she would think me foolish, I murmured the words.

She tilted her head. "What did you say?"

Miss Lillian was my friend. "I said, teach me. I want to learn." There was no reason to be afraid. "My Mama Emma, before we traveled the Trail, told me that she would teach me."

Lillian smiled. She giggled. She ran her fingers over the page, looking at the pictures, and then back at me.

I imagined myself holding the book, reading the words like she did.

She laughed again. "You want to read, Armentia?" She patted my arm. "Now, don't be silly. You can't learn to read."

"Yes, I can. I can learn. I know about the talking leaves, the Cherokee alphabet. My Mama Emma taught me." I began to write the letters on the dirt floor with my fingers.

Miss Lillian giggled again. "Why, those aren't letters, Armentia. Your Mama Emma must have been joshing you." She smiled. "Those are just squiggles. No one can read that." She patted my hand again. "Besides, you know it's against the law. Now, stop being silly and listen to me read."

I didn't mention reading to her after that, though she came to my cabin, again and again, to work on our blankets.

Maybe someday someone else, another child, would teach me.

She came one time and we stretched the blankets out before us. Miss Lillian pointed at them. "They can be Christmas presents!" We finished them before the first snowfall came.

"I'm going to give mine to my mother, when I see her again," I told her.

"Mine is so ugly," Miss Lillian said.

Her blanket wasn't perfect, but it was good for a first try.

"It's not so bad, Miss Lillian." Trying to make her feel better, I pointed out things that she had done well. "Look how tight these stitches are." I pointed at her blanket.

She still frowned.

"You'll do even better next time, Miss Lillian."

"But look at yours! It's so much prettier than mine!"

"The one you make next time will be even better." I tried to console her. "Your mother will love it no matter what."

"But yours is so much better!" She looked at hers, shook it, and then let it slip to the floor. "I can't give this one away as a present. It's too ugly!" Miss Lillian ran from my cabin crying.

When she came back, some time later, her eyes still red, she had a piece of paper in her hands. The paper had United States letters written on it.

She ran her fingers lightly over the flowers on my quilt. "So beautiful." Miss Lillian pointed to a place on the back of my blanket. "Sew these letters. Right there, in the lower corner."

I stitched the letters: L-I-L-L-I-A-N.

"Thank you," she said, smiling at me. She took my blanket, wrapped it around her shoulders, rubbed a corner against her cheek. Still smiling, she held my blanket while she twirled and danced on my dirt floor. "So beautiful," she sighed again. "My mother will love it!"

"Yes, she's going to love your blanket." I pointed at hers.

"That's not my blanket." Miss Lillian rubbed her hand over the blanket around her shoulders. "I'm going to give my mother this one."

"But that's your blanket over there, Miss Lillian!" I couldn't believe how my friend was acting. "That's my blanket! I made that for my mother!" I tried to snatch it from her.

Miss Lillian tugged back. "But I like this one better. You can have mine." She tugged harder. "And I gave you the cloth for the flowers. That material is mine."

I jerked harder, almost snatching it from her. "But it's mine! I made it! You have your own!"

Lillian jerked it again, planting her feet firm. She held fast to my blanket. Her face and eyes changed, distant from me, like right after she had combed my hair. Even her voice changed; it lost the kindness of my friend. It was stern instead. "It can't belong to you! You're a slave! You're my slave!"

I tried to hold on, but I could feel my grip loosening.

"Don't forget yourself, Armentia! You belong to me!" She stamped her foot, her voice quavering. "You belong to me, not the other way around!"

The words sounded unnatural in her mouth. They sounded rehearsed, like words someone had practiced with her.

I couldn't answer back what I wanted to say. I couldn't take my blanket back. I thought about Ephraim. I could feel my head starting to hang.

"Anything you make, anything you have, belongs to me." Miss Lillian jerked again, and I let go.

"I've been good to you, Armentia. Maybe too good. We're friends, but you must remember your place."

I closed my heart and, though I still looked at her, I closed my eyes.

She gathered the blanket that used to be mine in her arms and then walked to hers, lying on the floor. She stooped to pick it up, offering it to me. "Here, you can have this one. It's yours." She said it as though I was supposed to believe it was a precious gift, not something she wanted to throw away. "You can give it to your mother," she said like she was trying to make up with me, to be my friend again. "She'll like it."

I stood with my arms folded. I lifted my head, narrowed my eyes. I could feel my mouth in a straight line.

"Don't you look at me like that, Armentia. I'm your mistress!" She stomped her foot again, like she was trying to convince herself. "I'm trying to be nice to you. Don't be ungrateful! What are you going to do with a nice blanket like this down here anyway?"

She pleaded with me. "Don't be mad at me, Armentia. Don't be mad." She was a little girl again, like me. We were children again, and I almost melted. But then she tossed her blanket to me. I caught it. "Now, take that one. You said it was nice yourself. And you remember who I am."

I did.

We stood that way, my blanket in her arms, her blanket in mine, silent for some time. Finally, she smiled, a forced one to coax a smile from me. "We'll play tomorrow. All right?"

"Yes, ma'am."

Miss Lillian did come for me the next day and the day after that. I combed her hair when she asked. We even made more blankets together. But it was never the same between us.

No, I don't think that girl planned on stealing my blanket all along. I just think sometimes you'll do a lot of mean things when you got it in your heart that you got to be better.

I think it must be real pressing to be perfect.

Our friendship walked out the door that day with the words she said and when she carried what was mine out the door in her arms. Miss Lillian traded love for a blanket. But she ain't much different; people do it all the time.

But, the truth is, that ain't all that was stolen from me. There's the other that I have tried not to talk about.

CHAPTER TWENTY-SEVEN

*Y*OU REMEMBER, I TOLD YOU ABOUT THE TWO WOMEN that settled me in when I first arrived at the plantation, Miss Lula and Miss Bertha Bell.

"You just keep your mouth shut about it," Miss Lula had told me. Her skin was so fair, she almost looked like a White woman.

Miss Bertha Bell, whose skin was like coal, her eyes like large pools of cream, nodded at me. "Don't you think about it." Her accent must have sounded like Africa. "When it's going on, I think about my village, I think about my home, my mother and my father." She looked away.

Both of them were very young women, girls themselves. When I look back, I think they might have been sixteen or seventeen.

"I think sometimes that I am going to run away." With the same matter-of-fact voice she said, "Other times I imagine killing him," Miss Lula said.

"Hush, now, girl. You gone get us killed," Miss Bertha Bell said.

It got so quiet then, in the room where they were settling me in, that you could almost hear the candle flickering. Then the two of them looked around the room at the shadows while they giggled guiltily.

When they finished, Miss Bertha Bell said, again, to me, "You ain't nothing but a little baby. Your time ain't even come."

Miss Lula smiled and shook her head. "I bet he like your hair."

Master Cauley had come to visit me that night. That's when I learned what the two women meant.

That night when he came, he didn't say much. No, he didn't say nothing. He touched my hair, like a baby doll, but didn't look in my eyes.

I wanted to shout out to my father to protect me, when I understood what the master intended. I wanted to scream and run. How could something like that happen to me? With all that had happened on the Trail, my parents had still tried to protect me. Saving grown-up conversations until, maybe, they thought I was closer to the marriage my father imagined.

But I grew up right then, in that moment when Master Cauley touched me. I got a little older, and wiser than any child needs to be, each time he came to visit me. Right then, the words Miss Lula and Miss Bertha had spoken to me earlier came back to me. At that dark moment, some of their words began to make sense. I remembered what Miss Lula and Miss Bertha Bell said and got through it; when it hurt, I remembered the long walk and told myself I would survive.

That's when I thought about Abraham, and I let myself fall into the depths of the well. Other times, I was with Abraham fishing, or I would remember the slave boy Ephraim saying, "Jesus!" And sometimes I prayed. Not a words prayer, but like I let my heart be lifted up to the Great One, to Jesus. It was like my heart flew up like a butterfly where He could see me.

That's how my days were, working or playing with Miss Lillian by day, at night trying to have babies to work in her daddy's fields—pretending during the day that things weren't happening to me at night. That's how I thought my days would always be.

He sent a few other men, mostly slaves, to me. Like I said, he never said much to me at night, except sometimes he'd look at me. "What's wrong with you, girl? Why can't you have a baby? It's been almost two years." Then he would tell me I was no good, not worth the price he had paid.

The worse of it was with the slave men, them trying to act like they wasn't there too. If no one was watching, sometimes they didn't do nothing to me, since I was a child. But when they did, they were running someplace else in their own minds too. I could tell.

Like that queen bee in that hive laying eggs, I was supposed to be making babies he could use in the fields and whatnot, just like he used Miss Lula and Miss Bertha Bells's children.

I accepted that I was going to spend my whole life at the bottom of Abraham's well. I would just be happy where I could, like singing in the grove.

Days passed, summers passed, and I heard it over and over. "You are worthless!" He threatened to sell me to his brother.

I guess I tell this part of the story like I wasn't there, or like I was standing off someplace watching it happen to someone else. In a whole lot of ways, I guess I wasn't there.

You know children just nigh eleven or twelve, don't you? No differences between me, back then, and them—not much. I was just a baby trying to walk grown steps. And I didn't have an old soul, like my brother Abraham had, to help me.

That thousand miles had walked me from my home to someplace where the earth was red. But it had also walked me from being able to be a laughing, playing child. It had walked me from being my Mama Emma's spoiled baby girl to something she could lend out or sell off for a load of bricks.

Now, how is a child supposed to make sense of that?

I went from being my father's little girl, to someone that was supposed to be a breed-mother of field workers. A child can't think her way through that.

Sometimes I dreamed about him coming into my room. I wanted to run. I meant to run. But even in my dreams I would freeze, unable to run, or even to move, or breathe. I would awake panting, frozen in place.

The truth is, I was afraid. If I'd talked back, or tried to fight back, or run away, maybe I wouldn't be here to talk to you today. My bones, like sweet Johnnie Freeman's, would have been lying in some lonely woods.

That's how I felt then. It was like a dream, like it wasn't happening to me.

And no grown folks talked about it. What were they going to do or say? They weren't free either. "Master, that's wrong what you doing. Why, that's just a child." No, they couldn't say that. They would have been dead too.

They did the best they could, just trying not to make me shame. We didn't want to stand up; we chose to live.

It was a long time before I was free enough to think about it. When I did, a whole bunch of mad came rushing on me.

But what was I going to do? Wasn't no lynching party going to hang him for violating me, not even today.

That ain't the worst of it, though. When I got free enough to think about it, shame came too.

I've been so shamed, even after I was finished with the mad, the shame covered me. It covered me so, like a hand over my mouth, I couldn't even talk about it. I ain't told nobody, not even my family—except my mother. Nobody knew, except my mother and the ones that were there to witness it all.

Of course, Mama Emma and Papa knew. How could they

do that to me, to one of their own?

You might say that everybody did it back then, but that's not the truth. Everybody didn't do it. There was a lot of fight amongst our people about it; right up through the Civil War, Cherokee were divided on both sides, though most of our people said it wasn't right. But the ones with power, the ones with slaves, won out.

Lots of White folks said it wasn't right either. Wasn't nothing noble about stealing people's land or stealing people's lives, or stealing people's children. Lots of good people thought it was wrong, but I guess they were too busy being nice to say something. They were too busy being good to stand up and speak out. Or maybe they just didn't want to get involved. Could be, they were afraid too.

Besides, something I've learned, everybody can say something is right, but that don't make it so. And if a man wants an excuse to do wrong, he'll always find it.

Like I was saying, I haven't said anything about it until now. Shame kept my mouth covered for a whole lot of years. But, like I said, no more secrets. I'm telling the truth now, and I'm starting the telling with you.

You ask me why I didn't run away. Well, where was I going to go? Abraham taught me the way to run, the way through the forest from the stream. But the earth was black there and the bones of my fathers whispered the way. How could I find my way where the earth was red? And that man, Master Cauley, had a gun. He smiled, he fed us, and he gave us church, but he had a gun. And he told me he would use it. You remember that.

I don't think I was free enough in my mind to even think about leaving. Where was I going to run to? I could only imagine ending up someplace worse.

Tell somebody? Who was I going to tell? Who was going to believe me? Who was going to say that I was right and that he was wrong? Who was going to believe me over him? Who was going to put that man in a jail or hang him from a tree for me? Wasn't no crime, they would have said. Wasn't no proof. They would have beat me or killed me for opening my mouth.

A colored man will swing from a tree for just thinking about such a thing. But I ain't never seen a White man strung up for such a thing. Not even now and we free.

Miss Lula, Miss Bertha Bell, and all the people around me told me to keep the secret. We all kept Master Cauley's secret so we could stay alive. "Don't make trouble," they said. "Just make like it didn't happen and survive." That's what they told me, and that's just what I did.

No, I don't think all men—White, Red, or Black—are bad. I just think, like I said before, sometimes the good ones are too quiet.

Most times, the two women told me to be quiet. But there were moments when Miss Bertha Bell would not hold her peace. There were times when she said she was not a slave.

"We lived in a place of hot weather, tall grasses, and trees that bowed down to kiss the earth." She said that her people were African and Seminole, people from a place called Florida. "You must remember the name of the place that is yours." She said that she was stolen away and sold.

"But my people fight for me. They won't surrender us to make us slaves." She looked at Miss Lula and me as if she knew we understood. "My people—Wild Cat, Tall John, Tecumseh—they won't surrender us." She pointed at her black skin. "They fight hard. The White man wants to move us all to this place, to Indian Territory, to take our land." Her face froze. "But in the middle of the night, men stole me and sold me to Master Cauley to make him children, to be a slave." She raised her chin and shook her head. "But I am not a slave. No matter what they call me. We must stand up, some way, and fight!" She pointed to her forehead. "At least in our thoughts. Sometimes, I think about killing him."

Sometimes, we allowed ourselves to be angry for a moment. Then, we shushed it away. Most times, though, we all were quiet. Most times, we stayed in our place.

How could I stand up with all I had seen, Golden Bear's father dragged and then slumping to the ground? How could I escape, a lamb alone by myself?

Like the Red Bird said, could be Master Cauley didn't recognize that he was a wolf. Could be, he wouldn't let himself see that I was a precious little lamb.

It was so long ago, you are saying. Why can't I forget it? Why I got to tell? Well, it's just like those children of Israel that Red Bird told us about, those taken captive and carried away. They sang the truth to help themselves cross over. They sang the truth to help themselves survive. They sang the songs to help themselves remember they were once free. I'm just singing the truth so you'll know it. I'm singing the truth for my children, so they'll know the way they came. My guilt is gone, my people are gone; all I've got is these words. I'm not telling the truth to hurt anybody. I'm telling the truth to get free.

And I'm telling the truth to remind me there are wolves afoot. I'm telling it so I will remember to be a smarter sheep. I'm not keeping any more wolves' secrets. I'm going to stick closer to the shepherd. And if a wolf tries to bite me, or just get close to me, I'm going to open my mouth wide and bleat. "Baa! Baa!" I'm singing so I will learn to be a smarter sheep.

I'm singing my truth song 'cause someone's going to need to hear it, someone coming behind me is going to need to hear it so she or he can be strong.

CHAPTER TWENTY-EIGHT

$\mathscr{I}$ DIDN'T THINK I WOULD SEE MY MOTHER AND FATHER again. For all I knew, they could be dead. The whole time I was there at the plantation, it was like I was in a fog or like I was dreaming . . . like I was lost in the woods, or deep, deep down in the dark of the well.

One day, Miss Lillian patted a place on the bench where she sat. "I'm going to read you a story." I sat next to her while she read me a story about a girl in the woods picking flowers. She showed me a picture of a wolf that came along and tried to eat the girl. Then she read to me about a woodsman who came along and rescued the girl.

About that time, Miss Lillian's mother came walking by, her long skirt sweeping the ground. Her hair, golden like Miss Lillian's, was swept on top of her head in curls. She had an opened parasol held high in one hand. Her other arm was looped through and resting on Master Cauley's arm; he walked beside her.

She nodded at us. "Look at the children playing together."

She smiled up at her husband. "Aren't they lovely?" She nodded at Master Cauley. "It's so nice for Lillian to have a little play-friend. Almost like a baby doll." She looked at Lillian and me sitting together. "Sweet children. They must be about the same age, don't you think?"

The next day, I was in a wagon on my way home to my mother and father.

Just like that.

The Great One works in mysterious ways, don't He?

When the two women—Miss Lula and Miss Bertha Bell—packed me for the wagon home, they hugged me.

"The Good Lord sure watched over you!" Miss Lula said.

Miss Bertha Bell pinched me like they had in the beginning. "Home to your mother just in time. Just before your time."

They kissed me before they sent me outside. "Put this behind you, girl. Who knows? Something good might be waiting around the bend."

When that wagon drove me again past Abraham's well, it seemed like I woke up just when we pulled up in front of my mother's door.

CHAPTER TWENTY-NINE

WHEN I SAW MY MOTHER AGAIN, THOUGH HER HAIR WAS
not white, she had turned old. She held me in her arms. We sat
in the red dirt, clinging to each other, rocking and crying.
"Armentia's come home!" she kept saying.

It took a long time before she told me.

She told me that when my father woke after being hit with
the pistol, he ran down the road after me. He called my name.
"Armentia! Armentia!" He ran and then he cried.

"He could not take any more," my mother told me. "He
lost his hope and did not like this world."

Among those of us who were called slaves, there was always
talk that we were better off being owned by our own people,
by Indians. We fared better, most said. We ate better; we had
better clothes. Sometimes we married into the families of those
that owned us, sometimes we bought our freedom, or were set
free. It was rare for an Indian owner to beat a slave. We were
family. They were rarely cruel. We were people too. They were
not cruel like White masters.

But there's always somebody or something to make the rule a lie. The family that broke the rule was the Worthy family. The cruelest, the one most infamous of them, was Ben Worthy. There were tales told of him beating slaves. One, in particular, of him—while his wife screamed and begged for him to stop—beating his child's nursemaid because the baby's crying wouldn't stop.

It was said that the woman did not want to go there; she had begged her owner not to lend her out to the family because of how violent Ben Worthy was. But Ben's wife was too ill to nurse the baby, and the woman's master needed the money. People said the woman, Nettie, cried all the way to the house where the baby was, but those were her last tears. As she feared, she saw her last at the end of a rusty, metal shovel wielded in fury. The nursemaid was a woman from our original village, a woman my father knew.

There had been other stories about Ben Worthy, stories about people he had beaten, shot, or even set on fire. But this woman, Nettie, my father knew.

So, when my father had had enough, he knew just where to go, my mother said. "He looked down the road for you," she said. "But when he learned all the truth of where and how they sold you, I saw his spirit and his hope fly out the window." My mother shook her head when she told me the story. "He was a man of peace, but his hope went down the road in the dust after you. Not long after that, we heard the story about Nettie."

She said he vowed that he would not touch a brick to build Papa's house. "Not one!" he said.

"When the bricks came, it was too much for him. He held me and then told me good-bye."

My father walked out of our valley, past Abraham's well, to the clearing where the Worthys lived. He walked back and forth in front of the house, calling Ben Worthy's name. My father, who walked in peace, who made no trouble, taunted the man. He called him murderer.

Ben Worthy charged from the house and there was a fight. My father got the best of the other man, my mother said. He had him pinned to the ground, beating him. "Then, suddenly, your father rolled over and let go."

The crazy man killed my father. He shot him seven times.

"Your father died smiling," she said. "They say he said our names," my mother cried. "He did not want to be here. He could not save you, so he tried to honor her. It was a brave death."

Pride about my father stood up in me. He fought for me.

But then I remembered. There was no good death. Only being quiet would keep us alive. I was happy to see my mother and I did not want to add to her grief, so I kept my thoughts to myself and let her finish the story.

Two weeks later, when Ben Worthy attacked his own cousin, my mother said Worthy followed my father into the beyond when his cousin shot him dead.

Since then my mother had been alone in the small wooden hut. Now she spent her days, from dusk to dawn, working in the cornfields. Many days, instead of cooking, she was now picking cotton. Her hands showed the scars and the corners of her mouth turned down with tiredness and sadness. But her eyes lit when she looked at me.

I kissed her and held her in my arms.

CHAPTER THIRTY

$\mathcal{W}$E MUST KEEP YOUR FATHER'S DREAM," MY MOTHER whispered to me in the moonlight of our cabin. "Your coming home is a miracle. It is a sign. It is a sweet thing and it will make us well." From underneath her bed, she pulled a glass jar like one of the honey jars from long ago. Moonlight shined the jar. It had a red cloth wrapped around the top to cover it. Though it was not full, there were silver and copper coins shining in the bottom. "We will earn extra money and buy us some land," she said.

"Niggers don't own land. You know that." Miss Lillian whispered into my ears from far away. Who would sell us land? Dreams would get us killed. They had killed Golden Bear's father. Dreams had killed my father.

"We will make blankets."

I sat with my new doll beside me, the one my mother had given me after my return. "You are my little girl," she had told me. "Forget all that happened to you." Now, as I listened to

161

her, I thought of the blanket that Miss Lillian had taken from me.

"We will make beadwork." My mother's eyes were shining. "We will take our things to the trading post to sell, and we will sell until we have enough." She turned the jar in the moonlight. "I have been wrong to sit down in sadness. Your father is gone, but we must not give up. We must not let his dream die."

She taught me to string seeds of blue, red, orange, and white, along with pieces of bone, boiled to soften so the needle and thread would pull through. We separated the different colored beads into bowls, so that in the gray light of the moon we would be able to tell them apart. We imagined the colors as we worked in darkness. In the weeks and months that followed, we made beautiful patterns on bags, necklaces, and even soft leather shoes.

In the day—passing by Mama Emma and Papa's fancy house, by the unused bricks that had sent me away—my mother and I worked in the fields, tending the cotton. I watched her fingers bleed, watched her stooped back moving down the row ahead of me. Dragging bags behind us, we stood among the rows, wiping our brows and gathering crops for Mama Emma and Papa. But at night, we worked for ourselves, for my father's dreams, to earn pennies for our jar.

"We will never have enough." The money jar never seemed to fill, and I complained to her when my fingers ached.

She sat under the shaft of moonlight. "We walked the thousand miles. Our feet bled in the snow. This is nothing." She shrugged. "We will not surrender our dream."

So we bent our heads by moonlight, sewing one piece at a time. When we had enough fabric scraps, we made a blanket or quilt. Each time we finished a few things, we walked them to town.

We walked with our heads down, trying not to attract attention, trying not to look like we carried anything precious in the bundles we carried. We wrapped our treasures in rags, hoping to disguise them. Though buildings, roads, and schools had sprung up in Indian Territory, it had become a place without law. Maybe fellows thought if the United States could steal, then they could too. There were robberies and killings; desperate men in desperate times.

We walked to the trading post when we had things to sell, hoping that trouble would pass us by. No one seemed to be interested in our rags; it was not unusual to see people wandering around without homes, without food. But before walking home, we hid the precious pennies we earned. We knotted them in scraps of cloth and tucked them in our bosoms.

We passed by a whitewashed, wood-framed church. I pointed it out to my mother. "The one where I lived was bigger than that one."

She nodded but didn't answer. My mother never wanted to talk about when I was away. When I mentioned it, she looked away as though she was fighting back tears. "That is behind us," she would say.

It was behind us, but it did not trail far behind. We just did not talk about it. Not speaking of evil does not mean it is not there.

As we walked, we passed by the schoolhouse. I looked at it, at the children inside, and then looked straight ahead. It was another dream that would not come true. I was not allowed to go to school. No teacher, no schoolgirl, was going to teach me to read.

There were long stretches, as we walked along the dusty, rutted, red road, where it was quiet; just open fields and trees, and we were able to walk and talk together under the clear sky. My mother smiled at me. She held my hand.

"Keep your eyes down until we get home. Don't smile.

Walk so no one will see you," my mother told me.

"I remember, Mother. I remember."

We walked the walk from time to time, adding pennies to our secret jar.

CHAPTER THIRTY-ONE

$\mathcal{T}$HE TRUTH IS, MANY THINGS HAD CHANGED SINCE I HAD left. Some things had gotten worse. Pretending things had not changed, not talking about the changes, didn't mean they were not so.

It was the plan, we were told, that we would be free of the White man, free to live our lives in Indian Territory without interference. That is what they told us, but that is not what happened.

The White man came with us. He counted us; he listed us. We lived for many, many generations before he came, but he could not leave us alone. He insisted that his way was better; the only way to live was his way. We lived on what the land willingly gave to us, not forcing it to do more than it chose; the White man called us lazy. We hunted only what we needed, all game belonging to us in common; they called us uncivilized. Uninvited, he came to teach us, to sell to us. He forced us to take on his ways, to divide the land, to learn his language, to learn his words and forget our own.

Children—those of parents who resisted the new ways—were taken from their homes, from their families, and sent away to schools. If they did not change willingly, change was forced upon them. Their hair was cut, and they were forbidden to speak the language of The People.

The White man camped among us, watching us, guarding us as though he was afraid we would attack him if he left us alone. He bothered us because he had no peace.

When I returned, there were more houses. There were more churches—Mennonites, Baptists, Catholics, Methodists. They fought amongst themselves—*Who were the real Christians? Whose way was right?*—while they tried to teach us about peace, peace we had before they came.

Uninvited, they came to teach us their ways, to force us into their ways—children sitting in high, starched white collars, tight-fitting dresses and corsets so that they could not breathe. Their eyes were like caught rabbits.

Carrying my bucket, I walked past the school on my way for water. I stopped, looking at the new schoolhouse, looking through the windows at the children.

The teacher stood before them, her hair pulled so tight it cried out. The students were mostly mixed breeds. Those with dark skins—like me—could not attend. They bowed their heads over books with United States words.

I watched them, looking through the schoolroom windows. I had learned the Cherokee alphabet from Mama Emma, the talking leaves, though she had not taught me to read. I thought of the picture books that Miss Lillian had read to me. Maybe one of these children would teach me some day.

I stepped off the path, walking in the grass, to look closer. Hoping to see more.

"Welcome home, Armentia."

I turned. It was Mama Emma standing behind me. Her

expression, her mouth in a straight line, did not match her words.

She wore a shiny dress, a fancy hat, and held a parasol like Miss Lillian's mother. She wore gloves and her waist was tiny. She was cinched in, straight-laced, starched like the woman in the schoolhouse.

"You are home." She tugged at one of her gloves. "Your mother will need your help now that your foolish father is gone. He made trouble and now he is dead. I hope you are a smarter girl."

I swallowed the words I really wanted to say to her. "Yes, ma'am." I held my hands at my sides.

"If you are good, maybe you will be able to stay with her. Don't cause trouble like your father; don't be a pest like your brother. You see what happens to people who misbehave."

"Yes, ma'am."

"Now, come away from that window. The students won't be able to learn with your nose pressed up against the glass. Besides, slaves cannot learn to read."

I turned and took a step away. She had promised me. She had told me I would be able to learn. I lifted my hand to her. Maybe there was something left of the woman who had held me, of the woman I had thought loved me. But she shook her head and stepped away. I felt ashamed. I pretended that I had not reached for her.

"Right now, Armentia. You must come away."

I looked back at the window, then walked back to the path.

"Things are changing. It's the best for all of us, and you must obey." She stepped back onto her wagon. "And get home. It's not safe for you to be roaming about. The uneducated full bloods are burning crops, stealing cattle, and beating slaves . . . fighting to hold on to the old ways." She pulled at her gloves again. "You would do better to stick close to home." Mama

Emma drove away, dust flying from her wheels, and I made my way to the well.

The water bucket dangled from my hands behind me. I had heard all the stories.

"You keep your eyes open, Armentia. You watch out."

I had nodded at my mother's caution when I left, not really frightened. The people she talked about, that my father warned me about, were like the little people in the hills, stories I had heard as a child, but never seen. "Yes, Mother," I had told her when I left.

It wasn't little people that threatened me; it was those who had once been my people. I would have to remember this was a new place. I was no longer someone that Mama Emma held precious. I could no longer count on her old promises to me.

Red dust covered my shoes and the bottom edges of my skirt as I walked. Once there, my mind was only on drawing the water and getting home out of the hot sun. No little people were there. There was no one there that wanted to kill me.

I bent to fill my bucket. The darkness inside the well reminded me of home. It reminded me of The One Who Guards His Family. It reminded me of sweet Johnnie Freeman and Golden Bear.

Startled, I turned when I heard a horse behind me. Actually, it was four riders, each on a pony. "You are not welcome here! You make the mixed breeds fat!" a young man's voice yelled at me.

I froze, the bucket dangling in my hands.

They surrounded me, riding circles around me and the well. "What are you doing here?!"

The sun blinded me and I could not see their faces. I could only hear their voices, speaking a language I understood, but saying things that made no sense to me.

"You are not welcome here!" Their horses kicked more dust. "What are you doing here?" they taunted me.

"I have come to draw water from the well."

"But you are not welcome here!"

If not here, then where was my home? Was there no place for me? "But this is my home!" I told them. "I am Armentia. I walked the Trail Where We Cried. My fathers are your fathers! I have always drawn water from the well!" Though my mind was afraid, my heart stood its ground. Maybe being near the well gave me courage. "I have already lost my father!" I yelled at them. "I have already lost my brother, The One Who Guards His Family." One of the riders stopped short, steering his pony closer to me. But I did not stop speaking. I had had enough for that day. Let him strike me. I would not be quiet. "This is the language I know. I live among the people I know. I have already lost one home, the land of my fathers' bones. Where else can I go?"

Silhouetted against the sunlight, I could see the rider who had stopped his pony—a pony with three white socks—raise his hand. "Leave her alone," he said.

The other three riders slowed the pace of their circling. "Leave her alone," he repeated. "She is one of us."

As suddenly as they came, red clouds stirring behind them, they were gone. Shaking, but trying not to slosh water from the bucket, I ran home.

CHAPTER THIRTY-TWO

WE CONTINUED IN THE FIELDS BY DAY, SEWING AND stringing beads by night. It was a warm day, one of the last warm days before the leaves began to fall, when we made our way—with a new load—up the road to the store. I held my bundle with my baby doll tucked inside.

We talked along the dusty, rutted red road, where it was quiet, just open fields and trees, under the clear sky. My mother smiled at me. She held my hand.

"Keep your eyes down when we get to the store. Don't smile. Walk so no one will see you," my mother reminded me, just as she reminded me each time. "I remember, Mother."

When we neared the trading post, there was activity everywhere. There were farmers driving wagons, young men on ponies, and others in fancy dress clothes.

A few men—young and old, without life in their eyes—held bottles of liquor to their mouths. Drunk, they stumbled down the street and rotted in doorways. It was supposed to be a celebration, I suppose, but in their eyes I saw heartbreak.

The store smelled of dried, salted meat and spices like cinnamon and nutmeg. There were metal goods—horse bits and buckets. There were barrels of dry goods like flour and salt. In the back of the store, there were also bolts of cloth of all kinds, even fancy material that reminded me of Miss Lillian's dresses.

After sliding my doll out, I passed my bundle to my mother. And while she traded our goods for pennies, I wandered the store, finding my way past spices and candy, back to the fabrics. There were colors like the leaves in fall, like the sky in summer, and like wildflowers. I brushed the back of my hand along them. If I had tiny pieces, I could sew flowers on the next blanket I made, or I could make a dress for my doll.

I stopped.

Standing among the bolts of cloth were two White men, both with brown hair, one younger than the other. They fingered a piece of material that was smooth like glass, that was thin like ice on a running pond. Mama Emma had dresses made of the same kind of material. Hers was green, but the material they touched was blue.

Clutching my doll to my chest, I stepped backward toward my mother, trying not to make a sound, hoping they wouldn't notice me. They looked up and when they saw me, both of them smiled. They held up the material, waving it at me.

I made my way quickly to my mother's side. I leaned against her.

She had made a good sale, more pennies than we had made before. We tied them away and then quickly, my doll in my bundle, we left the store. "Keep your eyes. Walk so no one will see you."

"I remember, Mother."

When we were outside of town, when we were sure we weren't being followed, my mother and I slowed our pace.

"We will get our own land. Look what we got today." She

patted the place where she'd hidden her bundle. She nodded. "We will keep working hard."

"You two ladies have to be careful alone on this road!"

Startled, my mother and I turned.

It was the older White man from the store.

He smiled, drawing alongside us. "I was not the only one who saw you claiming money back there at the trading post. You need to be more careful."

My mother's eyes widened. Her mouth tightened, her lips pressed together. She did not answer the man; she would not look at him. She grabbed my hand. "Step to, Armentia!"

I clutched my doll and bundle tighter and stole a glance at the man, who was still smiling.

"So, your daughter's name is Armentia? She is a beautiful girl."

"Armentia, keep your eyes to the road!"

I stepped faster to keep stride with my mother's quickening pace. Her grip tightened on my free hand.

We were at an open place now, on the road to the farm where we lived. There was vacant land on both sides of us, no tended fields. There were few trees, just browning grasses, and dust puffing around our feet. Before, it was a safe, quiet place. Now we wished there were people around.

No one would hear us if we screamed.

The man stepped in front of my mother to stop her. "Slow down. There's no need to run!" The stranger was still smiling. No one would come along to see us, or rescue us.

My mother stepped around him, still squeezing my hand. "Pick up your pace, Armentia!" We were almost running.

The man stepped in front of her again. This time, he reached out his hand and grabbed her shoulder. "Stop running, Mother! You'll tire yourself out!" He grinned at her again.

My mother screamed! "Run, Armentia!"

CHAPTER THIRTY-THREE

My mother let go of my hand and screamed again, "Run, Armentia!"

When I heard her voice, suddenly I was back in the East. I was running through the forest, through the cornfield again, my heart pounding while a loved one called my name. "Run, Armentia!"

But this time, it was not Golden Bear chasing me. This time, it was not The One Who Guards His Family who warned me, who looked out for me. It was my mother and this time it was not a game. This time, on the dusty road in Indian Territory, I was frozen in terror, like in my dreams.

I was frozen too long.

When my feet finally began to run, his hand—the older one, the man that looked like a father—clamped on my shoulder, holding me in place. "Whoa, there, little miss. No need to run!"

My mother screeched and jumped for the man. "Leave her be!" She flailed at him with her fists. "Take the money, but leave her be! Take me, but leave her be!"

My mother pounded his chest, but he still held on to my shoulder, laughing. "Whoa, Mother! You've got it all wrong! I don't want anything from you!"

"You all right, Pa? You need some help?"

The sound of the second man's voice startled me. In the fight, I had forgotten about him. He stood out in the middle of a nearby field watching us; poised, it seemed, to come help the older man.

I looked between the two of them. The two men would overpower my mother and me. There was no point in fighting. Maybe, if we didn't resist, they would let us live.

My mother began to beg. "Take the money. Take me. Just leave her alone. She's all I have left."

Reaching for her, I dropped my bundle and doll in the dust.

She dug in her blouse for the rag that held most of our money, the seed for our land. She held it out to the first man as she dropped to her knees. "Leave her alone, please! She is just a little girl!"

The younger man, starting to walk through the field in our direction, called again. "You all right, Pa?"

"Quiet, I won't hurt you!"

My mother planted her feet. "Why are you talking to me, White man? I am another man's slave. I don't belong to you. My daughter does not belong to you. You cannot take us."

"You have it wrong."

My mother defied him. "You have no business with us, White man!"

The older man still held my shoulder, but waved his free hand at his son. He spoke gently to my mother. "You have it all wrong, my sister." He took her arm and tried to lift her, the rag still dangling in her hand. "I don't want to take from you. I want to offer you bread of life!" He lifted her again. *"Ho! Mitakuye Oyasin!* We are all related!" He nodded at her. "I'm your brother. I am Kituwah's son."

I looked at his blue eyes, his brown hair, his white skin. Kituwah's son? The words made me realize now that the White man and his son spoke the language of The People—though he spoke it in a way that was halting and sometimes unsure—the language of my people.

Kituwah's son? It had been a long time since I had heard anyone mention the Kituwah spirit, since I had heard anyone mention the old ways when we were all one family, when we were the Beloved Community, a beloved family.

My mother, her expression still guarded, let the man lift her to her feet. He pointed to his son. "We wouldn't hurt you or your daughter for the world. We followed behind you to watch over you." He nodded in his son's direction. "To maybe show you something to make you smile." He let go of her arm and then my shoulder. "We'd rather be on our way than hurt you." He shifted his weight to one foot. "We are part of your family. We are Kituwah's sons. We are ministers."

Since I had been home, my mother told me that it had been whispered about that there was a secret society, the Keetoowah Society, people who wanted to return to the old way, the Beloved Community—where things were owned in common, where all men and women were respected, where there were no slaves. It was said that many of the leaders were Christian missionaries—Black, White, and Red. Though the law forbade slaves to have Christ, the Keetoowah people welcomed all people.

He looked at the rag she held. "You put that away." The man used his hand to lift my mother's chin. "I can see you have been hurt, sister. But not by me. Not by us." He shook his head. "We'll just be headed on our way. We meant you no harm."

"No," my mother whispered. "No," she spoke more loudly.

She stammered. "Kituwah's son?" Her chin trembled as she wiped tears off her face.

I did not move, still not ready to speak or even breathe out loud.

"Yes, ma'am. We're preachers, my son and I. Evan Jones is my name, and we've been traveling all over the territory spreading the Good News." He looked toward the younger man. "That's John, my son."

The commotion over, John ran in the field, running away from where we stood. Evan Jones laughed, watching him. "We just wanted to show you something, and maybe invite you to a meeting." He turned, laughing, to watch his son. "Just wait until you see! It's a sight!"

Holding a string in one hand, John looked behind him as he dragged at a large scrap of material also tied to the same string. The cloth was the fancy, smooth kind, like Mama Emma's dress, like the kind they had held in the store. Only this piece was red, and it was held square by crossed wooden sticks. He ran, his brown hair lifting, and dragged the square flapping behind him.

Then the red square caught the breeze. The string tightened and the square swept into the air.

"Look at that thing fly!" Evan Jones slapped his knee. "Have you ever seen such a thing?"

My mother and I, our mouths open, stood mesmerized.

I had seen leaves dance on the wind. I had seen trees sway and flowers blow along the ground, but nothing swept so high into the air!

"It's a kite!" he said, trotting toward his son. He looked back at my mother and me. "You ever seen such a thing? Come on, follow me!"

Each time the wind blew, it tugged the kite higher. My heart soared with it.

I turned to watch my mother's face. At first her eyes and

mouth were round, then her eyes crinkled at the corners, and she smiled.

"See the red bird?" she said. "It is a sign, like before," she whispered to me. "Let us follow!" Captivated, my mother and I held hands, running after him.

She ran after the kite, giggling like a girl. I had not seen her smile since I returned. I had not seen her smile like this since we first saw the Red Bird.

When we caught up to young John—who held the kite taut by the string, like a rein on a wild horse—we stopped running. We panted, our eyes fastened on the dancing red square.

"Got a good wind!" John smiled. Brown hair hung in his face. He looked at me, extending his hand to me. "Want to hold it?"

I shook my head, no.

"Aw, come on. You can do it." He nodded to me. "Come on."

My mother smiled at me, also nodding. She pointed at the red kite.

I moved closer to him. We had been afraid so long, my family and I. We had been hiding so long. I had forgotten how to trust without thinking, to speak without thinking, to move without thinking. Slowly opening my fingers, I stepped closer, finally opening my hand for the string he offered.

"Oh! Oh!" There was a tug against my hand, like a fish caught on a line, only the clear water was blue sky. "Oh!" I looked at John, at my mother, and then back at John.

"Don't worry, you've got it!" John encouraged me.

The line tugged again. Something bubbled inside me. I held the red bird in my hand.

"It's a fine thing. Makes you feel like you're flying!" Evan Jones was smiling at my mother. "When he's flying that thing, makes me forget all my troubles. Reminds me of when he was just a wee boy." When he laughed, you could hear the joy down deep in his spirit, though—like his son—there was something sad about him.

The thing bubbling inside me spilled out. I laughed. I looked at my mother. She clapped her hands.

John and I followed the kite as the wind pulled it. When it began to pull in all directions, like a wild horse or a fish fighting not to be caught, I shoved the kite string back at him.

The sun on my face, the blue sky, the trees, the wind blowing—I closed my eyes and for a short time I was home. And it was not John, but Abraham standing beside me. Still smiling, as though she was back there too, my mother watched John and me while she talked with Evan Jones.

She spoke to him like he was her brother. Her head held high, she spoke like she was free.

When the wind gave out, the kite fell. John rewound the string. "Sure is a sweet pleasure, ain't it, miss?"

Miss? Not gal, or girl? I felt my heart tug again, upward, like the wind was pulling it. No one had ever called me "Miss." Kindness was one of the things left behind, in our village.

"My name is John." He bowed his head slightly. "What is yours?"

I looked at my mother, still talking, and then back at John. "Armentia."

"Nice to meet you, Miss Armentia." He bowed to me again.

Miss Armentia? I felt like Miss Lillian, like someone important, like he thought I was one of the princesses in one of Miss Lillian's books. I wanted to smile, but could not. He might make fun of me. He might take it back.

He bowed again, this time from his waist. "It sure has been an honor to fly with you, Miss Armentia."

An honor? Me? Finally, I risked it; I let myself smile. I nodded to him, then walked beside him to join our parents.

When we reached them, Evan Jones was speaking to my

mother. "I sure hope the two of you ladies can come to the meeting tonight. You'll have to find your way by the light of the moon, but it will be worth it. Brother Jesse is about as fine a preacher as there is!"

Brother Jesse? Maybe he meant Reverend Jesse Bushyhead, one of the Cherokee preachers we met! I remembered him from the Trail, how he spoke to us when we cried.

PART III

"*We can rest assured that whenever faces gathered around the campfire, there were Africans there to serve as spiritual guides into the wilderness. When there were dances to celebrate, lost children to mourn, or seasons passing to be marked, there were Africans present. In addition, we must never forget that on the 'trail where we cried,' there were also African tears.*"

—PATRICK MINGES,
historian, "The Keetoowah Society and
the Avocation of Religious Nationalism
in the Cherokee Nation, 1855–1867"

Chapter Thirty-Four

$\mathcal{I}$T WAS A SECRET MEETING, MY MOTHER TOLD ME. "NO mixed bloods. No slave owners."

There would be watch-outs posted to be certain the meeting place would not be discovered. After the lamps were out and there was no movement in the main house, we would have to travel quietly without lamps. None of the slave owners liked the Keetoowah Society meetings. The leaders didn't just preach Christ and salvation, but they also preached against slavery. They were spreading talk of something called abolition in Indian Territory. Mama Emma and Papa wouldn't like it if they knew, my mother said. Though some men, like Master Cauley, allowed it, it was against the slave code for us to hear preaching. They might beat her if they found out.

I remembered Abraham, beaten and bleeding, tied to a tree. "But, Mother," I protested. "You said that we should be quiet so we could avoid trouble." I saw the stripes on his back.

"We should go," my mother said as though her mind was settled.

"It is against the codes, Mother!" All of us knew that now there were slave codes, written laws that said slaves could not read, could not escape, could not marry. "We should be quiet; we should avoid trouble! That's what you told me!" There were even some laws that said we had to hide or straighten our hair. And there were penalties for breaking the rules.

"Maybe, Armentia, I was wrong. Silence has not kept back trouble."

Holding our breath, craning our necks from side to side, we sneaked out of our cabin, out of the compound, into the surrounding trees and darkness. We stopped when we heard sounds—some owl, some animal scurrying through the brush—like us, trying not to be seen.

I wanted to turn back. Every sound made me tremble, thinking we had been discovered.

We ducked branches, slid down hill and slope, and climbed through bushes and tall grass, until we heard a voice.

"Who are you?" It was one of the watch-outs.

"Tahlequah—who are you?" My mother answered as though she had planned what to say, as though she spoke special words, words that would get us past the watch-out and into the meeting.

The watch-out answered, "I am Keetoowah's son!"

Beyond the bushes, the watch-out ushered us into a clearing surrounded by trees.

There was a fire burning in the center. "It is the sacred fire," my mother whispered to me. "It traveled here with us from the East."

Once we were all settled, Evan Jones stepped out of the darkness into the firelight. "We are all Keetoowah people."

As my eyes adjusted, I saw many people, some I knew. Not far from us was what was left of Johnnie Freeman's family. They looked tired, even thinner than I remembered.

"We are all children of the Great Spirit, of God the Father, of the Breath Giver." Jones looked around the circle.

My eyes followed his around and I saw families that I had not seen since the Trail. Golden Bear watched the speaker while sitting close to his mother.

"He loves us all equally." The people murmured, agreeing with him. "We do not have to give up who we are, Keetowah's Children, the Beloved Community, to be His sons." He pointed around the circle at Black people—slave and free, at Red people—some married to Whites, their children mixed breeds. *"Ho! Mitakuye Oyasin!"* He repeated it. "We are all related!"

In the dark, I continued looking. I leaned, whispering, "There are mixed bloods here, Mother!"

Still watching Evan Jones, she whispered in response. "But their hearts are true. It is the heart that matters. They are full in the heart."

Evan Jones, his eyes and voice full of fire, nodded at the crowd. "I am White. My son, John, is White. But we are Keetoowah's children. We are part of the Beloved Community because we believe in the old way, in God's way, that all of us are His children. None of us greater than the other, none of us enslaving one another." He smiled. "Forgive my stumbling with the language. Reverend Bushyhead has, many times, translated for me. But tonight, I wanted to speak on my own."

Many of the elders, the old ones who had survived the Trail, sat in the circle. Their shoulders were slumped, but their eyes were bright watching him. They nodded at each other as he spoke.

"'It is easier for a camel . . .'" he raised his hand above his head to show us the height of the animal he spoke about, "'to go through the eye of a needle, than for a rich man to enter into the kingdom of God.' Our Lord said it over eighteen hundred years ago, but many of us still will not hear His voice." He shook his head. "By any means necessary, many of us tell

ourselves, we will get wealth; we will get more for ourselves by
any means necessary. If we have to steal or cheat for land, then
that is God's will for us. We make the Lord to be a liar. We
make Him to be a thief. But the truth is, He has no part in
what some of us are doing. We make Him ashamed.

"We kidnap people, or buy people that other ruthless
people have kidnapped. We are trading in stolen goods, stolen
souls, but we say it's acceptable to our Lord. He wants us to
prosper, we say. He takes delight in the prosperity of His people,
we say to excuse ourselves."

He waved the Bible in his hands. "And it's true. Those
words are in this book. But this book also says that we are to
prosper only as our souls prosper." His eyes blazed, his voice
shook with the power in his heart. And I wondered how someone who didn't know me, or my family, could care so much.
Why would a stranger, a free man, risk his life to help people
like us? Evan Jones was saying things that could get him beaten
or hanged. "How prosperous is the soul of a man who steals
from others to ensure his personal gain? How wealthy is the soul
of a man who steals lives, who murders other people's hopes
and dreams for the sake of his own?

"I would say that is not a prosperous soul, but a sick one. I
would say it is a soul that runs from the truth—that runs from
conviction." The things he was saying would make people
angry. The ones who owned us would not want to hear the
truth. "Those of us that do such things come up with all kinds
of ways of running from the truth, the truth that might indeed
give us a prosperous soul. So we give stolen people special
names—we call them slaves, niggers, redskins—so that we don't
have to acknowledge that they are human. So we don't have to
face the truth—that we have wronged Africans, Cherokees,
Creeks, Seminoles, Chickasaw—all part of God's Beloved
Community. We have wounded God's children." The mixed
breeds who owned slaves, the White people who owned slaves,

would say that this man—one of their own—was betraying them.

I could hear the sound of weeping around me. I could hear the sound of broken hearts melting.

"Long ago, we listened to the voices of our elders. We valued the teaching and wisdom of the wise women. We learned from the wisdom of Beloved Women like Nancy Ward, who we know as *Nan'yehi*.

"Now we have lost our way. Some of us even hold it up as a prize that we have White husbands or White wives, choosing mates by the status their color gives to us rather than choosing by the character of the heart." I could hear people murmuring as he spoke. "I'm not making it up. Those are not my words. Those are words printed in the *Cherokee Phoenix*." He looked around the circle. "And I agree with you. We know better— whatever our skin color—we know better. That is not love. Many of us, out of fear or ignorance, follow the ways of some White men who are misguided themselves. These misguided men teach that the acquisition of possessions indicates civilization. So, having more land, a bigger home, more livestock, and even more slaves, means that they are more civilized and superior to others. That is not the old way. That is not brotherhood. That is not love."

The elders, the wise women among them, nodded.

"Many of us pretend, right now, that it is a new moral question. It is a moral imperative, some of us say. We must take the land and make others slaves because we are intelligent and they are heathens. We must do this to teach the heathen about Jesus. We do it in His name, many of us say."

Evan Jones laid his hand across his heart. "But it is not a new question. It is not a question of evangelism.

"The issue was settled long ago. When Egypt oppressed the children of God, the matter was settled—riders and horses thrown into the sea." He waved his hand, as though outstretching it over an ocean. "When just the mention of the name of Ethiopia terrorized men's hearts; when powerful Cushite kings dominated, stealing land and stealing lives, God tore those kingdoms down. The issue was settled when we received the Ten Commandments that says to us, even now, 'Thou shalt not steal.' If we are commanded not to steal, does that mean only goods or oxen? Does it not also mean, thou shalt not steal land? How can it not also mean, thou shalt not steal men, women, and children? How can it not also mean, thou shalt not steal men's dreams?

"I come from across the waters, from a place called Wales. A place far, far away." I tried to imagine what his home looked like. Were there green trees? Was there a stream there, or a well? His skin was so pale. I wondered if all the men there—in Wales—looked like him. "Though it shames me that some of my brothers have come to the United States as slaveholders, the truth is that the matter was settled long ago in my country. The matter was settled in English law, which is the law of Wales, in 1772, almost a hundred years ago. It was settled in courts by wise men, by God-fearing men who outlawed slavery." A place with no slaves? I tried to imagine what that looked like.

Evan Jones stopped, still. He breathed deeply, and then spoke again. "There is a song we sing in my country." He sang the song in his language, in Wales, in words like the United States.

> Amazing Grace, how sweet the sound,
> That saved a wretch like me. . . .
> I once was lost but now am found,
> Was blind, but now, I see.

His high sounding voice was clear, like some bird I remembered, like the stream waters. As he sang, I grew thirsty for more.

He stopped singing to preach again. "Many of our brothers

keep slaves, saying, 'This one has slaves.' Or, 'That one has slaves.'" Evan Jones frowned and shook his head. "That other men steal and murder is no excuse. Each man must face God and truth for himself."

He sang again.

'Twas Grace that taught . . .
my heart to fear.
And Grace, my fears relieved.
How precious did that Grace appear . . .
the hour I first believed.

Something about the song was familiar. Like the waters, like something that I had been missing.

He paused his singing. "That song was written by John Newton, a slave trader who sailed the African coasts, stealing lives and selling them for a pittance. He wrote the song after he became a Christian, when he also still owned slaves of his own—when he still held God's children as though they were his possessions. His only thought, then, was his own salvation. He had not matured enough, in his love, to care for other men's souls. His love was still selfish. His love was still like a child's."

While he spoke, it came to me. I recognized the melody, though I did not know the United States words. Evan Jones began to sing again.

Through many dangers, toils and snares . . .
we have already come.
'Twas Grace that brought us safe thus far . . .
and Grace will lead us home.

Once I recognized the melody, I was even more thirsty for it—for the comfort that it gave.

"But truth set John Newton free. It convicted his heart. He realized the matter was already settled, and he began to speak out against evil he had done, against stealing other men and their dreams for profit. He joined other good men, like William Wilberforce, in the fight against slavery."

The Lord has promised good to me . . .
His word my hope secures.
He will my shield and portion be . . .
as long as life endures.

Evan Jones stepped closer to the fire. "My prayer is that the matter will be settled here in the United States without division, without bloodshed—without neighbor turning against neighbor, brother against brother. Without leaving wounds that may never heal. Let us pray that righteous men, churchgoing men and women, look into their hearts, like John Newton, and find the truth. Let us pray that the matter is settled with truth and love." Truth and love? Who loved us? The people who owned us were churchgoing. Was churchgoing supposed to be enough to change their hearts, to make Mama and Papa love us, to free us? I didn't believe it. Evan Jones laid his hand on his heart. "I pray my brothers will come closer to the Great One's fire and let Him change their hearts."

My mother squeezed my hand. I turned to find her crying. Then she began to sing aloud.

Ooh nay thla nah, hee oo way gee.'
E gah gwoo yah hay ee.

Evan Jones looked in her direction and sang with her in Cherokee. I did not believe that truth and love would be enough to set me free. But still, the song, hearing my mother's voice, began to melt the cold around my heart.

It was the same song from the Trail Where We Cried, "Amazing Grace," but in Cherokee words. It was the burial song we sang to honor those we lost. As others joined her in singing, I remembered Preaching John and the day at the stream—all from different places, from different languages, but singing the same songs. I began to sing with them.

Naw gwoo joe sah, we you low say,
E gah gwo yah ho nah.

My mother put her arm around me. We all sang the chorus through again, some in United States, some in Cherokee.

Amazing Grace, how sweet the sound,   *Ooh nay thla nah, hee*
That saved a wretch like me. . . .   *oo way gee'.*
I once was lost but   *E gah gwoo yah hay ee.*
now am found,   *Naw gwoo joe sah, we you low say,*
Was blind, but now, I see.   *E gah gwo yah ho nah.*

It was then that I understood it, what it meant to be Keetoowah. What it meant to be a part of the Beloved Community. We were all one. The Great One loved each one of us. He still even loved me.

The preacher Evan Jones nodded to each one of us, and then extended his hand. "Now you will hear from a friend of mine. He is a learned man, a compassionate man, and a wise one. He is a man who has spread the Gospel in the great halls of Washington, D.C., who has brokered for peace between the United States and the great chiefs of the Seminoles, he is Chief of the Cherokee Supreme Court. But with all his titles, greatest is that he is a champion for those who are the least among us. Reverend Jesse Bushyhead, come speak to us."

CHAPTER THIRTY-FIVE

REVEREND BUSHYHEAD STEPPED INTO THE LIGHT OF THE fire and looked as I had remembered him from the Trail, tall and powerful. Except that his hair was loosed now, flowing wildly and freely to his shoulders. He wiped tears from his eyes. "When I hear that song we were singing, 'Amazing Grace,' it reminds me of the Trail. It reminds me of when we could not bury our dead with honor. But that song was a place of comfort for us. That song helped us to move forward.

"My brothers, my sisters," he smiled, speaking in the Cherokee way. "The way has been hard for us. The Trail changed us—I know because I, too, walked the Trail. It tried to defeat us. Many of us lost our lives. But look at us, those of us who survived, here tonight." He smiled at us. "It has been hard. There have been many disappointments, many lost dreams. But look at yourselves. You have survived! We have survived!" He turned around the circle, his eyes stopping on each one of us. "And look at us, look at how beautiful we are. Many languages, many colors, from many lands—yet, we love one another.

There is no one here to report this story. No newspaper will tell our story. What we do, gathering like this, is forbidden. So, it will be up to you to tell this story, to tell it to your children so that they will know that we gathered together here in beauty and in love, the Beloved Community."

He wiped more tears from his eyes. "You are wounded; even still, there is trust here. So, in trust, I share with you my true name—*Dta-ske-ge-de-hee*. I share it because you are my brothers and sisters, because we are family."

He stood strong like a tree, his eyes piercing. "You are God's children. You are the ones for whom He sacrificed His only begotten Son, Jesus Christ. You are the sons and daughters in whom the Breath Giver is well pleased. We are all one. We are all one family, one Beloved Community. And He has not forgotten you."

I fought back my own tears. I wanted to believe that the Breath Giver remembered me. It was easy to believe His love with the eternal fire giving light and warmth. It was easy to believe with my mother and so much love around me. My heart believed, but my head asked, what about tomorrow? What about tomorrow when the sun watched us stooped over in the fields?

Tonight, though, Reverend Bushyhead reassured us. The firelight covered him like a blanket. "These are troubled times. Our land was stolen, the place of our fathers' bones. But it does not stop there." He stared ahead, as though he was looking through space, looking through time. "We lost the land; many of us have not received the money promised to us." He shrugged. "If a man steals your land, why would he not steal your money?" He looked at my mother and me. "So, many of us are not just heartbroken, but hungry and homeless. And what of our brothers and sisters who are called slaves? There is nothing for them to start over with, not even a promise. Like us, they have shared in the suffering; many of them also lost their lives.

"Yet, even with this loss, we have gained. We have learned of the Lord who died for us. We have learned about reading, writing, and created our own alphabet. We have learned some new ways that are good for us. But we choose, also, to hold on to who we are, to the best of who we are. We are not confused. The best, we have chosen—that is eternal salvation. But we reject a culture that enslaves other men based on lies. We choose Jesus as our Savior, but we choose the Beloved Community as our culture. Christianity is the religion we choose—it is the relationship we choose with the Breath Giver—but Keetoowah, the Beloved Community, is the relationship we choose with one another.

"It is our culture. It is the way we live with our brothers and sisters, sharing in common, respecting each soul. We choose brotherhood. *Ea Nigada Qusdi Idadadvhn!* You are all my relations in creation!"

Reverend Bushyhead pointed at Evan Jones. "My brother, Reverend Jones, talked about selfishness and greed. The country may split apart because of men's greed. They fight for money, they fight for property, they fight for land that is not theirs, and they fight for souls that are not theirs—making free men into slaves. They turn their backs on what is true—that we are all related."

As he spoke, I thought of the Trail Where We Cried. I thought of the family I had lost, of the friends and family that we had left behind. I also thought of Mama Emma and Papa. I had lost them too. They were not here tonight. They had separated themselves from us. Now we separated ourselves from them. We had loved one another once. Mama Emma and Papa once had treated me as though I might be their daughter.

I thought of the nights I spent in their home, the meals we had shared. Now we distrusted one another. Now we feared one another. Now I was no longer their daughter; I was their slave, to be bought or sold.

"It is hard not to despise our brothers, but as Pastor Evan has said, we are children of grace and we must extend that same grace. As he has said, we have been matured by God's love."

Reverend Bushyhead's words, so much like the wise woman's on the Trail, called me back to him. They both spoke with passion. But now his words seemed more urgent. "Like a child, the young spirit takes what it wants, pushing others out of the way, and then makes excuses before the Father. 'They are heathen,' the young spirit says, pointing at our clothes. The young spirit believes that the one who is wealthier and who has more possessions is better, more civilized. 'They are not my color, so you like me better,' the young spirit says, pointing at our skin. They look at how we live together—sharing together—and call us ignorant. They forbid many of us to read and call us ignorant."

As he spoke, it was as though I was back with Miss Lillian, combing her hair, listening to her read.

"Teach me to read."

"What did you say?"

"I said, teach me. I want to learn."

Reverend Bushyhead's words washed away the image. "Intelligence is the ability to learn, to see a new world and learn from it. Civility is the ability to see people who are different, and respect and love them. The spirit is young and does not know that it is not judged by fancy clothes, but by the beauty of the spirit. Maturity is judged by the compassion and love of the heart."

The preacher cautioned us. "People will talk against us because we speak truth. They will say we are ignorant and heathens because we speak against their greed, because we speak against their crime, against owning others, of making their brothers slaves. But I ask you, how can a civilized man own his brother? How can a child of God mistreat his brother? How can one man sell his brother for money?" Reverend Bushyhead's glance returned to the circle. "What have we gained from all this stealing, from this greed? I even fear that the church may split apart—people choosing things, thirty pieces of silver, over spirit and truth."

There was so much love lost. Love traded for land and money. Even Miss Lillian had traded our friendship for a blanket. I thought of Abraham and Ephraim, Golden Bear's father and my father.

The night birds, the frogs, the crickets made music around us while Reverend Bushyhead spoke. Darkness shrouded our backs while the fire lit our faces.

"I hope that we will not have to choose bloodshed. But somehow, we must stand up. We cannot allow this evil to go on—we cannot allow them to continue to abort the dreams of men and women and children, and of even the unborn—born without choice into lives without hope, into lives of slavery even before they take their first breaths."

I looked at my mother, at the sadness she wore each day. But Mama Emma and Papa were sad too. They wore fancy clothes, but it could not cover their trouble. We had all lost each other for land, for bricks, for things that really did not matter.

"I fear that bloodshed is coming. If the church splits, the church that has God's grace, how can we expect that the nation will survive without a fight?" He shook his head. "Washington, Jefferson, Jackson—they are men who walk in greatness, but they walk with blood on their hands, they walk with the burden of theft bowing their backs.

"The way has been hard. I may not be with you long. I have seen too much. Heard too many lies, seen treaties broken and people dying." The group quieted, deep in thought, listening to Reverend Bushyhead. "But hold fast to the truth. Hold fast to your faith. Hold fast to the hope within you."

In a deep voice, he began to sing. Only, now, he sang in United States words.

Amazing Grace, how sweet the sound,
That saved a wretch like me. . . .
I once was lost but now am found,
Was blind, but now, I see.

When he finished, he wiped his eyes and then extended his hand. "Now, hear a friend. I have been with him, to see him lead many people—White, Red, and Black—to Christ. If we are to judge this man by his fruit, as the Bible says, and not by his color, as others want us to do, then he is a great man. A great man!

"He is called slave, like many of you. But if we judge him by his service, then he is among the greatest men in the kingdom—seeking to save those who would enslave him!"

Reverend Bushyhead, his tears now dried, smiled, pointing in the darkness. "Hear my brother who has preached in our churches, who risks his life daily here in Indian Territory for the Gospel." Reverend Bushyhead walked from the circle. "Brother Jesse, come forward."

Another man, a Black man, came and stood before us.

CHAPTER THIRTY-SIX

$\mathcal{B}$ROTHER JESSE? HE WAS NOT WHO I HAD EXPECTED when Evan Jones had spoken with my mother and me on the trading post road. Brother Jesse was not the Reverend Jesse Bushyhead, but a slave like my mother and me. He was a Black slave who preached the Gospel in the midst of the Beloved Community, in the midst of Indian Territory.

Reverend Jesse Bushyhead and Brother Jesse embraced, Bushyhead towering over the shorter man. Then the Cherokee preacher went to his seat.

Though his face was without lines, Brother Jesse stooped like an old man. It was like heavy burdens he had carried bowed him, not age. He held a Good Book, the Bible, in his hand.

The noise of the crickets, the bullfrogs, and the owls seemed to hush as he spoke. "You know that I am a prisoner in chains, a prisoner for Christ." His voice rose above him, made him seem taller. "But when I can steal away—some of you know me, I recognize your faces—I steal away to share the Good News." Who were these people? Who was this man? It was hard to believe that he ran away to help other people. It was even harder to believe that, having run away, he kept coming back—even though he might be beaten—just so he could help more people. I was afraid to run to save myself.

"Those of you who know me know that I have been persecuted. I've been strung up, hung from trees, beaten." He tapped his back. "I bear the scars to prove it."

His words made me think of Ephraim, of that day long ago when I first met the boy. Those were days before I had seen anyone beaten, days when I knew nothing of scars. Those were the days before I knew fear.

Brother Jesse's voice lowered, full of quiet assurance and power. "I've been beaten and bent, but I'm not broken. As the apostle Paul said, 'We are troubled on every side, yet not distressed; we are perplexed, but not in despair; persecuted, but not forsaken; cast down, but not destroyed.'"

As I listened, I was reminded of meeting the Red Bird on the Trail, but this was something even more strange to me. This man was like Ephraim, only he held his head high. He spoke confidently. He spoke the language of The Principal People. There was power in him, like sacred fire burning in his bones.

"We've been hurt, lands stolen, families stolen. Because of the color of our skin, because of the language we speak, because of the way we dress, there are people who think we are less than them. Many of you, like me, are even another man's slave."

I thought of Preaching John on Master Cauley's plantation, a preacher like this man. Only, this man held a Bible in his hand. This man spoke not only to slaves, but he spoke boldly to free men.

"But, like the apostle Paul, I want you to know that we are prisoners for the cause of Christ. We have no reason to be ashamed." He rubbed his hand over his short, wiry hair. "Before I was stolen and forced into slavery, I was an educated free man, like the apostle Paul. And, like the apostle Paul," he held one finger in the air, "I don't mind what I have given up for the sake of the kingdom. I have come to remind you that we are all joint heirs. We are not slaves as some call us, but we are joint heirs with Christ. We are part of a royal priesthood!"

Royalty? I thought of the princesses in Miss Lillian's books. They all looked like her—blue eyes, blond hair. In the darkness, I touched my own hair, touched my skin. Royalty? Me?

"Those that want to hold us in chains, they just don't recognize us. They mistreat us because they don't know that we are the Creator's children, that we are royal heirs. I have come to remind you that you may be in chains, you may be poor and homeless, but this present suffering does not compare to the glory that will be revealed in us. One day, people will recognize us for who we are! God will claim us as His own beloved children, children in whom He is well pleased!"

Brother Jesse spoke as though he had heard what was in my heart. It was hard to believe, that one day Mama Emma and Papa would remember who I was. It was hard to believe that one day Master Cauley would recognize who I was, that I was like his Lillian, a princess too. It was hard to believe that the Great One would claim me as His own.

"I came to tell you that you are not the first ones, the first royalty to be mistaken for a slave." He held the Bible open, flipping through pages. "In ancient times, there were others. They came before, to tell the story, to show us the way."

"To show us the way . . ." I thought of Abraham, who went before us. And I thought of the many things that Red Bird had told us, about the songs of the ones who came before us.

"The Breath Giver and the ones who walked before you, whose bones have been left on the Trail away from the places they loved, who have cried until the road ran with tears, they know. They cry an ancient song with you, and God hears."

I could hear the words he sang to us.

By the rivers of Babylon, there we sat down,
yea, we wept, when we remembered Zion.
We hanged our harps upon the willows in the midst thereof.
For there they that carried us away captive required of us a song;
and they that wasted us, that plundered us,
*   required of us mirth, saying,*
Sing us one of the songs of Zion.

Now, in front of me was a Black preacher, and I heard the words of the ancient song as he spoke. Crowded around him were Black freedmen—like what was left of Johnnie Freeman's family—and Black slaves; full bloods like what was left of Golden Bear's family; Whites; and Black Indians, like my own family. Crowded around him, I felt in my heart, was all the pain and hope of those who had bled and died, even that of the ancient ones who came before us.

He opened the book, opened his mouth to read, and then stopped. "Oh, my brothers and sisters! I wish that all of you could read. I wish that you could read this book for yourself! Then you would know that this book, this letter of love, was written for you!

"If you read this book, you would know that Christ came down from glory, where He was with God and the Holy Spirit from the beginning. Though we are sinners, He came that our sins might be forgiven, that we might have a right to the tree of life! He came so that our names might be written in the Book of the Lamb!

"If you could read this book, you would know Him so much more! You would know that He walked among men. If you could read this book, you would know that Jesus washed the feet of the unclean and the unlearned. He touched those who were untouchable and He loved those that were rejected and despised. He taught those that others considered unteachable, the poor, the women—He gave the best seats to those who matter least to men. He even blessed the aliens among them. With love, He held them in His hands."

As Brother Jesse spoke, I leaned my head on my mother. I wanted to crawl onto her lap. I knew the shame, the shame of being untouchable. I knew the shame of being touched without love.

How could there be a king, or even a prince who loved me? How could there be someone who cared to hold me in his arms? How could there be king or prince who was not ashamed of me?

"If you could read this book, you would know that He loves you. That though He was royalty, King of kings, He came to earth as a poor baby born to the poorest of the poor. You would know that He believes in justice because He was born into a nation of oppressed people, people just like you and me. If you could read this book, you would know that Jesus was beaten, just like some of us. He was bound, just like some of us. He was spat upon, just like some of us. And He did it all for each one of us, so that we could have better lives—everlasting lives. If you could read this book, you would know that He teaches that we must love one another; that whatever we do—or don't do—to the least of people, we do it to Him. When we starve the poor, we starve Jesus Christ. When we neglect the homeless, we neglect Jesus Christ. When we abuse the children, we abuse Jesus Christ."

I squeezed my mother's hand. How could a prince care about people like us? Why would anyone give up what they had to comfort us?

"If you could read this book, you would know that it is not God, it is not Jesus that holds you down. You would know that He came to heal the brokenhearted, to bind up wounds, and to set the captives free! He came to comfort His people. If you could read this book, you would know that God says, 'Thou shalt not oppress a stranger: for ye know the heart of a stranger, seeing ye were strangers in the land of Egypt.'" He held the

Bible to his chest. "Oh, I wish you all could read this book. You would know that the Lord has given you power, power to overcome, and power to be all that He says you can be. I wish you could read this book, because you would know what God's promises are for you. If you could read, you would read the words of the apostle John's Revelation."

He flipped through some pages and began to read, "'After this I beheld, and, lo, a great multitude, which no man could number, of all nations, and kindreds, and people, and tongues, stood before the throne, and before the Lamb, clothed with white robes, and palms in their hands. . . .'" He paused.

He pointed to Golden Bear and what was left of his family. "All nations, all kindreds, all people, all tongues!" He pointed to what was left of sweet Johnnie Freeman's family. "All nations, all kindreds, all people, all tongues!" Each time he spoke, his voice rose louder and louder, until it shook the air like thunder! Brother Jesse pointed at Evan and John Jones. "All nations, all kindreds, all people, all tongues!" And, finally, he pointed at my mother and me. "All nations, all kindreds, all people, all tongues!" His voice dropped to a whisper. "Oh, my children, I wish that all of you could read it." He turned one shoulder toward us, so that we could see the curve of his spine. "Some people don't want you to read because they don't want you to know the whole truth. But it's worth every stripe I bear on my back. It's worth every beating I get to tell you the whole blessed truth! Because the truth is, our sweet Prince wore stripes just like mine—stripes so that we could be healed!"

In the firelight, I could see tears pooling in his eyes. He wiped them, and then read again. "'And one of the elders answered, saying unto me, What are these which are arrayed in white robes? and whence came they? And I said unto him, Sir, thou knowest. And he said to me, These are they which came out of great tribulation, and have washed their robes, and made them white in the blood of the Lamb.

" 'Therefore are they before the throne of God, and serve him day and night in His temple: and he that sitteth on the throne shall dwell among them. They shall hunger no more, neither thirst any more; neither shall the sun light on them, nor any heat. For the Lamb which is in the midst of the throne shall feed them, and shall lead them unto living fountains of waters: and God shall wipe away all tears from their eyes.' " He wiped his eyes again, not with soft hands, but with strong, callused hands. "He knows our suffering! He feels it! He knows our pain! But God shall wipe away all tears from their eyes . . . from your eyes. . . . All nations, all kindreds, all people, all tongues!"

CHAPTER THIRTY-SEVEN

*I*T WAS NOT WHAT WE HAD BEEN TAUGHT. WE HAD BEEN taught, since we'd left our home in the East, that Jesus was the White man's God. He was not for us. We were not to learn about Him. Learning about Jesus, like reading, was against the law. The missionaries had been wrong to teach us, we were told. We didn't have souls, we were told. Jesus was not for us, and we could not read. We were animals.

All nations, all kindreds, all people, all tongues? My heart wanted to be glad, but I would not let it. I was afraid. How could I believe it with all that had happened to me? I was untouchable. How could I believe that the Breath Giver wanted to wipe my tears, to hold me in His arms? I burrowed closer to my mother.

"I came to tell you that you are not the first ones, the first royalty to be mistaken for a slave," Brother Jesse repeated. He turned pages, slid his finger down a page and began to read. "'Now Israel loved Joseph more than all his children, because he was the son of his old age: and he made him a coat of many colours.'"

I listened to him, not believing my ears. How could a slave read? He was not supposed to be smart enough to read.

"'And when his brethren saw that their father loved him more than all his brethren, they hated him, and could not speak peaceably unto him.'"

I listened to Brother Jesse, not believing my eyes. No one snatched the book from his hands. It was against the law now in Indian Territory for him to read. Yet no one in this circle forbade him to read. No one beat him here, among the Kee-toowah people.

"'And Joseph dreamed a dream, and he told it his brethren: and they hated him yet the more.'"

Reverend Evan Jones, his son John, Reverend Bushyhead, the people in the circle—they all listened to Brother Jesse. They listened like what he said might save their lives.

"This boy Joseph was his father's favorite son. He was only seventeen. Not much older than this child here." He pointed at me.

When the circle of eyes turned on me, I was not sure whether to run, or to stand. My mother held my hand, re-assuring me.

"Joseph's father, Jacob, had his other sons when he was younger—when he was wild, when he was jealous, when he was a trickster and a thief. And his older sons were just like him. When he looked at them, they reminded him of the sinful man he had been. His older sons reminded Jacob of his ugly past. When Jacob looked at his older sons, he saw manipulators—like him; he saw boys willing to betray their brothers.

"But Joseph was the son of Jacob's transformation. He was the son born after Jacob took a cold, hard, honest look at him-self. Joseph was the son of Jacob's purification. Joseph was beau-tiful, obedient, honest, pure, and in his dreams he heard the

wisdom of God. Jacob liked his younger son, Joseph, because
he reflected all the good that Jacob had become in his old age."

Brother Jesse tapped the Good Book with one finger. "So,
you remember, sometimes when people don't love you, it's not
because of who you are, but it might be because of what you
show them about themselves. Joseph's brothers hated him
because they did not understand that their father did not like
them because he did not like remembering who he once was.
His brothers hated Joseph because *his* goodness revealed *their*
faults.

"Jacob, the father, might have been able to make all of his
sons beautiful and loving, if he had taken the time. But isn't that
the wonder and goodness of God? He gives all of us—men and
women, young and old, Black, Red, and White—the chance
to be a favorite, to be a joint heir like His Son. We only have
to choose."

I listened to him, wondering if what I saw was real, wondering if it was a vision, if I would wake and find myself in my
mother's cabin, or wake and find myself on Master Cauley's
farm.

"So the older brothers hated Joseph because of his coat,
because it was a symbol of his father's affection. But they also
hated him because he had a dream.

"He didn't make himself a dreamer; he simply was. It was a
gift. But they hated him for it, just as one woman will hate
another woman because of her beauty, or a man will hate
another because of his strength, or as one man will envy another
because God has given him beautiful land."

He looked back at the book, and I wished that I knew the
words. I wished that I, too, could read them with him. It was a
wonder to see. It was a miracle to see!

"Joseph was a dreamer, and because he was without guile,
he honestly told his dream to his brothers. He even shared a
second dream with his whole family. He didn't keep his dream

from others, because he didn't know that his fellow men would kill him simply for having a dream. He didn't give himself the dream; it was a gift from the Breath Giver. Having a dream isn't sinful; having a vision isn't a thing of pride, but men will hate you for it just the same. When men hate you, you remember that. They'll hate you just for having a dream."

Brother Jesse tapped the book again. "Young Joseph told his brothers a dream of twelve sheaves in the field, where they, the eleven, bowed down to him. And, because he was too honest to hide, he told them another dream of the sun, the moon, and stars—and of them bowing down to him. His brothers never thought a good thought about him, so they hated him. They never considered that his dream might be for their good.

"So they went about their daily lives—being jealous and disobedient. Instead of tending sheep, they went to the big city. Instead of staying on the path, tending their sheep in Shechem, they strayed and went further north to Dothan. When they saw Joseph coming, having found them and wearing the symbol of his father's approval, they came up with a plot, first, to kill him. By the by, they decided to sell him into slavery. The royal one, the favored one, the beloved one sent away in chains because his brothers hated him, because he had something they wanted. They hated the goodness, the innocence they saw in him."

Brother Jesse held his hands in front of him, as though they were bound or in shackles. "The brothers sold Joseph, took his beautiful coat, dipped it in goat's blood and gave it to their father when they returned home." He shook his head. "And the truth is, two of his brothers didn't want to go along with it, but they didn't have the courage to stand up. They hoped that good intentions would save their brother Joseph." He frowned. "Their lack of courage, not being willing to stand up, got Joseph thrown in the pit, sold into slavery. Good intentions without action are never enough. Good intentions without action left their father brokenhearted."

He began to read again. And when he read, it was like the kite flying, something tugged my heart higher.

Brother Jesse read clear and loud, like he could be a school-teacher. "'And he knew it, and said, It is my son's coat; an evil beast hath devoured him; Joseph is without doubt rent in pieces.

"'And Jacob rent his clothes, and put sackcloth upon his loins, and mourned for his son many days.

"'And all his sons and all his daughters rose up to comfort him; but he refused to be comforted; and he said, For I will go down into the grave unto my son mourning. Thus his father wept for him.'"

Like the kite after the wind, I hung on Brother Jesse's every word.

"Those boys stood around watching their father's heart break. They watched him weep, knowing that they had strayed from the path, knowing they had harmed their brother. Jealous men, evil, wickedness in high places, will try to bury you and your dream and deny they have done wrong." He tapped his chest. "But it is mercy inside of me, mercy that wants to forgive, mercy that wants to help them. It is that same mercy that lets me know that God is at work inside of me.

"Don't blame theft of land and slavery—this sad state of affairs—on the Giver of All Good Gifts. It is satan that wants to destroy dreams, satan that conspires to have you thrown in the pit to kill you and your dream. But don't lose hope!" Brother Jesse held his finger in the air.

"Poor Joseph—from the pit he was sold into slavery, into that ugly institution in which many of us find ourselves. Oh, what a vile thing that men try to lay at the feet of God, at the feet of our loving Savior.

"Taken from his home, from his family, from the land he knew, Joseph—just like us—was sold into slavery in a foreign land. But even in dark places, the Father's bright dreams will not die if we don't give up."

I thought of my own father, of the nights in the cabin when he spoke to my mother and me. *"One day you will marry a man, a man with a brick house. And you will have a big wedding, with many blankets, with big food, and relatives from all over. You will be a beautiful maiden. We will own land of our own. You will not carry the water. You will own the well."* As I listened, I wondered if those dreams, my own father's words, would live again. I wondered if his words would come true.

Brother Jesse looked up, pointing at the sky. "Darkness could not hide that young Joseph was royalty, that he was favored." He looked back at us. "Even slavery could not hide the fact that he was blessed. Even darkness can't keep goodness and light from showing up around you."

He shook his head. "But Joseph's troubles were not over. The man who owned him in that place called Egypt, a man called Potiphar, had a wicked wife who wanted to use the boy. She owned him and she could do whatever she wanted with him, she thought. Her shameful fantasies were more important than young Joseph's dignity."

I looked at my mother, then back at the sacred fire. My face warmed with shame remembering Master Cauley's visits to my cabin.

"But Joseph said no. And his no landed him in prison." Brother Jesse shook his finger at us again. "You remember this. Being submissive doesn't mean giving yourself to wolves. That's what that woman was, a wolf. We are to submit to the Good Shepherd, we are to know His voice, but that doesn't mean that we're supposed to be deceived or used by vicious wolves."

I had wanted to say no to Master Cauley. I wanted to cry out. But who would have heard me? Where could I have run?

Brother Jesse's words made me think of the Red Bird, speaking with us on the Trail Where We Cried. *"The one who does not protect his lambs, he is an imposter, a wolf in sheep's clothing. The one who leads the lambs astray, who devours them, is not the shepherd. The one who gets fat while the sheep suffer, he is a wolf."* I was a lamb, separated from the flock, unable to protect myself from the wolf.

Brother Jesse stood in the light of the fire, shadows and light covering his face. "We are to resist the devil, resist the wolves, even if sometimes it might mean death." He paused. "Some things are worth dying for."

"Some things are worth dying for." His words . . . I could feel them piercing my heart.

"We have to find some way of standing up!" The short preacher shook his fist. "Even if we only, first, stand up in our hearts!"

He did not understand. Brother Jesse was a man. Men had no fear.

But I was a child. I had walked the Trail. I had seen what happened to people who stood up: They were taken away, never to be seen again. They were forced to march a thousand miles. The ones who stood up were shot and dragged away.

I was a child. I had to stay alive.

CHAPTER THIRTY-EIGHT

Brother Jesse walked the circle, the light of the flame on his back. He continued with the story. "The boy Joseph stood up inside himself. He ran from that wicked woman and ended up in jail. Even when you do the right thing, sometimes the wrong thing will happen to you. Just like poor Joseph." He pointed at me. "He was a boy. Not much older than that child."

All the faces turned to see me. I didn't want them to see me. I didn't want them to see the shame the story opened in my heart. I touched my hair. I lowered my head until his voice called their eyes away.

"Even in jail, Joseph didn't give up hope. Even in jail, he didn't give up faith in the truth of his dream. Jail squeezed that boy; it ground him like grain in a mill. What came out was faith, because that's what was in his belly, that's what was in his heart. Faith and hope was the seed inside the husk. If bitterness had been at his core, he would have come out of prison angry. He would have denied his dreams. If pride had been at his core, shame over his situation would have kept him silent and he would have given up hope that he could interpret and believe in dreams—he never would have gotten out of the pit."

The preacher was wrong, I argued in my heart. Only fools tried to have courage when they were bound. Only those who wanted to die fought for hope when they were bound. Only fools kept believing. I kept quiet to stay alive.

Brother Jesse came to stand near my mother and me. "But Joseph held on to his faith. Even in prison, he was honest, open, and trusting. He was there many years, but he kept believing in his dream, in his ability to interpret dreams."

He looked at me. "No matter how long it takes, you must not give up your dream. You must not give up who you are. You must remember who you are, child."

Why did he keep pointing to me, looking at me? Why did his eyes seem to see my shame? I was angry with him. Yet, as he spoke, I could still feel the tugging in my heart.

"It can take a lifetime, but we must have faith that God's promises will come to pass. Being broken and robbed of his family, to have his dream stolen from him could have finished Joseph. But faith and righteousness, even in the presence of his enemies, even surrounded by wolves, brought him out."

It was just a story. Why was I supposed to believe that my life would change for the good? Change had taken Abraham away, had taken my father away. Change had brought me shame. It was safer to hold on, even if it was bad, to what I knew. It was easier to stop fretting, as Miss Lillian had warned me.

Despite my thoughts, Brother Jesse persisted. "Joseph believed the dream, instead of believing that he would be in prison forever. Instead of doom, he kept his eyes open for God's goodness, he kept looking for God's mercy to find him. And what he believed is just what happened to him. Word of his gift, like God promised him, brought him before a great king. Hope kept him believing. Hope kept him alive! Hope, faith, and his gift conspired to make Joseph a great man—even in a foreign land."

He threw his arms open wide. "One day those prison doors swung wide open. Joseph didn't give up hope. He didn't go in a corner and die, and one day he stepped from the pit to the palace. It didn't happen without heartache, it didn't happen without having to fight back doubt, it didn't happen without tears." Brother Jesse raised his finger again. "If people tell you that you will be able to make it without effort, then they lie. Success comes with much business, with much hard work that will bend your spiritual back."

I looked at the curve of his spine. Close to me now, I could see his broken, scarred hands. "Finally, Joseph connected with someone—someone who also had confidence in who he was—a king who was not afraid of Joseph's dreams. Finally, Joseph connected with someone who could let him shine and not be threatened by his light.

"Joseph's dreams said he was a leader, he believed them and acted like one. No matter what anyone said, he knew he was not a slave, so he didn't act like one. He didn't see himself as a prisoner; he saw himself as a star. He believed the dream God gave him rather than believing what men said, or what his circumstances said. In his heart, Joseph believed the dream, and so it was."

He stepped even closer to my mother and me. "One day, Joseph saw his dreams come true. One day, his brothers came to him, bowing as he had dreamed. In the story, that is when we learn that the dream was never about pride. It was a dream about Joseph, because of his position, saving his brothers' lives. There was a famine in their homeland, and that famine brought them face-to-face with the brother they had betrayed."

Brother Jessie turned and began walking away from my mother and me. His voice softened, trailing behind him. "Mercy and love in his heart, despite his pain, made him forgive them and restore them. The dream in his heart, the dream his brothers despised, had freed him and saved their lives. It was a dream about a good plan, a dream of hope and a future."

His voice rose, the sacred fire glowing around him. "Dreams are worth living for, worth dying for. Dreams are worth running for, my children!

"There is hope, if we can acknowledge who we are. If we can come face-to-face with ourselves, and wrestle like Joseph's father, Jacob, we can change. We can walk with transformed hearts. We can find peace and joy with renewed minds. We can become great people, like Joseph.

"No man wants to look and see that he is broken, that he is diseased or disfigured. But if he will be brave, if he will judge himself, then, like Jacob, he can change and even raise a child of great beauty like Joseph.

"It was not easy for Jacob to change. It is a hard thing to see yourself—to recognize that you are broken, to see that you are wrong. It is painful to see that you are diseased. It is painful to recognize that you are diseased when you see it in your children, when you see the footprint that you have left on the ground.

"Stepping into the water to be baptized is easy—but honest confession of what is wrong with you hurts right down to the depths of the soul." He balled his fist and hit himself in the stomach. "I know. I'm telling you what I know. It hurts so deep, like a wound to the mortal body." He doubled over with the blow.

Then he stood up, staggering. His face contorted as though he struggled with great pain. "And it is even more painful— after you know it must be done—to rip out that thing about you that is evil. And, my brothers and sisters, don't let anyone fool you. It is not easy!" He stood, holding out his arm. "That diseased part of your soul, it hurts like disease in your arm. You can feel it." He shook his arm at us.

"Most people run from it. They are not brave like Jacob. They don't want to feel the soul's disease, the soul's pain. They try to pretend, like Jacob did for so long, that the sickness is not there. So they try to cover it by acquiring more things. They try to cover it by drinking too much."

I thought of the men I saw—the women too—the ones who drank too much. The ones I saw falling down, lying down on the road.

"It would be wrong of me to deceive you, to tell you that changing is easy. Cutting that disease from your soul is painful. It means you have to cut away a piece of who you are."

Brother Jesse held out his arm again. "It's like hacking away a beloved arm." He wielded the Good Book against his arm as though it were an ax. My mother and I flinched with each blow. "It's like plucking away a beloved eye." He paused, his gaze burning into us. "It takes great courage. Great, great courage indeed! It is like putting oneself up on a cross." He lowered his voice. "But the man or woman who has the courage to do it, to change, that man or woman can be made whole. Though he loses the diseased part of himself—an arm or even an eye— that man or woman can walk away changed and made whole."

Brother Jesse rubbed one hand over his Bible. "We know that Jesus was great because He transformed the people. We know He is King of kings because of the children He leaves behind, He makes them whole!

"We can choose to be courageous people. We can choose to stand, to fight against what is wrong inside ourselves. We can choose to be made whole."

Brother Jesse turned, once again, and looked directly at me. He looked at me as though he knew me. "No matter what happens, daughter, hold on to your dreams! No matter what chains men bind you with, hold on to your dreams! Don't let bondage and oppression break you! You remember I told you, my daughter." He looked around the circle and pointed at Golden Bear. "You remember I told you, my son." He looked back at me. "Choose to be made whole! Then run for your dreams, my daughter! Run!"

CHAPTER THIRTY-NINE

WHEN THE MEETING DISBANDED, MORNING WAS NOT FAR away. There was no time for talking to those we had not seen in a long time. So we nodded to them, moving quietly into the shelter of the trees.

When I saw Golden Bear walking away, I raised my hand to him in salute. He smiled and nodded in return.

My mother and I made our way through the trees, the moon our light. When we stepped into the clearing, I saw Golden Bear, his belly still like his father's, riding away on a pony.

He rode a pony with three white socks—a pony like the one ridden by one of the riders at the well.

My mother and I stooped, tipping softly, hugging the trees, staying in the darkness of the bushes and high grasses. When we reached our compound, all the windows in the main house and in the cabins were still dark.

Safe inside our cabin, my mother plaited her hair into one long braid. As she braided, her black curly hair and her face moved in and out of the moonlight coming through our window. "We will work harder!" she whispered to me. "We will make double so we can buy our land sooner!"

My heart pounded. What was she thinking? "Mother, we have to be careful!" I spoke softly, trying to keep the sound of fear out of my voice. It would be daylight soon. The angels of tonight's dreams—Evan Jones, Reverend Bushyhead, and Brother Jesse—would be gone.

"I think Brother Jesse is right. We have already been careful, Armentia. Now I think we must be brave."

We undressed quietly, putting on our night clothes, and climbed into bed.

"We have to be careful, Mother. Trouble will come to us!" I could not stop my voice from quavering. We could not let tonight's dreams get us beaten . . . or killed.

"Trouble has already come to us, my daughter. And we have allowed trouble to bully us, to make us frightened, to make us weak.

"That is not who we are. We are from proud women. We are from women who fight alongside their men. We are from strong women who own land. We come from wise women, from women who know the voice of the Breath Giver." She spoke quietly, but her tone was fierce.

"Especially you, my daughter. You are not a tortoise, a *u-la-no*, hiding your head. You have always been like a panther, a *tlv-da-tsi'*, fighting whatever comes against you. You are your father's daughter, so you are a child of peace. But we also carry the blood of our mothers—so we are like porcupines, like the *di-li tsu-tsa-o-s-di*, leaving those who come against us with a reminder of their trespass. Remember that. You're your mother, so I must help you remember who you are."

She slid underneath her sheets. "You and I are the only two

left standing. There is no one else to be strong. We are of the Deer Clan, but sometimes even deer must stand and fight."

I went for water early the next morning. The sun rose golden, the sky yellow and rose around it. All that I had seen the night before—Preacher Evan Jones, Reverend Bushyhead, and Brother Jesse—stirred in my mind.

"There is no one else to be strong." My mother's words walked with me. *". . . sometimes even deer must stand and fight."* How could she forget what had happened to the brave ones on the Trail? How could she forget Golden Bear's father? He had stood up strong, he fought like a panther, and we saw him die by the side of the Trail because of it.

What I had seen had excited me, but it had also frightened and confused me. Brother Jesse—the image of him preaching out loud to White, Red, and Black people, the image of him reading boldly and unafraid—I would have believed it when we were still in the East, but it was hard to believe in Indian Territory.

"So, I see it is Kituwah's daughter!"

Turning to see who sneaked upon me, I dropped my bucket.

"You walked more quietly when you were a girl!" It was Golden Bear, sitting on his pony. He smiled. "You are still a little girl; you are no woman!"

"Golden Bear!"

"It is my name." He nodded. "Don't yell it out, surprised, as if you do not know me, little girl."

"I am no little girl."

I walked, him on horseback, as we talked. He looked me over. "So you say, Kituwah's daughter. But if you are to remain to grow to a woman, you will have to listen more closely to who rides up behind you."

He was older, taller. His voice was deeper, but it still

reminded me of when we were young. "Don't be so proud of yourself. You are still no man!"

"So you say." He laughed out loud.

"So I say!"

He stopped smiling. "You are home again. I heard that you were sold away."

Shame pressed my head down. "Yes."

We stopped in front of the schoolhouse. "Don't worry, Armentia. The One Who Guards His Family still watches over you." His pony started at the sound of a wagon coming up the road. He reined it still. "Lift your head, Armentia. You are still strong. You are still good." He looked back over his shoulder at the wagon. It was closer. "And don't worry. You will have no more trouble at the well!" He slapped his pony and galloped away.

I watched after him, a plume of dust following him. I watched until the wagon, Mama Emma's wagon, pulled alongside me.

"What are you up to, Armentia?" She frowned at me, holding the reins in her hand.

I shook my head.

"There is trouble brewing and, if you're not careful, you'll find yourself right in the midst of it." She looked up the road, toward where Golden Bear disappeared from view. "Behave yourself. You and your mother. I would hate to see something happen to you. I would hate to see something happen to your mother." She pointed after Golden Bear. "That one is like his father—trouble. And he will end like him." She frowned. "Kee-toowah Society! They are all trouble!"

I said nothing.

She looked toward the schoolhouse. "Didn't I tell you to stay away from here, Armentia? Are you hardheaded? Don't you understand?"

"I was fetching water."

"Water?" She looked around. "Well, I don't see a well here. You have no business stopping here." She frowned. "Move on. There is nothing for you here."

She flicked her reins. Without thinking, I stepped near her wagon. "Don't you know me, Mama Emma? Don't you know who I am?"

"Of course, I know you, Armentia! Don't talk crazy! Now step away from the wagon, and move away from the school."

I stepped closer to her, whispering, as I had to Miss Lillian. "Teach me."

"Armentia, don't be silly. Go home. The sun must have burned your head!"

"Don't you remember when you loved me?"

"Don't talk foolish, girl!"

"Remember when you called me your daughter?"

"I remember no such thing!" She looked away, then quickly back at me. "You are a slave. I remember no such thing!"

"But you promised me you would teach me when I was older. You taught me the alphabet, and you said you would teach me to read when I was older." I stepped closer. "I'm older." I remembered Brother Jesse holding the Good Book in his hands. I wanted that feeling. I wanted to know the words, to read the stories.

I reached for her skirt. "I'm older. Teach me." I grabbed the hem. "Touch me," I whispered.

Fear in her eyes, she leaned away from me. "Don't be foolish. Go home!" She snatched her hem away from my hand.

I stepped closer. "But I want to be like you! Mama Emma, teach me," I whispered to her. "Don't you love me? I was your daughter. Remember?"

She jerked away and then flicked the reins. "You are a foolish girl! A troublemaker like your father and your brother. Get away from me!" She rode off, yelling over her shoulder. "Go home! You foolish girl! Go home!"

CHAPTER FORTY

$\mathcal{I}$T WAS A FOOLISH THING TO DO, TO SPEAK UP, TO QUES-tion Mama Emma. I was ashamed, shamed that I had asked her for anything . . . especially love.

I expected trouble to come. Weeks passed, we harvested the cotton from the fields, and we added more pennies to our jar. Still nothing happened.

My shoulders lowered, I stopped looking behind me for trouble.

"See," my mother told me, "we must not be afraid."

When we came in from the fields that evening, Mama Emma was standing in the doorway of our cabin, our money jar in her hands. When she saw that we were watching her, she lifted it higher in the air. The light of the setting sun caught the copper of pennies, shining like honey. "I see you two have been busy!" She shook the jar; the pennies rattled. "I know your son stole my honey." She stared straight through me, then looked back at my mother. "But I didn't know you were a house of thieves."

"We did not steal it!" My mother's eyes followed the jar, as though, if she watched closely, it would not get away.

Mama Emma smirked. "How did you get it then?"

My mother's chest heaved. "We earned it. We made goods and sold them."

"That is what you say, but I am missing this exact amount of money." Mama Emma shook the jar again. "There is no way you could earn all of this."

"We worked hard, we worked double!" My mother moved closer to me, her eyes still focused on the jar.

"I own you. I gave you no permission to work or earn money. If you labor and keep the money, you steal from me."

My mother, silent, looked at Mama Emma. I put my arm around my mother's waist, pressing close to her.

"Either way, you steal. And do you know what I do to thieves?"

"It is not stolen!" my mother insisted.

"I say it is!" Mama Emma stepped from our doorway and came to stand in front of us. "You think I don't know what you're doing? You think you—two slaves—are smarter than me? You think I don't know where you've been going? You think I don't know about the secret meetings?"

Others gathered, slaves and those that worked for Mama Emma and Papa. They watched from a distance.

Mama Emma hissed her words. "You and your stinking Keetoowah Society! You think I don't know you plan to kill us and steal everything!"

She hit my mother then with the jar, and my mother slumped to her knees. Pennies scattered about us.

"Mother! Mother!" I cradled her in my arms. Blood dripped down the side of her face.

"I told you not to make trouble! I warned your pretty daughter!" Mama Emma spit at us and then she stormed away.

"Mother! Mother!" I held her and cried.

My mother's voice was weak; it sounded far away. She raised a hand, grabbed my blouse, and pulled me closer. "Don't be afraid, Armentia. You are strong. You are strong." Her hand dropped from my shirt and she closed her eyes.

Some of those watching helped me carry her into the house. I held her and gently washed her face. Through tears, I washed the matting blood from her hair. I watched her chest rise and fall as she breathed, until it rose no more. I held her until they came for me.

Two men loaded me, my hands tied behind me, into a wagon.

That was the last time I saw my mother.

CHAPTER FORTY-ONE

WHERE THEY TOOK ME WAS TWO DAYS' WAGON RIDE from where we lived with Mama Emma and Papa. I cried all the way.

"Shut up, gal! We're not listening to that caterwauling no more!"

But even when they struck me, I would not stop crying. My family was gone. What more could they do to me?

The plantation they took me to was even larger than Master Cauley's. The owner was Master McDowell. His wife was Mistress Gail. When we pulled up in front of the main house, she rushed out to meet me as though I was a long-lost friend. "Untie her!" she demanded. "She is not a criminal!"

The two men obliged.

When I got to the ground and stood in front of her, she hugged me. "Don't you worry about a thing, now, girl. You are home!"

Her hair was brown and her curls jumped when she walked,

her wide skirts rustling around her. She did not look much older than me.

Mistress Gail took me to the kitchen. Smiling, she showed me around. There was a black iron cooking stove. Pots and pans hung from the ceiling.

She pointed. "This is your mammy, Susie!"

Susie smiled wide as the Mississippi River. "Well, come on in here, child! You know I'm mighty glad to see you! If you ain't as pretty as a picture!"

Mistress Gail kind of curtsied. "You are just going to love Mammy. She is the best cook in the whole wide world, I do believe!" She smiled at Susie. "You teach her how to make those butter biscuits, now, you hear?"

"Yes, ma'am. You know I will!" Mammy Susie grinned.

Before Mistress Gail's scent was out of the room good, Susie was rolling her eyes. "Mammy my foot!" The old toothless woman cussed a blue streak. She cussed so, it was like sparks flying off a fire. She cussed so, I went from being shocked, to being scared, to snickering under my breath. "You call me Mammy and I'll be serving your missing body up for their Sunday dinner! I'm grown, you not; you call me Miss Susie!"

"Yes, ma'am."

"Now, wipe your face. Whatever you're crying about, looks like you've cried enough. If tears were gone fix it, it would be fixed by now." She waved her hand and began to move around the kitchen. "I don't want none of that falling in these here pots!" She tapped one with a big spoon. "I got to eat out of 'em."

"Yes, ma'am." I wiped my face with the back of my hand.

Miss Susie was always moving. She talked while she stirred, while she measured, while she fried. "Ain't no good place to be a slave, if you ask me." She rolled her eyes. "Some crazy people here say they wouldn't never leave." She smacked her lips. "But me? The first chance I get, I'm taking me on up out of here."

She looked at me. "You one of those crazy people can't stand to leave their master?"

I thought about Mama Emma. "No, ma'am."

"By that look on your face, I guess you ain't!"

I tried to make my face like stone. "No, ma'am."

"Well, you don't have to tell me. All us got our stories." She grabbed a rag and shook a cooking pot. She put a lid on top, and then looked at me. "Pick up your lip, girl. You gone trip over it!"

Miss Susie was still in motion. But not fluttering like a butterfly—she was more like a boat moving water and everything out of her way. She looked down the hall after Mistress Gail. "That girl ain't worth the salt it took to make her!"

"Yes, ma'am, Miss Susie." It was all I knew to say.

"Now, get on over here and rinse your hands so I can show you something about making dumplings." While she kneaded the dough, Miss Susie talked about Mistress Gail. "That girl ain't got the sense God give a chicken, and worth even less. Can't cook, can't clean, can't think. Lord, have mercy!"

Miss Susie did it all the time, grinning at Mistress Gail when she was present and then laughing at her when she was gone. It got so it was like we had a sweet, sneaky secret between us. After all I had been through, I took a laugh wherever I could find it.

As days passed, I got to see that Mistress Gail spent most of her time smiling and patting her "children"—that's what she called us—on the head. If she wasn't doing that, then she was running after Master McDowell. Her skirts flying, she always seemed to be too late, to have just missed him as he rode away on horseback or in a wagon, his blond curly hair shining in the sun. "Jacob! Jacob!" she would call after him. When he was out of range, she would turn to whoever was near. "He's a busy man. He's a good man." She said it as though she was trying to convince us.

In between Mistress Gail's hugs, Miss Susie mocked her and taught me to cook by day.

CHAPTER FORTY-TWO

$\mathscr{I}$T WAS SUPPOSED TO BE A SECRET THAT MASTER JACOB McDowell came to my shack by the light of the moon. Baking was my job during the day; trouble slept with me at night. He didn't ask my permission and he didn't ask my pardon when he left. Nobody was supposed to see him creeping around, not even me. It was all a big secret, except that everybody knew about it. I wasn't supposed to make no noise or talk about it. I was supposed to pretend that what was happening to me wasn't a man, wasn't a ghost, wasn't even a figment of my imagination. None of us that saw him coming and going were supposed to talk about it; I guess if we didn't talk about it, it wasn't so. If we pretended the truth was a lie, the lie the truth, then even the good Lord wouldn't know.

I was older now. My childhood was left behind on Master Cauley's plantation. I was practiced at not being hurt. I had promised my mother that I would be strong.

'Course, I couldn't cry out. I couldn't tell nobody. I had already learned that. It wasn't even happening; that's what I was supposed to pretend. If I said or thought anything else, why, I would be doing the master a great injustice.

Funny thing, though, about secrets; pretty soon the secret was pushing my dress out in the front and in nine months' time that secret was out and born into this world screaming and shouting. Looking just like him, that thing that was done in the dark came to the light with curly blond hair. That secret crawled. Then he started tottering around while he sucked his thumb. That living secret, smelling like milk around his mouth and holding on to my neck for dear life, gave me so much pleasure.

You may not believe it, but when I looked in his eyes, I saw Abraham smiling back at me. I hadn't been so happy in so long. I would kiss his little forehead, his little fat hand would lay on my cheek, and sometimes I would forget all that had happened to me—about losing my sweet brother, about the Trail I had traveled, about losing my father, being lost to my mother, about traveling down that road on that wagon while my father's hopes dripped down the back like melting ice. Sometimes he even made me forget how he came into this world.

Oh, he was sweet sunshine. He made everybody happy; and it didn't hurt that he was proof for me, he was proof for everybody, that we was being mistreated. He bounced from knee to knee. Everybody pinned their hopes on him.

"Lord, that child could pass for a White man. He could get up one day, get away from here, and make something of hisself."

"That child is smart as a whip! He gone be somebody. Ain't nobody gone be able to hold him back." He was a light-skinned piece of possibility.

In a few more months, that secret was speaking a few words. For a long time, I just called him Little Secret, but then I decided that he deserved a proper name. So, I called him Abraham Proof.

He was the cutest little thing, and smart too. When no one

was watching, I showed him the Cherokee alphabet and my Abraham Proof traced those letters in the dust on the ground. I couldn't teach him to read because Mama Emma hadn't taught me that, but I gave him what I knew.

I told him stories about the great people we came from— some on ships from far away—and that we lived among and were part of people who walked the beautiful land of our fathers. I told him about the stream, about the green mountains, and about the well. I told him about the chiefs and about the seven clans. I told him about when everyone owned everything, about my mother, my father, and about his uncle Abraham. I told him that we were Cherokee.

"It seems hard to believe now, but someday we'll have our own land. Land with a well just like this one. And when we get our well, we will call it—Abraham's Well." I whispered to him in the language of our people.

I showed Abraham Proof the scar on my ankle. He'd point at that scar and then at the sky, and laugh. "Momma got a star on her ankle," he would say. It was like a dream, hearing my own baby call me Momma!

And I taught my baby to run.

Oh, it was a sight to see! I would get all full of laughs on the inside, like before we walked the Trail.

You should have seen those stubby, fat little legs a running, his arms just a pumping. We weren't free and we couldn't run far, but pretty soon my baby was running well, running like the wind! The One Who Guards His Family would have been proud. "We come from good people, smart people, proud people," I told him.

"My name is Abraham Proof," my son would tell people. "I can run. See?" He would get wings on his little feet and fly around.

"We are The Principal People. We are Cherokee. We come from free people, people who own the land. And my father said we will own the land again, and we will own our own well. We will call it by your name. It may not look like it right now, but it's going to happen. Wait and see," I told him.

"We are Cherokee. We are Aniyunwiya! We are going to own our own land. We are going to have a well that bears my name, Abraham's Well," my little Abraham Proof would say. He would smile—he had dimples like his daddy, Master McDowell—and made everybody laugh.

Some time in the night, when he was asleep, when only the moon and stars were still awake, I even whispered him the words in the language of my birth.

Finally, I had me somebody.

I had somebody that loved me, somebody who touched my face. He woke up in the morning just to see me. He twisted his fingers in the curls of my hair.

The hole in my heart—the one that had been left by the loss of my brother Abraham, by the loss of my mother and my father, by the loss of sweet Johnnie Freeman—had gotten so big I thought it was going to swallow me up someday. Then my sweet Abraham Proof came along and, like a baby, I buried myself in his arms.

"Always together," I whispered in his ear. "We are going to have a well."

"And we'll call it Abraham!" His little hands patted my hair.

CHAPTER FORTY-THREE

$\mathcal{M}$ISS SUSIE LAUGHED UNTIL SHE HAD TO FAN HERSELF. "Abraham Proof, boy, if you ain't a mess! Get your little self on away from here!" She smiled at him while she stirred and sifted a mile a minute.

Abraham Proof stood on a chair next to her, white flour on his chin and cheeks. He smiled at Miss Susie while he held some dough in the air. "You like it, Miss Susie?"

"Well, child, I sure de-do!"

"You think I'm doing good?" He squeezed the snaking strand of dough between his fingers.

Every day, he came with me. When we walked through the door, she held out her arms to him. He would run and jump into them. She held him, breathing him in like sweet, hot cinnamon. She held him like he filled her empty spaces too.

Miss Susie looked at me, like she was just thanking me for even giving birth to him. "I ain't never seen nobody with so much talent for making crust," she told him. Then she winked. "Exceptin' me, of course!"

His blond, curly hair like a crown, Abraham Proof had Miss Susie tied around his finger. He could smile at her and suddenly she'd get the notion to bake an apple pie or one of his other favorites. She still raised her eyebrows at me, but Abraham Proof could do no wrong. When he wanted to cook, she stood him atop a stool. Otherwise, when he wasn't cooking, he laughed and talked, tangling himself in our skirts.

In the time that had passed since Abraham Proof's birth, though Master McDowell still ran from her, Mistress Gail had pinned him down long enough to give birth herself. She had the sweetest baby girl, baby Molly, with pretty eyes like hers and blond hair and dimples just like her daddy.

Since that time, Mistress Gail didn't have much time for me. She brushed by me when she saw me alone. Most of her time she spent bouncing her baby in her arms. But who could blame her for that? I was right partial to my baby too.

Molly on her shoulder, one late morning, she swept into the kitchen. She nodded to me, but beamed at Miss Susie. "Mammy, I've been feeling like I want some of your butter biscuits." She licked her lips. "And a big plate of summer squash."

Miss Susie put on her smile. "Why, sure, Mistress Gail. My pleasure. Anything else you like?" Abraham Proof pulled at her skirt, hiding himself behind her.

Mistress Gail reeled off a list of things for the dinner menu. She smiled, kissing Molly, and twisted so that her skirt rustled around her. When she was happy, when she smiled, she was such a pretty woman. Her cheeks were pink; her hair bounced when she tossed her head. But I already told you that, didn't I?

But then when she saw Abraham Proof, her smile cut short. "Well, that's all, Mammy," she said. She held Molly closer to her. She looked at Abraham Proof and spoke to Miss Susie as though I wasn't there. "I don't think he should be in here." She pursed her lips. "It's dangerous, don't you think?"

I could see Miss Susie's face twitching; she was working so

hard to keep the smile plastered on her face. "We keep a might good eye on him."

"I don't think he should be in here," Mistress Gail insisted. "Do you?"

The smile was still on Miss Susie's face, but her shoulders slumped. "No, ma'am. I guess not."

When Mistress Gail and Molly left, Miss Susie looked after her, and then down at the floor. "Lord, I don't know what I'm going to do if my baby has to go. But don't you worry. We gone work something out."

I looked at Miss Susie, who looked all fussed up like she was about to cry. "Don't worry, Miss Susie, you can always come by the cabin."

She lifted Abraham Proof in her arms. "Lord, I don't know what I'm gone do if they take this child away!"

CHAPTER FORTY-FOUR

MAYBE I SHOULDN'T HAVE NAMED HIM. OR, MAYBE IT was because Little Secret, Abraham Proof, talked so well. Maybe I shouldn't have taught him about the land, or taught him the alphabet.

Pretty soon, like Miss Susie said, he had to go.

When he was six years old—just when I thought I had somebody that would be with me forever, they took Abraham Proof from me and sold him to a woman from New Orleans.

Losing one Abraham was bad, but two was more than I could bear.

When they sold my baby, they didn't say a word to me. They just grabbed him up.

When they sold my baby, he was a secret, so it was supposed to be a secret that it hurt me right down to the bottom of my feet.

It wasn't supposed to hurt me, so I didn't even cry. Not out loud.

But I was sad on the inside. So, so sad, I thought I was going to die.

"You pick your lip up, now, girl," Miss Susie told me. "Don't walk about here sad, looking like something been done to you. You'll just make it harder on yourself. You know that. You ain't no little girl no more. You probably all of eighteen now." She was right, even though I'm sure I saw tears in her eyes too.

She was right; so I tried to make my face stone, but inside my heart was bleeding, bleeding, bleeding. I didn't think I could hold on.

I sat in the road and waited, then, to die.

CHAPTER FORTY-FIVE

New Orleans, 1855

ABRAHAM PROOF FOUGHT AGAINST THE EMBRACE OF the woman that tried to hold him. She smelled too sweet, like too many flowers, but there was also something in the smell that burned his nose. After all this time, it still burned his nose.

"Oh, don't fight me, little one!" She tried to hold him. "Your momma loves you, *mon petit!*"

She was not his mother! His mother was far away!

They had snatched him from his mother's arms. He had watched her, her face frozen, when they had carried him—kicking and screaming—away. He had stretched his arms to her, his hands grabbing for her but only touching air. "Momma! Momma!" He could still feel how his lungs, throat, and face had burned.

He had watched his mother stumble to her knees, her face still frozen. He saw her—dust flying around her—when she stumbled to the ground.

Holding him tightly so that he could not run back to her, they loaded him into a wagon, and he had cried all the way.

"Momma! Momma!"

"Shut up that noise!" one of the men said, raising his hand to hit him.

"Don't hit him!" the other one said. "Just turn him and let him look behind. No marks, Madame Beauview said. She has paid a lot for him."

Abraham Proof only quieted, some, when they let him face away, face toward the mother from whose arms they'd snatched him.

So he faced his mother's direction while he rode in the wagon, and then on the boat. When he could not find her direction, he focused on the moon. "Momma! Momma!" he called to her.

Now Madame Beauview tried to hold him. "Oh, *mon cher*, I am your momma now!" He pushed against her flowery softness, against the stiff bustle of her gown. "You are Momma's little prince!"

"No!" he yelled at her. "I am Abraham Proof. I am *Aniyun-wiya*, one of The Principal People. I am Black and I am Chero-kee!"

Madame Beauview, her chin trembling, looked around her, pink with embarrassment. "You must not say such things! You must not try to hurt me! I am your momma! You are my child, *mon enfant!*"

"Take me home!" he insisted.

He knew she would not. Too many days had passed. Madame Beauview had paid a great price for him. She had paid so that he could be her son, one of her maids had told him. She would never let him go.

But, in turn, he would never forget. "I am Armentia's child! My mother has a star! One day I will return to her! We will buy land, we will dig a well!" He could not stop his tears. "And we will call the well Abraham!"

They might steal him away, but they could not take her memory from him. They might take him away, but he would never forget.

He would never, ever forget.

CHAPTER FORTY-SIX

I THOUGHT I WAS GOING TO DIE RIGHT THERE. THEN Willie Saunders came walking up the road.

I ain't never seen a slave walk so free.

I think I fell in love because when he was around, I felt free too.

And about then, with Abraham Proof gone, I needed all the free I could get.

Willie Saunders was from a farm not far away.

"Hey, girl," he said when he saw me. "You got a name?" He spoke United States words.

"Armentia." I didn't even try to hide that I liked him. I needed to drink in that freedom that washed around him.

"Where you from?"

I told him about the mountains, about the land of my fathers' bones.

"Tsalagi," he said, and began to speak our language. "Aren't you afraid to speak it out loud?"

"They can beat me if they want to, but they can't own my

mind, my heart, or my tongue." Willie Saunders was crazy free.

He smiled. "Can a girl named Armentia dance?"

My porcupine quills came out. "Well, I expect if anyone can, I can."

He was right to ask me. I didn't know what I was talking about.

But Willie Saunders did. In the quarters on the farm where he was, they had a dance every harvest time. There were people playing stringed instruments and one man blowing a jug. Mistress Gail let the slaves from our plantation go, those that wanted to.

People danced like they were dancing for their lives. I stood against a wall, holding it up—hoping it would hold me. Willie Saunders walked up to me and stuck out his hand. "Will you dance with me?"

I looked at all the people smiling. I thought of the Green Corn Festival, and of the dancing.

We were slaves now. What was there to celebrate? "It doesn't seem right."

He smiled and pulled me to the dance floor. "We may not be alive tomorrow. Better grab your joy and move your feet while you can!"

He swung me so that my feet lifted off the floor and the lamplight twirled around me. I could hardly catch my breath.

He was one crazy, dancing man!

"I ain't been here long, either." Walking home, he danced around me. "You did pretty good for a little girl that never danced before."

"You don't look much older than me!"

"Maybe not, but I can dance!"

"Hmph!"

He told me that he had lived near Creek country. "A bunch of us got free for a while."

He grabbed for my hand and I snatched it away. "Stop lying!"

Willie Saunders kept smiling. "I'm not lying. A good number of us stole food, guns, clothes." He laughed. "We locked Old Man Vann, all the masters and their families, in their rooms!" He waved his hands in the air. "We could hear them hollering as we went down the road! *Let us out! Let us out!*'" He shook his head. "Like we were going to turn around, go back, and let them out!"

I laughed at the way he told the tall tale. "You lie!" He reminded me of Abraham.

"I'm not lying. We headed for Mexico. We hightailed it across the desert. It was far from here. Sky so blue, and mountains red, purple, and orange." He breathed deeply, like he could smell the air, like he could smell being free. "Do you know Mexico?"

I shrugged. I didn't know where I was now, let alone some strange faraway place.

"They've got a place down there where men can live free. I tell you the truth!"

"If what you say is true, you would be dead!" I laughed at him.

"No, they caught up with us and brought us back." He stopped smiling, and for a moment, I almost believed him. "We almost made it. You could almost see Mexico from where they caught us." He pointed as though it was just ahead. "Red and purple mountains, orange mountains sticking up ahead like fingers. We almost made it." He sighed, then he smiled again. "When I get a chance, I'm going again. Next time I'm going to make it. I'm going to take enough water and food."

He jumped in front of me and bowed. "Of course, if they hadn't caught me that time, I never would have met you." He took my hand. "I never would have had the chance to marry you."

CHAPTER FORTY-SEVEN

𝒯HERE WASN'T MUCH COURTSHIP, JUST A FEW VISITS UP the road. We couldn't live together, but they would let him come up the road once most weeks to see me after we married. It wasn't much, but it was something.

Mistress Gail thought it was a good idea. Her face seemed to brighten. She hugged me and smiled like she had when I first arrived.

Mistress put honeysuckle in my hair, and I wore a new dress she made for me. A preacher of sorts spoke some words, then Willie Saunders and I jumped the broom. I wrapped him in a blanket I had made, and all of us ate molasses cake. It was about as fine a time as a slave could have, I guess.

When it was over, Mistress Gail took me to my cabin to light the candles and make ready. "Now, you know you and that boy Willie are not really married," she said while she fluffed our hay-filled pillows. "It's against the law for slaves to marry. At least that's how it was in Virginia, so I expect it's the same here." She smiled like she was telling me some good news, like she was telling me she was expecting a light summer rain. "It's not legal, you know that. The master could sell any one of you away at any time. The Good Lord's marriage is just for White folks. But I don't see any harm in a little fun!" I could tell the way she was grinning that she thought we were sharing something special, a secret between good friends, like we were playing with corncob baby dolls.

It's hard when people are hurting you to remember that maybe they don't really mean you any harm.

"Look at these clean sheets! Almost as good as any White woman's!" I know in her heart she thought she was being good to me, forgiving me for Little Secret, or maybe making up to me for him. Maybe she thought me having a husband, even an illegal one, would make things better for all involved. "There's even a tin tub of steaming water out back."

I didn't have nothing to say and was stiff as a board, but she pulled me to her. She was still giggling when she pinched my cheeks hard enough to make my eyes water. "There, now, some color!" she said. "Don't be scared, now. You know all about men, don't you?" She giggled. "Of course you do. Silly me. Don't worry." She hugged me again. "It's not real, but sometimes pretending is so much more fun!"

She scurried out and my husband Willie came and stood in the doorway. He walked in, one arm behind his back, and gave me a big old hug. He kissed me on the forehead.

I told him what I could not tell her. "She said it ain't real. Our marriage ain't real. They might sell us whenever they have a mind."

He brushed his lips to my ear. "Hush, little baby."

"It ain't right!" Tears burned my eyes—not wedding tears, but Abraham tears, Johnnie Freeman tears, Little Secret tears.

He whispered in my ear again. "The Great Spirit knows who we are and where we are. We planting and growing where we are just as good as we can. He let us love as much as we can.

What we can't," he kissed my neck, "we don't bear the blame. In front of the Lord, with all my heart, I vowed to you and to Him. The Breath Giver makes marriage real." His lips covered mine.

The talking was over. Legal or not, it sure felt real, sure felt like the Lord was smiling on us. Some preachers might argue different, but the Lord will make it clear on that great gittin' up morning.

My husband dropped the little bag he was holding behind his back and carried me to the bed. Truth is, for a time, I forgot what the mistress said.

It was like I was swimming awake through a dream. When evening came, Willie got up from the bed, grabbed me and the bag on the floor and headed outside, round the back to the tub. The sky was a beautiful blue—deep blue, to purple, to a little darker than cornflower—and the fireflies mixed with the sky stars.

First he reached into the bag and pulled out a purple ribbon. Then he held that bag up over the tub of water, and big white flower petals tumbled out. Cream-colored flowers, heavy and sweet-smelling, floated on the black water. Willie took hold of my hand and helped me step in.

Naked as a baby, covered in the flower water, I soon couldn't tell the flowers in the sweet water from the stars shining in the sky above me.

Oh, buffalo gal, won't you come out tonight
Come out tonight
Come out tonight . . .

My husband sang to me soft and sweet. I had never heard Willie sing before. He ran his fingers through my hair. He scooped handfuls of the flowered water into it, then tied my hair back with the purple ribbon.

*Oh, buffalo gal, won't you come out tonight
And dance by the light of the moon.*

If I ain't ever knowed I was beautiful no other night, well, I knowed I was a beautiful bride that night. Yes, sir.

He had a little piece of rag made out of old sheeting, but I swear it felt like satin or silk. While I sat on my knees in the water, he washed my back, dripping fragrant water on my face and hair. It dripped on my lips and into my mouth, sweeter than any of Mama Emma's honey.

Willie eased me to sitting while he stooped beside the tub. He washed my hands one finger at a time and then followed on up to under my arms. He washed my feet and in between my toes like I was a little bitty baby. He washed places you would think a man wouldn't know to wash. Then he kissed all my scars, all the places shriveled up from having my first baby, all the places I tried to hide.

It didn't matter what Mistress Gail or the law said. I looked up in the heavens, and at that man's hands, and I knew I was married.

When he raised me up out of the water, he wrapped a clean sheet around me. He carried me in the cabin and sat on our one chair, me on his lap. "Don't worry, little baby." He tied my hair with a shiny purple ribbon.

He kissed my forehead and my fingers. "Don't worry, little girl."

I didn't. And it wasn't until I stopped worrying that I realized that I was.

We fell asleep. When the sun came up, we were still sitting in that chair.

CHAPTER FORTY-EIGHT

$\mathcal{N}$EXT TIME, WHEN I LEAVE, I'M GOING TO MAKE IT. I'M going to get clear away to Mexico."

I swatted at the gnats flying around my head, and tried to fan away the heat of the day. Willie Saunders was doing what he always did—laughing, smiling, and talking about getting away.

He walked next to me. "I've been thinking about it. Going over what we did wrong, and what I'll do different next time."

Free was all he thought about. "Well, I don't see why you're waiting. If freedom was the most important thing on my mind, why I'd just pack my roll and go." I kicked at the dust as we walked. If he was going to leave me, sooner was just as good as later.

Smiling, Willie Saunders grabbed my hand and spun me around like we were dancing. "Don't be mad, now, sugar!"

He kissed at the side of my face, but I moved away. "I'm not mad. It don't make no never mind to me." I looked around to make certain that nobody was watching. "I just don't know why you have to talk about it all the time. We only get to see each other once every week or so, and that's the only thing you can talk about. Why can't you be satisfied?"

He pulled me onto a tree-lined path that was shady and cool. Shrubs laced with white honeysuckle wove themselves among the trees. "I don't want to leave you. I want to be free. Don't you want to be? Don't you want to choose your own life? Even what we had before was better than this."

Of course I remembered—I remembered the stream, I remembered Abraham, I remembered before they took us away. But how did that make life better? How did holding on to dreams make life more livable?

"I can't give up, Armentia. I can't live life thinking this is all there is." Hugging me, he lifted me off my feet. "I can't live letting this be the best you ever have."

I don't know why I tasted bitterness on my tongue, but that's what happened. "Well, then, I guess you'll be dying soon." It surprised me how mean my words sounded. What I wanted was for him to stay alive, to stay with me. I'd lost everyone else.

Willie Saunders lowered me, slowly, to my feet. He hugged me, stroking my hair. "We aren't supposed to live this way. No choice. No freedom."

I held him, my fists balled up in his shirt like I was going to hold on to him and never let him go. "If you run, you'll die." Burning tears squeezed from my eyes. Didn't he remember the Trail? I did; I remembered Golden Bear's father.

He held me tighter. "I can't help it. If I have to, I'll have to die trying." He grabbed my hand. "Come on!" He pulled me along behind him. Running, looking behind us, we ran further down the path. He stopped when we came to a small clearing. "This here is the place. Someday it's going to be the right time to run, and this is the place where you'll come to meet me.

You'll come by the light of the moon." He began to sing to me softly.

> *Oh, buffalo gal, won't you come out tonight*
> *Come out tonight*
> *Come out tonight . . .*

I laid my head on his shoulder, swaying in his arms. How much could he ask of me? I'd lost everyone who tried to run or stand up, or even speak up. How much more was I supposed to give? "Why is this so bad? We're alive, aren't we? We get to dance sometimes, to see each other sometimes. Why can't that be good enough?"

I held him and prayed that he wouldn't go. Prayed that he would change his mind. When he went home, I was still praying.

All week long, I waited for him again.

Maybe a few days would pass and he would change his mind—he would forget about thoughts of running, I hoped.

I thought about the sound of his voice. I thought about his arms around me, and I waited for him to come. But when he came, it seemed like I couldn't let myself get close to him. He hadn't forgotten; freedom was still on his mind. "Can't you be satisfied?"

He held me close, his lips pressed against my hair. "This is not the way it was meant to be. Some just ain't enough." He kissed the top of my head. "I want freedom. I want all of it. I can taste it. I go to sleep thinking about it. I wake up thinking about it. I want freedom and I ain't never going to have it if I wait on somebody to give it to me." He held me. "We don't have much time, Armentia. Let's don't waste the time that we have fighting. We'll talk about it when the time comes."

Week after week he came to see me. Nothing changed. He whispered about freedom, and I fussed in response. The more time passed, the meaner and hotter my words got.

CHAPTER FORTY-NINE

ONE DAY, ONE EARLY MORNING RIGHT OUT OF THE BLUE, while Miss Susie and I headed for the house and Willie Saunders headed back to his master's farm after our weekend visit, she stopped short. She looked after him, her hand on her hip. "The way you treat that man, if I was just a little younger, I would be waiting for the chance to come along so I could take him right from you." Miss Susie watched my husband walk away like he was the butter for a hot biscuit she was about to eat. "Seem like sometime you think you better than him. Seem like you think that if he love you, then he should let you treat him bad; whenever you mad at the world he let you take it out on him. But it seem like to me, if you love him, then you treat him right."

I cooked for him. I cleaned his clothes. Wasn't that enough? I didn't know that anybody watched that close or heard that sometimes I misspoke to him. Sometimes when people sneak up in your business, business you don't even want to talk to yourself about, it just cuts you on the inside, down deep. It wasn't her business, I thought, and I would have told her so except I knew she was handy with a rolling pin.

"When I was younger, I didn't have no trouble taking a man from a woman like you. She might have been prettier, but when the Lord was handing out sense, women like you forgot to get in line." She laughed herself silly over that one. "Don't be frowning at me. It's your choice to be silly and lose him. He's a good man. You may not know it, but other women hungry and they watching that man all the time."

Miss Susie went to the barrel just outside the door, scooped some water and rinsed her hands. Then she scooped more into a pitcher and brought it in to the table where she made the bread. She pointed. "Get the fire going." She went to another barrel and scooped flour into a bowl.

"I seen women like you before. Men too." She grabbed a metal sifter and dumped the flour in, catching the drifting white powder again in the bowl below. "You want life and love to come with no trouble." She frowned when she said the last word. "You want it to be easy." Shaking the sifter by the handle, she shook her head. "Ain't nothing easy about our lives. If you going to wait until it's a perfect time to love or to do, then you'll wake up gray-haired, bitter, with nothing at all."

When the flour was finished sifting, she reached in a jar, and to the bowl added two pinches of salt. "We born into a world without much choice, a world that say we got to ask someone else before we take any step. If you gone do anything wonderful, you got to wait on someone else's say-so."

I added small twigs to the oven fire. I fanned it, watching the embers glow.

"Well, waiting on somebody's nod works for some people. Some people get the 'go ahead' all the time." Miss Susie took a fork and used it to lightly stir the powder. "But some of us, we got to take it by force. If we wait for someone to say we can, we gone be waiting until kingdom come." She looked at me as she stirred. "Ain't nobody gone say yes to you. If you want it, you gone have to do it anyhow. That's what your man knows."

Miss Susie walked to another jar, opened the lid, and scooped out baking powder. She walked back to the bowl and dumped the scoops in the dry mix. Flour puffed into the air. "You got to take it by force, and you can't wait for the perfect day. That day ain't never going to come."

The way she was talking, the frown on her face, I knew it wasn't a time for me to answer back. It was a time for me to hear what she had to say.

"You gone wait until slavery is over and the foot is off your neck? Well, that day may never come. You gone wait until the man won't die, be killed, be sold, or run off, before you'll give yourself all the way? Well, child, when is that going to be? You better grab hold of it; tomorrow might not get here."

I added more sticks, larger ones, to the fire. I wouldn't say it to her, but I'd already been through enough. I wouldn't say it out loud, because I didn't want to taste the back of her hand, but I didn't need her advice. I had already cried enough tears. I'd had my heart broken enough.

Miss Susie went to a large metal tin can and scooped out a large amount of lard, the pork fat that gave her biscuits so much flavor. She brought the lard and scraped it into the bowl. "You got a man with an itch for freedom. If I remember rightly, that's the thing about him that caught your eye in the first place." Using her fork, she began to cut the flour and the fat together. "We people are funny, ain't we?" She looked at me briefly, and then back at the bowl. "The very thing that attract us to somebody, we spend all the rest of our time together trying to get it out of them."

I went to the pile of logs near the oven, and added three of them to the fire. I tried to keep what I was thinking off of my face.

Miss Susie looked over at me. "Careful, now. Don't get it too hot."

"No, ma'am. I know. Just right." I added two more logs.

I walked closer, watching the mixture turning to dough. She continued pressing the fork into the flour and fat while she talked. "You got to know when it's your time. You got the chance—even though tomorrow you may not be alive, or he may pack his roll and go—you got the chance to love today. So, what you gone do today?"

She scooped water from the container nearby and drizzled it into the bowl. She laid the fork to the side, and stuck her hands in the bowl. "See these biscuits, here? Now, no doubt, there is a perfect time to make them. A time when the flour is just right, the baking powder is just right, no meal worms in them. There is a time when the perfect pig comes along with the perfect fat to turn into the perfect lard that will make the biscuits just right." She began to gently knead the dough. "There is a time when the oven temperature is just right, the weather is just right to help them be nice and fluffy."

She lifted her hands from the bowl, flexing her fingers. "There is a time when I'm feeling fine—my hands are warm and don't hurt, and when my back doesn't bother me when I bend over." She placed her hands back in the bowl. "But the truth is, I don't know if I ever seen that perfect time. Every day, I just show up and make these biscuits. Happy or sad, hands or back aching, flour or powder ain't right, I still make do and make the biscuits. The same way with life. The same way with love. You got to keep showing up. If you gone win over the evil that tries to kill you, you got to keep doing it anyway."

Caressing the dough like a loved one, she formed the soft mixture into a ball. "If you gone love, you got to love even when it don't make sense." She held the ball in one hand and used the other to sprinkle flour on the place on the wooden table where she rolled the dough. "If you gone be free, you gone have to run or stand up when it don't make sense."

"You been through too much. More than a child should have to bear up under. You ain't got a lot. But what you gone do with the little you got?

"If you want to love, if you want to live, you got to take it by force and you can't wait until the perfect day to bake your biscuits. If you don't take your chance," she stared at me—hard—"somebody else will. If you don't love that man, somebody else will. I'm too old, but somebody else will."

It was hard to keep from pouting. I didn't want to hear what she had to say. What Miss Susie said hurt me. It hurt me like cutting off that arm that Brother Jesse had talked about that night by the campfire. Her words made me have to face up to and feel all the times I had been mean to my husband. It made me think about when I was too afraid to run, or even stand up. Wasn't nothing about it that felt good. It hurt. But that woke me up, and I declare I did a lot better. I tried to.

I don't know why I treated that sweet man like that. Maybe I was trying to see how far I could go before he would leave me. Truth was, sometimes, I was just mad and I took it out on him. And, maybe, the truth was, that a little of what I had been through, people being better and having more because they were more White, or more Cherokee, or lighter, maybe some of that had rubbed off on me. Maybe I was hurt and I needed somebody to hurt with me.

It was also just as true that it didn't occur to me that somebody else was watching, that he really might leave, or that somebody might take him from me.

"Treat him mean and that's what you'll get back," Miss Susie said to me. "Some other starving woman will grab him from your plate."

I still couldn't believe she was saying it to me.

"Close your mouth, girl, before a fly gets in. You just wasn't thinking, because you're young and dumb."

I followed behind her, thinking hard.

"You can't get to joy being mad. Take it from somebody who knows. Being mad will kill everything around you. The madder you are—the more mad you plant—the more mad you'll get. It's just like adding salt to a pot. The more you add, the more you'll get in the end. Too much salt won't never make a cake turn sweet."

She laid the dough on the board, patting it gently. She rounded it with her floured hands. Miss Susie grabbed her rolling pin, dusted it with flour, and then began to roll it back and forth on the ball. "Things are changing. War is coming. I can smell it in the air. But if you want that man, if you love him, you don't have time to wait. You got to love him now. You got to run when he says it's time."

The truth is, I didn't know anything more than Mistress Gail about living or loving. Neither one of us had the sense God gave a chicken. If things would have been different, been like the Good Lord planned, both of us could have been learning from all Miss Susie was cooking in that kitchen. And I don't mean just cakes and pies, but all that wisdom she was stewing up about life.

Maybe Miss Susie and me shouldn't have made fun of Mistress Gail, but ain't no doubt she shouldn't have used the life out of us. No doubt at all.

But two wrongs don't make a right.

All of us needed to be in the kitchen, together, talking. But slavery didn't allow it. To some people, slavery maybe seemed like a good thing. But it kept Mistress Gail unhappy and from learning how to be a grown-up, a take-care-of-herself woman. It kept me from having pretty dresses and a house and a husband who got to be all of a man without running away. I could have been easygoing sometime. And I could have had a real marriage, a for-real, for-life and law marriage, and babies that weren't secrets.

Mistress Gail could have had all the real love she wanted from Miss Susie, for-real-Mama love instead of make-believe love, because that's what she really wanted. That's why Mistress Gail was always in the kitchen. Miss Susie loved her some, but how can somebody love you all the way when you got your foot on her neck? Can't be. Just can't be.

If you are loving somebody that way, controlling them, and you think they are really loving you, you are just fooling yourself.

The Civil War is long over now; the century has turned, as they say. I see pictures painted nowadays of White ladies wearing fancy dresses while they hold parasols, and of smiling White men in dashing gray uniforms. You can put all the pretty colors on a lie you want, but it's still an ugly lie. There wasn't anything good about slavery, and the evil it did is still walking around grinning today.

I'm an old woman and I saw it for myself when the evil was young and I see it now, old and crafty. Same old evil, painted pretty, keeping its clawed foot on people's necks. Some people get good schools and medicine and dreams and guilt, while other people get nothing and anger. Same old ugly wearing new lip rouge. Some work and get poor while others get rich off the ones that work. That ugly is still walking around in some people thinking they are better, in people thinking they got more because they're better, in people snickering behind others' backs, in some having and some having not. Some live in big houses, brick houses, while others live in shacks. It just makes for a lot of hurt and hate.

Maybe if it wasn't for slavery, me and Gail could have been friends, real friends. It might have been hard, because sometimes the best friendships take a whole lot of work. But we maybe could have been friends. Slavery wouldn't let us be friends. We could have helped each other be better women and better wives. But maybe, after I'm gone from now, it won't still have the power to keep people apart.

When you meet me in heaven, you'll have to let me know how things turned out.

But that morning, Miss Susie just kept on talking while she made her way around the kitchen. "If you don't love him, somebody else will."

CHAPTER FIFTY

*M*ANY SUMMERS PASSED, ENOUGH THAT I STOPPED counting. I kept working in the kitchen, and got pretty good at baking biscuits and such. And every week or so, Willie Saunders came walking up the road. We kept hoping for a baby, but it seemed like Abraham Proof was the only child I was ever going to have. Maybe the inside of me was scared to have another baby that somebody might take away.

Things went on that way. Things stayed quiet and trouble seemed far enough away.

There were rumors about war coming, about skirmishes between the North and the South. There was fighting, some said, between those that wanted slavery and those that wanted men to be free. There was news that there was division among my people, the Cherokee, about which way we would go. Then somebody said that the Cherokee had sided with the South in the war.

But all of that was far away, so I settled into loving him, even though Willie kept talking about leaving. I didn't fight it; so much time passed, I thought we would never go. I thought he would never go.

One night, late, I heard his voice. He was singing outside my window.

> *Oh, buffalo gal, won't you come out tonight*
> *Come out tonight*
> *Come out tonight . . .*

In my sleep, I smiled and waited for him to come in the door, to kiss me and crawl into bed beside me. I kept waiting, but he never came inside.

> *Oh, buffalo gal, won't you come out tonight*
> *Come out tonight*
> *Come out tonight . . .*

It was not a dream. I shook my head. He was singing because he had come for me. He was singing because this was the time.

I grabbed my roll of clothes. The ones I had packed, the roll I never thought I would use.

> *Oh, buffalo gal, won't you come out tonight*
> *And dance by the light of the moon.*

I grabbed the bread and pork I brought and wrapped away each week. I grabbed the food I never thought I would use. I grabbed the wedding ribbon I kept tucked under the mattress. My heart was beating so loud in my ears I couldn't think. My hands were sweating. I stumbled, scared someone would hear me, trying to get out the door.

I met him in the place we had planned, the place in the woods. My bowels, I could feel them loosening. My heart beat so loud I was sure that my husband could hear it. The back of my shirt was wet from fear.

Whispering, he grabbed me to him. "We gonna make our way to Fort Gibson in Kansas. They'll give us food there. You can stay there, maybe get a job cooking. I'm gonna join up. They're signing people up for the war."

"The war?"

Willie Saunders was so excited. Though he was whispering, he was glowing like the moon, like a star in the sky.

He was so excited, he didn't see that I wasn't going.

I knew it the minute I saw him. It just wasn't my time. I pressed the bundle with the biscuits and fried cracklings into his hands. "You go on ahead. You take this with you."

He looked up at the moon. "Come on, honey. We got to go!" He took a step forward, turning his back to me, and held his hand stretched behind him, reaching for me.

"No, you go on, Willie Saunders. I'm staying behind." My feet were moving side to side, like they wanted to go, but my heart knew I was going to stay.

"No. No. You're just scared. You're coming with me." He turned to look at me. We both knew then I wasn't going to go.

"You go on. It's for you. It ain't my time. I'm not ready now. I'd just slow you down." After all that had been taken from me, here I was letting him go. "You'll come back for me."

"I'm not going without you. I'll stay right here." He came and stood in front of me. I looked in his eyes. We both knew he wasn't going to stay.

"Yes, you are. You've been waiting for this. You are going on up the road, now, you hear?" There I was, in the middle of the night, sending the sweetest thing in my life away. But he couldn't any more stay than the moon could keep from rising.

He looked down at me, and then back up the road. "I'm gone come back for you."

"I know you are. I'll be looking for you." Somehow, we both knew he wasn't coming back. "I'll be so proud of you." I stood on my tiptoes to kiss him, fighting back tears. "You'll have on a fancy jacket and shiny gold buttons. You'll come marching along with that rifle on your shoulder. And I'll shout out, 'See that good-looking man, the one with the pretty smile? Don't you touch him, now!'" I stepped away and waved him down the road. "'That man is mine!'"

He started making his way down the road, taking a step or two and then turning back. "I'm gone come back for you."

"I know you are. I know."

"I'm gonna come by your window. Singing

'Oh, buffalo gal, won't you come out tonight
Come out tonight
Come out tonight . . .'"

"I know you will." I was crying by then.

"I won't go if you tell me to stay!"

I ran to him and pressed the purple wedding ribbon he gave me into one of his hands. "I know, but it's your time. Who's going to free us, if not you?" I kissed his sweet lips and then I pushed him away.

A cloud moved in front of the moon and it was hard to see him. But I could hear tears in his voice. "I'm coming back for you."

It was getting harder to see him, but I could still hear his voice whispering to me. "But you go on, now, Willie Saunders. Go on before the sun catches you."

I could hear him moving away. "Baby, I'm gone be looking for you. I'm gone be looking out my window! And when you come back, we gonna dance!"

Then he was gone.

For the first two weeks, I know I shouldn't have, but sometimes I stood out in the moonlight watching for my husband to come back. I would wake from my sleep thinking I had heard his song. But I knew in my heart that he wasn't coming home.

A week after that, Master McDowell started packing to take us south to Texas.

CHAPTER FIFTY-ONE

MASTER MCDOWELL SAID THINGS WERE GETTING TOO dangerous. There were too many runaways.

I knew one of the runaways he was talking about was my Willie, but I kept my face like stone.

He called all of us together, from the house and from the fields. Mistress Gail and Molly stood close behind him.

The Pin Indians—a group that opposed the new ways, that were against the Treaty men and slave owners—were rampaging, burning farms, and killing people, especially slaves. Master McDowell looked each one of us in the eye. He appreciated each one of us being loyal, being faithful. "They're especially killing slaves," he repeated.

The only way he could keep us safe was to move us all to Texas.

Miss Susie whispered under her breath, "The only way he figure he can *keep* us is to move us all to Texas. He stay here, most everybody will steal away."

We packed everything and everybody, all that we could

take, into wagons. The wagons were filled to busting with sacks of flour and sugar, blankets, furniture, pots and pans. Horses were tied to the front of the wagons and cattle trailed behind.

Everybody was in motion, but Miss Susie said she was staying behind. For once she stopped moving. She sat in the kitchen on her favorite stool. "I'm too old to go. My bones don't want to go bumping down no road."

Master McDowell tried to reason with her. "I can't leave you here. I told you that they're killing slaves."

"You can't stay behind!" Mistress Gail was pink in the face with worry. Tears wet the collar of her dress. "Don't let her stay behind, honey!" she pleaded with her husband. "Make her come!"

Miss Susie, gray and heavy, wouldn't budge. "Well, I guess what you need to do—if you care about me like you say—you need to 'mancipate me so I won't be a slave. That way, won't be no reason for nobody to kill me. Because I ain't going nowhere." She folded her arms. "What time I got to live out, I'll live it out right here."

Master McDowell had met his match. As we prepared to leave, Miss Susie watched us, leaning on the front gate. Mistress Gail cried like she really was leaving behind her own mother.

This time, there was room for all of us to squeeze on the wagons, or ride on horses. On top of a wagon bundle that seemed to most reach the sky, I sat on a chair lashed by ropes that held the whole thing down. "You sure you gone be all right, Miss Susie?" If anybody would, she would. But I was sure going to miss her. I was even going to miss her on her most contrary days.

"There's plenty of crops in the ground. I know how to scrounge around for myself. There's enough sticks and wood to make do. I been cooking for all you all, so I surely know how to cook for me." She set her mouth resolutely in something akin to a smile. "Today, I'm making my first free choice. I'm choosing not to make another move."

As we pulled away, I wondered if Willie Saunders would find me. And I wondered about my son Abraham. So many years had passed since I had seen him. I wondered if he still remembered my name.

Mistress Gail wailed, her arms outstretched, until we couldn't see Miss Susie and the plantation faded from view.

CHAPTER FIFTY-TWO

South Carolina
July 16, 1863

ABRAHAM PROOF CINCHED THE LEATHER STRAP OVER HIS shoulder and tightened the one around his waist. He knocked sand off his boots and off the hem of his uniform slacks. They were muddy and torn, though he had not had them long—just in time for a fashionable death.

He would not think that way.

He stood up, flexed his arms, then checked his sword, his rifle, and bayonet. *Don't shoot until you see the whites of their eyes, boys!*

If this was his moment—he looked up at the blue sky and the bright yellow sun—then it was a glorious day for a good death.

He looked at his brother soldiers, the other colored men of the 54th Regiment Massachusetts Volunteer Infantry. Hardly any of them were from Massachusetts. Like him, they had been recruited, had found their way from all over the country.

"You don't have to go there. You don't have to fight. If you told no one, no one would know that you are Black or that you are Cherokee." His wife, tears in her eyes, had turned him to face the mirror. "Look at yourself," she said. "You're as White as anybody. Look at your blue eyes. Look at your blond hair!" She turned him, again, to face her. "You don't have to go off to war. We could take the children and go north. Maybe we could go to Canada, or to England. We could leave all this behind!" She pleaded with him. "You're an educated man. You could get a job teaching. No one would have to know."

Abraham Proof watched his daughter Portia walk by the door. "I would. I would know."

He had kissed his wife and their two children good-bye. "Who are you?" he had asked them as he mounted his horse.

"We are the grandchildren of Armentia, Armentia who has a star. We are Black and we are Cherokee. . . ."

They were so young, but he knew they would remember. So would his other children, children born of slave women. They would remember just as he had. Abraham Proof looked out on the waters of the Atlantic, up the narrow stretch of South Carolina beach to Fort Wagner that lay ahead on what seemed a mountain of sand. No doubt, the cannons and howitzers of Sumter and Cummings' Point were also focused on the narrow path. As his wife had advised, he could have walked away, but now he stood on the beach, surrounded by his brother soldiers.

How could he go free with the one who had borne him left behind? So, he fought to free his mother. He stood on the beach, waiting for the call to assault, so that no other child would be stolen from the arms of the mother he loved. He stood and fought so that his mother, so beloved, would have her land.

He and all the other men had been warned by their officers that many of them would die today. If he fell, he would leave behind his sweet wife and children, but he knew that they would remember. . . .

It was a beautiful day to die.

CHAPTER FIFTY-THREE

$\mathscr{W}$E WERE ON OUR WAY TO TEXAS, TAKING BACK ROADS, hiding from anyone that might come along. Abandoning the plantation, we were supposed to be avoiding trouble. They might burn the house, but they wouldn't get us, Master McDowell said.

We tried to avoid anything in uniform. If they came across you—blue, brown, or gray—they were as likely to take any provisions you had. *"We're confiscating all you have in the name of . . ."* We had heard the stories, so we were careful to stay out of the way.

But we fought all the way there anyway—either the weather, critters, or the roads. At first, we tried to travel only at night. But it was too hard. There were sinkholes on the trail, just waiting to take a chunk out of a wagon wheel. In the dark, with no lamps, it was too hard to see. So, we traveled in the day's heat. Babies cried, mad, as though they knew something was wrong. From time to time, Mistress Gail cried like the babies, still missing Miss Susie. This time, all of us rode. But we were a moving feast for horseflies, mosquitoes, hornets, and anything else that wanted to taste human blood.

Sitting atop the wagon, all I had time to do—besides swatting at critters—until we stopped for the night, was think.

When we stopped for the evening, the other women and I made fire. I filled a large kettle with whatever water we could find. While it boiled, I skinned and butchered, or scaled, or plucked and feathered whatever meat the men could find. Like I had seen my mother do, I added beans to the water, stirring in the meat, some salt pork, and dried corn. Like Miss Susie had taught me, I made a rough sort of biscuit dough and flipped it back and forth between my palms to make flatbread. Because there was no oven, I fried it up in a skillet.

But, until evening came, I rode and thought of all I'd been through. I thought about all the people I'd lost. It seemed that each step closer to Texas brought back memories of all I'd left behind.

My brother, the land, my father, even Golden Bear's father—all lost to me. I'd told myself that if I was quiet, if I disappeared, maybe the pain would go away.

But it didn't. I was quiet, and trouble still found me. I didn't fight, and evil still made me its prey. I'd lost my mother, my son, and my husband. Now, there I sat on top of a wagon forced somewhere else I did not want to go. Forced—as though I did not have my own dreams, my own hopes and love, a place that I wanted to be.

When we stopped for the evening, I climbed down from the wagon.

I heard the voice of my mother calling to me. *"Trouble has already come to us, my daughter. And we have allowed trouble to bully us, to make us frightened and weak.*

"That is not who we are. We are from proud women. We are from women who fight alongside their men. We are from strong women who own land. We come from wise women, from women who know the

voice of the Breath Giver." I blew at the twigs to start the fire.

"Especially you, my daughter. You are not a tortoise, a u-la-no, hiding your head. You have always been like a panther, a tlv-da-tsi', fighting whatever comes against you. . . . Sometimes even deer must stand and fight." They were words from my mother, but what of all the people that we had seen killed? What of all the people who had stood, but who were now lost?

Once the fire burned and the water was ready, I stirred beans and salt pork into the pot. Who was I to fight? Weren't they more powerful? Hadn't the Great One chosen them to rule over us? Who was I, what strength did I have?

The voice of Reverend Bushyhead spoke to me. *"We choose Jesus as our Savior, but we choose the Beloved Community as our culture. Christianity is the religion we choose, it is the relationship we choose with the Breath Giver, but Keetoowah, the Beloved Community, is the relationship we choose with one another.*

"It is our culture. It is the way we live with our brothers and sisters, sharing in common, respecting each soul. Ea Nigada Qusdi Ida-dadvhn! You are all my relations in creation!"

I stirred the dried corn into the water. Those were big ideas, ideas from a man who had power, who was a preacher and a judge. It was easy for him to talk about dreams and community and love. But who was I? I was trying to stay alive.

"Dreams are worth living for, worth dying for. Dreams are worth running for, my children!" It was as though Brother Jesse was standing near me while I tended the fire.

What power did I have? I had seen my mother killed by a jar that held her dreams. What could I do? As I tended the dough, Miss Susie's voice whispered to me. *"But some of us, we got to take it by force. If we wait for permission, we gone be waiting until kingdom come."*

I stared into the boiling pot. All the voices swirled around me. I was sad in my heart. Through the voices, something heavy pressed on me. I tried not to hear them. There was enough for me to worry about, enough for me to tend to now.

CHAPTER FIFTY-FOUR

As scared as we were of soldiers on our way to Texas, there were plenty of wild things to fight along the way too. Snakes. Polecats. But I had too much to worry about. Maybe it was too much time on the wagon. Maybe it was heat talking to me. There I was in the middle of nowhere. There I was with too much foolishness in my head.

Stopped by the road, after a long, hard day's travel, while the food cooked, I watched a young mother take her babies to a nearby stream to bathe. After the fire was started and the pot boiling good, after I finished the bread, I went to join them.

When I stepped out of the trees, I saw her.

There she was, hunched by the water, her babies in her arms. She was frozen, her mouth open, she couldn't even scream.

That young mother was no more than twenty feet from me.

In between us was a big brown, hungry-looking bear.

I don't know what came over me. Maybe I'd lost so much I wasn't worried about losing my life. Tired out, maybe I was too tired to care. Or maybe that day, I was just too crazy in the head from all the voices to care. I had been pushed just too much too far.

I grabbed a big old stick and, yelling, I charged that old bear. Before it could turn, I smacked that hairy thing square on its backside! "You get on away from here, now, unless you want to be somebody's coat!" I hit that creature harder than it deserved. I hit it for all the mad I had been carrying around inside!

That bear turned around, confused like. And looked at me like it thought I must have lost my mind.

I raised my hands high, waving that stick in the air; standing tall I forced out the words as I backed slowly out of reach, "You come on, now, if you got the nerve! I'm tired of folks pushing me around!" It was just like me to make my stand with mankind by facing off with a bear. "You come on! I'll take this stick and bust you in your pie chopper!"

I know people are all the time talking about dumb animals, but that bear sure eyed me like he was trying to figure me out. Lord, I must have looked like a fool to him. Honest to goodness, he sat down on his haunches, started scratching his head and blinking his squinty eyes.

That day, he had tangled with the wrong sister. "What more are you going to do to me that ain't already been done?" I was screaming so that my throat was hurting. I pounded on my chest. "You may take me down, but before I go, I promise I'll lay you on your dead side!"

I jumped up and down, pointing and shaking. "If you know what's good for you, you'll get your big self on out of here!"

That poor bear stood up on all four of his feet like he was deciding whether he would charge or not. It scratched at the ground.

"You come on! I'm ready for you!" Hot swelled up inside my head. I could hear my mother's voice speaking to me.

"Sometimes even deer must stand and fight."

Right then and there, I decided I was going to be like Miss Susie and make a decision. I was going to listen to Brother Jesse. I was going to listen to my mother. I decided I wasn't being scared no more. "Right here, old bear, this is where I'm making my stand."

Well, I think that bear, looking at me jumping around and jabbering away, decided it wasn't worth it. He figured it was better to try again on a better day. He lumbered off, looking over his shoulder—I guess to make certain I wasn't following behind.

I gathered up the young mother and her babies, though she kept stealing glances at me as we walked—as though this was a me that she had not seen before.

When we got back to the wagons and told our bearish tale, nobody believed it. "Go on, now, Armentia. This is no time for tall tales!"

I was too winded by the face-off to argue. Let them believe what they wanted to believe.

They just kept on laughing. They even put the woman's little boy up to recounting the story. They stood him up on the back of a wagon.

"That bear was goin' like this." The boy made his hands into claws and hunched his little back over. "Grrr-grr!" The little boy stood taller. "And then Miss Armentia swung her stick and yelled at that old bear! And he took to the hills!"

At first, I was kind of prickly about it. But after seeing the little fella do it so many times, I got to where even I was smiling about it. Like I said, let them believe what they wanted to believe.

Until two days later. The men spotted that bear trailing us. A few of them took off after him.

That's why I can tell you, bear meat ain't bad to the taste. In fact, it's kind of sweet. That's why, when we rode into Texas, I rode in the proud owner of a large, brown bearskin throw.

CHAPTER FIFTY-FIVE

$\mathscr{I}$ DIDN'T KNOW THERE WAS A PLACE WHERE MEN WALKED that was as hot as Texas. But Master McDowell found us all a place there near a place called Tyler, not far from Palestine, not too far from Cherokee County. "Watch out for the soldiers," he continued to warn us. The place was hidden away, far off the road.

It was hard going at first—we slept on the wagons or under makeshift tents. But this was not new to us. Most of us had resettled at one time or another, so we adjusted. It was not long before we were planting fields with seed that we had brought with us. We planted cotton and the three sisters—corn, pole beans, and squash.

We sewed and mended. Men hunted while we spun thread and used looms we carried with us to weave cloth.

Like my mother, I stirred the cook's pot. Like my mother, I worked in the fields.

With each drop of the spade, I knew more and more that I did not want to be there. Each time I bent my back, I knew I needed to change my life. One day, I would leave Texas. I would go back to the Territory and find my husband. I would go back and find my son. Then, we will buy land, I told myself—land like my father dreamed.

I walked the rows, sweating underneath the hot sun, scooping into the mouth of a large bag tied over my shoulder. My fingers curled around the dried kernels of corn. I scattered them in the furrows, tossing a handful at a time. But every seven times, or so, I hid a handful in a pocket I had sewn in the folds of my skirt.

It would be seed for planting my family's own ground. I had been taking the little bit I stowed away, knotting it in small rags like my mother and I carried our money, and sewing up the tiny bundles in the hems of my skirts when I was alone.

"Soldiers! Soldiers!" A woman behind me began to yell.

We had been hiding so long, we had talked about it so many times—we moved without pausing to think. Each of us ran to our houses to protect the people and the things that were ours.

By the time we got to the cabins, soldiers on horseback had called everyone outside. Master McDowell stood in front of them, his arms around Molly and Mistress Gail.

One of the soldiers blew a bugle. Another one held a flag. One who appeared to be the leader waved to us, calling us from the fields.

"Come on in, now. Come on! We've got something you need to hear."

What was there to hear? We already knew what it was. They had come to confiscate our rations, to take our livestock, and other things. They would leave us to starve, as Master McDowell had told us they would. They would take anything valuable that we had, then, most likely, they would kill us.

I pushed my way to the front of the crowd. If this was it, if they were going to kill me, I wanted them to look me in the eye. I was through with hiding, and I would not go easy. I would not lie down and die.

The man who was the soldier chief began to speak. He did not speak to Master McDowell; he looked past him as though he was not there. Instead, he looked at us—all of us who had been invisible for so long.

"The war is over now, ladies and gentlemen. But it looks like you people haven't gotten the news." He looked briefly at Master McDowell and then back at us. "He doesn't own you anymore. Stay if you want to and work for wages. But you're free now; you can go your own way. Today is June 19th, 1865. War's been over for almost a month now. You're now free to go your own way."

He pointed at the cabins, the cows, the horses, and all the things around us. "This belongs to you as much or more than them. You've earned it, I suspect. Take it with you."

We were all quiet.

"Do you understand me? You're free!" He shook his head, looking at the bugler. "We'll set up here and get your names, then you can get started. You can get on your way." He leaned forward on his saddle. "And those of you from Indian Territory, well, since they seceded and joined the South, well, you just might have some land waiting for you—160 acres—when you get home."

We still stood quiet, waiting for Master McDowell to speak for us like he'd always done. Free? We were waiting for the sky to open up wide, for angels to take us away.

The soldiers in blue took the table from the main house and set it outside. They lined us up, and as we walked past, a soldier asked each of us our name. Then he wrote it down. "You sure you want to keep that name? You're free now! You don't have to keep the master's name. Why, you should change it. We *recommend* you change it—to Evans, or Jones, or Washington, or even Lincoln!" Who was going to argue? Most of us changed them right then.

It is a funny thing to get what you've been praying for—most times you're too stunned to cry or yell. Now that we had freedom, what were we to do with it?

We stood quiet. "Where will we go?" people whispered. "What will we eat?"

Those of us who walked the Trail wondered if it was true, or if they were here to fool us, to kill us, or steal us away.

When it was my turn in line, the writing soldier asked my name. He kept his eyes on the book in front of him.

I thought for a moment, not sure what I should answer.

"You understand my words, miss?"

Finally, I answered. "Mrs. Saunders," I said. It was my first time taking on my husband's name. I claimed it as my own, like any other wife.

"Like I told the other folks, you'll need to change your name." He held his pen, ready to write, but still looking down.

"It's my husband's name," I answered. "He's a soldier just like you. He's away fighting in the war."

He still did not look at me. "Yes, ma'am. And your first name?"

"Armentia."

He froze, and then looked into my eyes. "Would you repeat that, ma'am?"

"Armentia. Armentia Saunders."

His eyes still on me, he opened his mouth to speak, but another soldier cut him off. "Write it down, now, and move them all along." He wrote on the paper. Truth is, I don't know what he wrote. None of us did. He didn't ask us how to spell our names. We didn't know—and if we did, we'd be afraid to say.

I left the table to stand with the other people.

We were no longer slaves.

When the writing soldier finished, the soldier chief spoke to us again. "Get up, now. Get going."

Some people, free people, moved for wagons—including the mother and the children that had escaped the bear. I watched them piling in—one or two beginning to smile. They were leaving. One of the men laughed, "We's free!"

My feet would not move. "Where are you going?"

"They're going to lead us north to Fort Gibson," the mother said to me.

Fort Gibson? The place where my Willie Saunders had run off to?

"Get a move on, now!" one of the soldiers said.

They were leaving.

My head was light. My knees buckled, but I managed to stand. I looked at Master McDowell and Mistress Gail. "Wait!" I said.

It was like the kite string tugging at my heart. My feet moved. I lifted my hand. "Wait! Wait!" It pulled and tugged. "Wait for me!" I was afraid, but laughter came out of my mouth. I clamped my hand over it as I ran. Inside my cabin, there wasn't much to grab—some clothes, a coat, a blanket, and the bearskin—to remind me. I bundled them and ran.

I jumped aboard, my feet dangling off the edge.

Master and Mistress McDowell looked brokenhearted, like something had been stolen from them. She didn't cry this time. Maybe she was all out of tears. She just lifted her hand. I raised my hand to wave in return, then lowered it again.

We began to bump away from the Texas campsite, leaving Master McDowell, Molly, and Mistress Gail behind. There were people still standing with them, people I knew would never leave. They were the kind of people who would say there was nowhere else on earth they'd rather be than with their masters, the kind of people who would say slavery was the best life they ever had . . . probably because they were scared like me. Scared to try something new, even if it might be better.

I didn't want to be like them. That's why, even though part of me was scared and thinking I ought to stay, I grabbed my things and made that scary part of me get on the wagon anyway. Every breath I took, as we bumped along, I felt a little better, a little freer.

Riding with me on the wagon were people that seemed to get hotter and madder with each bump. Maybe getting free gave them the courage to speak up, yell names, and feel the anger we had all been hiding behind smiling faces and eyes that always looked down.

If you had asked me, before we started bouncing down the road, I would have thought I would have been one of the mad ones. I had every reason to be angry—lost my home, my father, my mother, my son, my brother. No real family or home, just moving here and there with people going in and out of my life. I had cause to lift my fist and shake it at Master—at Jacob McDowell and everybody like him.

But that was one of those moments, my head jiggling from side to side at every dip in the road, one of those moments I couldn't explain if there wasn't no God. "Wait! Stop! Wait a minute!" I yelled over my shoulder at the driver. When the wagon slowed, I jumped down and ran back. I ran up to Mistress Gail—to Gail, still standing there looking lost. I hugged her real hard. Only the Great One could have done that. On my own, how could I hug the neck of the woman that sold my baby away? I don't know any other way to explain it.

"You gone make it," I told her. "You gone be all right." I guess it was fitting. We had a strange kind of friendship for a whole lot of years.

But that's all there was. After I hugged her, I ran fast as I could back to that wagon and never looked back.

That night, when we stopped further up the road, the men caught a wild pig. They dug a pit and roasted it. While it cooked, we danced and sang by the fire.

I watched the people laughing.

There was no one to tell me when to come or go.

I didn't know how to feel.

There was no one to make me cook or work in the field.

I tried to remember how it was long ago. Then I began to sing.

In dat great gittin' up mornin'
Fare you well, fare you well

While I sang, I noticed the writing soldier still watched me.

In dat great gittin' up mornin'
Fare you well, fare you well

I smiled and looked away from him. I was married and he was too young. I was on my way to find my husband and my son. I was on the way to claim our allotment of land.

That night was not the first time I tasted roast pig. But it never tasted so sweet before.

It was not the first time we traveled hard road. We made our way to Fort Gibson—still fighting sinkholes, snakes, mosquitoes, and roving bears.

But this time, we traveled with hope and dreams in our hearts.

This time, I traveled with love in my hand.

CHAPTER FIFTY-SIX

$\mathcal{W}$HEN WE APPROACHED THE FORT, THE GATES WERE LIKE I remembered—wooden gates, lines of logs that swung open. But it was not Fort Butler. There was food for us, and there was activity around it and inside. Like Willie Saunders had told me, it was easy for me to find work as a cook. Watching all the people, I kept my eyes open for my husband, I inquired of every person that I met.

In the same way, the writing soldier kept his eyes on me.

Finally, one evening, he approached.

He stood in front of me, looking down, and then he looked at me. "I have something for you."

"No, I'm married, you see." I couldn't help smiling. It was flattering, all the attention the soldier was giving me. But there wasn't nothing on this earth that was gone tempt me away from Willie Saunders. When I saw him again, I was going to put my arms around him and never let him go. If he had to fight in a war, or run to Mexico, I was going to be going with him.

He reached inside his jacket. "No, ma'am, it's not like that."

He was so young. I touched my hand to my hair, still smiling. I couldn't wait to see Willie's face when I told him the story about the young soldier that couldn't keep his eyes off of me.

"I've been carrying this letter," the soldier said. The envelope was stained, bent and folded. "I've been carrying it a long time. Never thought I would really meet you. Then there you were in line." He shrugged. "It didn't seem like the right time before. I just didn't know how to tell."

He handed the letter to me.

CHAPTER FIFTY-SEVEN

South Carolina
July 16, 1863

WILLIE SAUNDERS GRIPPED THE BUTT OF HIS ARMY-ISSUED bayonet rifle. They had waited all afternoon, all day; dusk was now approaching. With every step he took, his canteen slapped against his backside, his heels sinking deeper in the sand. He held his head high.

He was probably never going to see his pretty wife again, bless her no-dancing heart. He was probably never going to hold her again in his arms. The purple ribbon that she had pressed into his hands when he left her was tucked inside his jacket, smooth against his chest, against his heart. He had left a letter for her with a corpsman and told him her name and how to get it to her, to her people in Indian Territory. "Just in case I don't return."

The sergeant called out the cadence as they marched the sandy strip of the South Carolina beach. *Ayup! One! Two! Three! Four!*

Willie Saunders marched among a proud unit—the 54th Regiment Massachusetts Volunteer Infantry, colored soldiers, a

Negro unit, buffalo soldiers his people called them. The men in blue marching with him were all shades. Some were so light, if they had chosen, they could have passed for White. Some were dark.

Some had accents, like Tippoo Saib, that said they were not long from Africa. Or, like the one who said he was from an Atlantic whaling ship, kidnapped when his crew was ashore. Sold into slavery, both of them were now on this beach far from home. They would rather die than live in bondage anymore, they said over and over again.

There were men who had escaped from plantations. Among them, a man named Ephraim who showed Willie his back, lifting his shirt to show brown skin all striped, full of scars.

And there were others like him. Those that were Black, but who had the look, the ways, the language of the Cherokee, the Choctaw, the Seminole, the Creek, or the Chickasaw.

Few if any of them were from Massachusetts. They had been recruited from all over the country. *Come join us! Let's show them that we are men! Let's fight and, once and for all, earn an equal chance!*

They would soon be out in the open and the bullets would start to fly. He could have headed for Texas, or maybe made it to Mexico. But how could he go and not fight for his wife?

From the corner of his eye, he caught a quick glance at the ocean waters, dark now. Mostly he could hear the rushing waters, the ebb and flowing tide—sometimes a flash of white-cap. He remembered this water, this beach. Vague memories from when he was a boy. He had memories of this sand, and of a time when it belonged to his people, when they were brothers—a time before the Trail. At least, he thought he remembered. Or was it just recollection of a story his mother once had told?

Double time, now, you soldiers! Show them what you're made of, boys! Show them colored is as good as any! One! Two! Three! Four!

Fire from Fort Sumter—red flashes, gold trailers—booms that shook the air—shells crashed about them! The first fire just missed the columns of men.

It was too dark now to see Colonel Shaw—the young, soft-spoken White man, their leader, who looked younger than he was—now up ahead.

Willie's breathing was shallow, quick and shallow. If he died, he died for freedom. He died for liberty, for his and for his wife's. If he died, he died for his people and for this land that once was theirs.

But he wouldn't think about death now. He didn't want to die.

Howitzer fire, sputtering bursts of white light from Cummings Point hit the line. Men fell like cornstalks under a scythe.

He would think about singing outside Armentia's window.

Oh, buffalo gal, won't you come out tonight
Come out tonight
Come out tonight
Oh, buffalo gal, won't you come out tonight
And dance by the light of the moon.

He would think about bathing his wife by moonlight. He would think about holding her in his arms.

Quick time, now, you boys! One! Two! Three! Four!

When the trumpet sounded, those that had avoided the early fire began to run. His rifle drawn, his bayonet in position, he jumped over men who lost their footing in the heavy, wet sand.

Shots cracked around him. Fire from Fort Wagner rained down on them. Men fell . . . in the gunfire he could see red dotting their faces—some all dark red and running where brown skin once had been.

Yelling, he ran for the fort, avoiding the scream of shells and fighting for footing in the sand. He could see the rebel flag atop the fort above him, ahead of him up the dunelike hill. It was the flag that said he did not have the right to life, a right to liberty, a right to simple happiness.

More men fell around him. Men he had shared meals with; men who on quieter days had laughed at his tall tales. One of the men, now on the ground, had a gaping cavity where his stomach should have been.

When he stepped over the man, he felt the fellow grab his leg. *Help me! See! I'm bleeding! Don't let me die!* He had to go forward. Willie jerked his leg away.

Don't fire until you see the whites of their eyes, boys!

If he waited until then, he was never going to get off a shot. His unit was in a bad position. The enemy, their flag flying high, looked down on his unit—on their march up the narrow strip of beach—from their position high above.

The enemy picked them off like hogs in a pen, like lambs.

Willie raised his rifle when he saw a shape. He raised it, focused, and fired—not sure if he hit his mark.

A hot fireball, out of nowhere, knocked him backward off his feet. He spun like he was dancing. *Well, there she goes.* It burned like nothing he'd ever felt, hotter than the brand that had fried his skin. Willie lifted his head, struggling to get to his feet. *Umph! There goes another one!* He spun again, falling harder. There was no way he could stand now. But he could feel a hot, sticky wetness bubbling up through his mouth, running down the side of his face onto his neck.

He saw the feet and legs, tasted the wet sand of men stumbling over him. *Go get 'em!* Other men would get further than he had. *We're comin' for you!* He thought it was Tippoo Saib's voice, his legs that stepped over him. Maybe Tippoo would be the one to pull down the rebel flag.

Willie turned his head to see a young man, one of his comrades, lying near him on the ground. It was a young one, one called Abraham. Blue-eyed, blond-haired, a very young man.

The men from the fort above still fired on those already

fallen—making certain they were not just wounded, but dead.

Willie rolled onto his stomach—a white flash from inside his head almost blinded him. Then there was another pain, like a knife that flashed from his lower back to the top of his head. *Don't move!* his body screamed to him.

He couldn't wield his rifle, but maybe he could shield the young man from any more pain. It was over for him, but maybe Abraham, if he could cover him, had a chance.

If I die, at least she will get the letter. Willie ground his elbows into the sand to grind his way forward. *She will know how much I loved her.* Each inch was so much pain. *A letter to his sweetheart, a letter to his buffalo gal.*

When he reached the young man, he stuck out his hand to comfort him . . . leaving splotches of dark blood where he tried to wipe away sand.

Willie coughed, choking. He was dying. He knew it. But it was worth it to die for Armentia . . . for freedom . . . for truth . . . and for love.

CHAPTER FIFTY-EIGHT

THE WRITING SOLDIER PRESSED THE LETTER INTO MY hand.

"I don't read, sir," I told him.

He said my love, my Willie Saunders, had dictated it to him for me before he stormed the beach. "I'm sorry," the writing soldier whispered to me. "He was a brave man, that's about all I know."

He tore open the letter and slowly read to me.

My Dearest Wife Armentia,

If you are reading this, then I have died on this beach in South Carolina. But having gone, it is worth it, because I believe that you now are free.

Don't cry for me, my buffalo gal. Next to my life with you, this is the best thing I have ever done. I only wish we had danced one more time.

All my love to you, my darling, until again we meet.

Your faithful and adoring husband,
Willie Saunders

Now it was my turn to look away. "Thank you, sir." I took my letter and walked away, looking for a dark place so that no one would see me cry.

When I found a place, I lay down. I balled up like a baby. I hugged the letter to me. I rocked it in my arms. Between my tears, I sang myself to sleep.

> *Oh, buffalo gal, won't you come out tonight*
> *Come out tonight . . .*
> *and dance by the light of the moon.*

I stayed at Fort Gibson after that, just long enough to make passage money. When I located a party leaving, I headed back to what had been my home.

CHAPTER FIFTY-NINE

*W*HEN I REACHED INDIAN TERRITORY, I MADE MY WAY to the bureau, the office that decided on claims for land.

As I walked along, there was less clay and more dust—too many people planting too much on too little land.

There were even more strangers now. There were more wagons to sidestep, more horses to dodge. There were men who came through the land to drive cattle, and others who came to steal from other men over the Territory border because the United States law could not reach them there. There were *Aniyunwiya* and plains people who complained about the disappearance of the buffalo.

And as I walked, I walked past the bricks I had paid for—the brick my mother and father had died for—they were still sitting in piles on the ground.

It was busy in the bureau office. Dark inside, except the light coming from the window, there were families clustered at the counter, who were talking to clerks.

"You'll have to fill out this form," a man said, not looking at me. He lifted it, handed it to me.

"I don't write."

He lifted his head, looking at me over the rim of his glasses. "I guess I'll have to help you, then." He said it like I was a bother. While I stood, he sat writing down my information. "Your name?"

"Armentia. Armentia Saunders," I said.

He wrote it down. "Where are you from?"

"From the East. I walked the Trail of Tears."

He flipped open a large book, a book full of names—name upon name upon name. "No Saunders here," he said. "No Armentia Saunders registered here." He slapped the book closed. "No Saunders in that book at all. If your name is not in the book, you can't claim any land."

He waved his hand for me to step aside.

"But I am one of The People. I am Cherokee."

He tilted his head back to look at me. "Don't appear so to me."

I spoke the language for him.

"Anybody could learn that." He tapped the book. "If your name is not in the book, you get no land."

"But I was a slave and the soldier chief told me . . ."

"I don't know anything about war, and a soldier doesn't know anything about my job. A soldier can't tell you anything about claiming land. Do you see that man in this office?" He looked around the room.

"No, but—"

"Then I think you better listen to me instead of that man. We have counted the Cherokee and taken their names down on rolls. If your name is not on the roll, then you have no claim."

"Once I had another name. I was married and my name was changed to Saunders, and before that I had another name."

He squinted at me and waved his hand. "Seems unlikely.

You don't expect me to believe you when you continue to change your story."

"But there is someone here, someone, I'll find someone. There's someone here who knows who I am. Someone who will remember my name."

"You're free to try. I don't know what good it will do. But if it pleases you, then go ahead. I don't think you'll have much luck. Every bit of land given to a slave, to someone who doesn't deserve it, is land that's taken away from The People. Government is really sticking it to them for backing the South in the war." He snorted. "And they already think they've lost enough land."

For a long time, I stood on the road in front of Mama Emma's house. I walked back and forth. So many memories, so much hurt, so much anger. The loss of my family, I laid at her feet. It was her hand that had killed my mother. She hadn't been sent away for any of it. Instead, her wickedness had got her a house, land, and fine clothes.

Her house was like I had remembered it. There were still some small wooden cabins that people walked in and out of, still heading for the fields with bags in their hands.

I hated her for what she had done to my family, to me. It was hard to think of seeing her, of asking her for anything— even just to ask her to say that I was once her slave. It was shameful to have to admit that she still had any part in my life. But as much as I hated her, there was also part of me that was afraid. I didn't want her to still be able to make me afraid, but I had seen her kill my mother and not look back. I knew Mama Emma would do most anything.

I hated her. I hated her house. And if hate was all there was, it still would have been easy to make myself go to the door, to get the land for me and for the son I hoped would come and find me.

What held me out on the road, what I was most ashamed of, was that there was still something in me—with all she had done to me and my family—that hoped things would be different now. A part of me, a little girl part of me I guess, still wished that she would love me again. Or hoped that she really had loved me at one time, that I had not just made it all up in my head. *"Oh, Armentia, my daughter! I am sorry! I have been so wrong. Can you ever forgive me?"*

Part of me wanted to say yes, and put my arms around her. With all that had happened, I still wanted to hear her say it. *"Things will be different now, my daughter."* She would hold me in her arms. Mama Emma would cook for me, draw bath water for me, and give me new clothes. *"I am sorry, my daughter, for all you have been through."* She would throw open her door and spread her arms. *"Welcome home!"*

I forced myself toward her door. I needed the land, a place for me and my son.

When I knocked at the door, it barely opened.

"Mama Emma?" She was still dressed fancy, but her face was old and tired. She did not look happy.

Her eyes widened when she recognized me. "Get away!" she squawked. "I don't know you."

"You know me. Come with me to the Indian Bureau. Tell them who I am. Tell them that I am one of The People. Tell them that I belonged to you."

Mama Emma pressed to close the door. "I do not know you." She frowned. "Don't come here trying to steal our land. I am not your Mama Emma, you lazy girl."

I held it open. "Has it been so long? You remember my father, my mother Sara, The One Who Guards His Family, and me. Remember? You know us."

"Move out of my doorway! I told you, I do not know you."

Through the door opening I could see Papa sitting at a table. His hair was also gray. His body was with us, but his spirit was gone. He stared straight ahead.

"You know me, my name is Armentia!"

"I know no such thing! We had no slaves," Mama Emma insisted and slammed the door.

It was what I knew would happen. It was what I should have known would happen. Still it hurt. Still I was ashamed.

I thought then to find Golden Bear. But I learned that only his mother was still in Indian Territory. When I found my way to her place, sheltered by trees, there was no one there with her. She did not have much to show. She was not so thin anymore. "Sit with me." She fed me *pashofa,* like my own mother once made, while we talked, sitting on stools under a tree.

She had been quiet for so many years; it was surprising to hear her voice. Maybe she had stood up to her bear too.

"While you have been away, much has changed. It is not like the olden days when women gave the counsel for war. Now men fight all the time." She shook her gray head as she dipped the steaming corn and peas into my bowl. "The United States War between North and South came to us and split us even more apart." She filled her bowl and then sat beside me. "Many of us wanted no part of it. What does the White man's war have to do with us? But those with slaves wanted to keep them. The rich win, so we sided with the South." She nodded at me to eat, then dipped her spoon in her bowl and took a mouthful. "Almost good as home?"

"Almost."

"Yes, almost. I think there's something missing in the earth here. To me, things are not as sweet." We ate in silence until she spoke again. "Golden Bear was like his father. He could not make peace with the new ways." She looked at the leaves on the ground in her yard. "He was not alone. He joined with the Pin Indians. You know, they wore crossed pins on their lapels." She sighed and then took another bite.

"During the war, we fought amongst ourselves—those that had slaves against those that did not—the Treaty men against the Pins. Golden Bear was caught in the fighting—men fighting like badgers, not brothers. Even the Baptists split over it, just as Reverend Bushyhead warned."

I waited for her to tell me, knowing all the time.

"One morning, he did not come home." She looked at me. "My family is gone now." She pointed at the small, weathered wooden cabin behind her. "The people who own this land have taken me in, so I can stay here until it is time to go home to our fathers." She stirred in her bowl. "And the Great Spirit still sits with me. He talks to me."

Golden Bear's mother, with all that she had been through, was still like stream waters. Peace sat with her, peace I didn't think would ever come to me again.

I asked her if she would come with me to the Bureau.

"If I could help you, I would. But they have denied my claim, too, for treaty violations. I guess that means because Golden Bear would not be quiet about what he believed. My voice, to them, would be like the wind talking. They would not hear. And I am a woman . . . and that means nothing now." She patted my hand. "And you are lucky to be here, my dear. They have made many people, like Johnnie Freeman's family, leave the Territory. Even the preacher, Evan Jones, had to go. And Reverend Bushyhead has gone to be with the Breath Giver."

There was no one to remember me. No one who would claim me. I wandered about. Mama Emma turned away when I saw her. Others, besides Golden Bear's mother, would not answer when I called their names.

My name was not on the rolls. So, I gathered up my things and sat by the side of the road, like so many people, until I found someone who would take me in.

In return for cooking, the Erwins gave me a little one-room shack on their land. And when there was a moment free, I got reading lessons from their girl, a schoolgirl. Her name was Emma. She wore fancy clothes, and spoke and read the United States words pretty well. But she wasn't like Mama Emma; there was nothing stuffy about her. Before the war, she attended school in Tennessee at the Clarksville Female Academy, she told me. Now that the war had ended, she would soon be going back to school again.

She and I traded what little we had. She pointed out the United States letters, taught me to write them, and helped me learn the words. In exchange, I told her about the old days, about how it was before. It was all she wanted to know about. "They will not let us speak the old words. They do not want us to remember." So, we met out by a tree, trading letters and words for memories.

I didn't have land. I didn't know how things would go, but I was free now and I wanted to read. She was patient, that child, sitting on the ground—leaves falling around us—and teaching me.

My little shack was only big enough, mostly, for my bed. Behind it, I planted a few seeds—some of the corn I had tucked away in my skirt hems. At night, as my mother had taught me, I strung beads and made blankets—working by the light of the moon.

Like my mother before me, when I had made a few things, I made my way—past buggies, past wagons, past cowboys, and other lost souls. Wild men, drunken men, and sad-faced women had multiplied while I was gone. I wondered if they had lost their families. I wondered if they had lost their land. Carrying Willie Saunders's letter in my hand, I picked my way around them, and sold my things at the trading post, keeping pennies in a new jar.

At night, I counted my pennies, looking at the sweet copper

in the jar, pennies that would buy my land. Land that would be waiting when my Abraham Proof came to find me.

I shook the coins, shining in the moonlight. "You're going to make my father's dream."

It was on one of my trading post visits that I met him, standing inside, seeming to take up all the room in the store. His skin was copper-colored, like he was a mixture of everything.

He grinned, his arms folded, standing with one hip higher than the other. "No need to get your feathers flustered, mister. I'm just looking for a little work." He wore a broad-brimmed hat, and two guns on belts that crisscrossed on his hips.

The shopkeeper was red-faced. "It's not work you're looking for, young fellow. What you're looking for is trouble. Now, you get yourself on out of my place!"

The cowboy moseyed out of the door, tapping with one finger on one of his guns.

I sold my goods, tucked my money away, and then I followed after him.

I know you're already thinking this is foolishness. But I told you I would tell you the truth, even all the bad.

That day, maybe for the first time, it came to me that I was free. I'd lost my husband; I was brokenhearted. But at least I was free. I jumped on it, not looking where I was going, landing feet first.

I'd been running, all the years from trouble—now I was staring it in the eye.

His feet splayed out in front of him on the dirt road, he sat on the wooden board sidewalk.

"I've got some money, cowboy. You want to work for me?"

He looked up at me, tipping the brim of his hat to keep the sun out of his eyes. "You talking to me, ma'am?" He smiled, like he knew a funny story.

"I've got trees and firewood that needs to be chopped."

"That so?"

"And I need me a pen built so I can get me some chickens."
I tried to put a calm in my voice that I wasn't feeling. "While
you are working, you can bunk out around my place . . . with
me."

Oh, now, don't act too shocked, like you ain't never done
nothing you think back on as crazy.

He was still grinning. "You don't know me. I may not be
trustworthy."

"I can trust whoever I choose to, thank you very much."
Oh, I was feeling very, very free. I was talking a lot and hadn't
even asked him his name.

He wasn't anything anyone would have chosen for me. I
wasn't long in the tooth, but he was still way too young for me.
Even if he wasn't, people probably would have said he was too
short, or too tall, or too dark, or too wild.

But I didn't have to ask anybody what he or she thought. I
didn't have to ask for anyone's permission. Most of my life,
other people had been making choices for me. *Do this, gal. Do
that, gal.*

Now I was choosing for myself.

Being free is good. But if you're not careful, free will let
you do crazy things.

"So, you coming, or not?" he said to me, getting up from
where he sat. Well, I wasn't anybody's gal anymore. I was free
to choose, so I chose to put my feet in the road behind him.
"Get a move on there!" I yelled to him. I was plucky about it.
I wasn't chasing behind him; just making my choices known.

He walked ahead of me, kicking up dust, his chin and chest
high like he was king of the world. Newly free, to me it was a
mighty attractive thing.

"Hey, there!" It was hard to keep up. He took mighty big steps and I trotted a little just to keep up. It sounds foolish now, recounting this. But it sure felt fun and free back then. "Hey, there!" I said.

The young man stopped short all of a sudden. I almost tripped and ran right smack dab into the back of him.

He turned around with a big ol' pie-eating grin like it wasn't the first time some girl had almost tripped herself up over him.

I reminded myself that I was a woman, a free woman. I started asking questions I should have asked before we started down the road. "Are you from around here? I've never seen you before. Do you have a name?"

He looked me over. "My American name is John William."

Wasn't that something? Every man I ever had a spark for was named John, William, or both. It looked like a sign to me—like a red bird or a rainbow in the sky. Maybe I thought it was a sign because I wanted it to be one.

I reminded myself that I was getting to be an old hen, so I tried not to let him see that my feathers were getting bunched together. "So, where are you from?" I covered my eyes so I wouldn't get sunblinded when I looked up at him.

"From some of everywhere. I'm from anywhere I please."

"Well, that's nice."

People passing by looked at us—at him, like they knew him, and then at me like I was stupid, crazy, or both. They looked at me like I should have known better.

But I didn't care; I was free.

"I'm just trying to make a little money so that I can go back there."

"Well," was all that I could say.

"Yes," he nodded, still smiling like he had a joke.

"So, you are not staying here long?" We started walking again.

"No, I am not, Miss . . ."

"Oh, my name is Armentia."

So, he came to my place and stayed—bunking out back beneath my window.

He chopped trees and built a pen—always laughing like he knew something funny. "You sure you got enough money to afford me?"

"Oh, I got it."

He folded his arms and tilted his head back. "No offense, but you don't look like a rich woman to me." He pointed at my cabin. "You're a pretty woman, but you sure don't look rich."

"Don't you worry." Oh, I was grinning all over myself like a fool.

For the next few days, after everything he did, he asked me about his pay. "You sure you got my money, buttercup? You wouldn't be stringing this old country boy along?" He would smile. "You aren't going to fool me, are you? Are you going to have me working just to see your pretty eyes and all your curly hair?"

Oh, he was a sweet-talking, pretty young thing. It occurred to me that he might be nice to have around. It crossed my mind that if he worked with me, we could get us land—land for us and Abraham Proof—that much sooner.

So, that night, I showed him my jar.

There it was, almost full, gleaming in my hands.

"Well, stars!" He asked to hold it. "You got enough, all right! You really had me fooled."

He sat inside and talked to me.

"We'll buy land and grow our own. We'll have chickens, a pig, and a cow. Then we'll get us a well." I talked and talked until sleep rushed up on me.

In the morning, that pretty young cowboy was gone.

He took my jar, and all my hope with him.

I paid for a hard lesson. The thing I learned about freedom is, you're free to make bad choices too.

After that, all the people that wouldn't talk to me suddenly remembered my name. "You should have known better, Armentia. You were too old for him."

"Didn't you know he was a cowboy? Didn't you know he was a bad man?"

Other than Emma, I'd had no visitors. Now they flocked to be by my side.

"Didn't you know how foolish you looked? I thought you had more wisdom than that!"

"Didn't you know that was Cherokee John? Baddest man in the West!"

They kept up the parade until nightfall. I kept up my chin until then.

It seemed like people had just been coming in and out of the door of my life—so many people, none of them able to stay. The only one always there was me . . . and Mama Emma. I guess I was just trying to grab ahold of someone—someone I could keep. Maybe people can't understand that if they have a family or a settled place. A man that's got groceries can't understand a hungry man stealing food. Maybe you think I'm just making excuses. Maybe I am. But I just wanted somebody of my own. I needed somebody.

Underneath the moon, I cried into my arms. What a fool I had been.

I cried until I realized, I wasn't really crying for him, for some Cherokee John. It wasn't even the money.

I was crying for my family and my son. I was crying for my husband, for the hope and the dream that I had lost. Willie was never going to stand outside my window. I was never going to hear his voice singing to me again.

His letter was under my bed. Opening it, I read the words—this time by myself—again. Then I folded it, laid it on my heart, and cried until sleep came.

CHAPTER SIXTY

$\mathcal{I}$ DIDN'T HAVE THE STRENGTH TO START AGAIN, TO earn again what I had lost.

So, I planted the three sisters—beans, corn, and squash—behind my shack and kept cooking for the Erwin family.

That shack, on their land was where—I finally accepted—I would die.

There was plenty of time—moons, summers, many years—sitting on the porch, to think about what might have been. I turned gray thinking and feeling regret.

While I sat, time did pass. Little Emma went back to school in Tennessee. She wrote me letters. There she met a man, a former slave, named Newton Ewell. They married and moved to Texas, near Cherokee County, near where Jacob McDowell had hidden us.

She had nine children—Valcris, Ara, Elijah, Ruby, Audrey, Thomas Jefferson, Georgia, Otha, and Jewell—that last time I heard.

Emma was brave to go there, so far from her family. If I had

been that brave, I often wondered, what would my life have
been?

My family could have been like those that hid away in the
mountains, or some of those who watched us as we marched
the Trail—their native blood disappearing into White or Black.

Or, I could have run away. I could have grabbed ahold of
Miss Lula and Miss Bertha Bell's hands. What did it matter that
we didn't know where we were going? Some night, I could
have grabbed my Abraham Proof and run clean on away. That
night, when he came for me, I could have followed my husband. I could have held his hand and run with him up the trail.

I could have listened to those who loved me, who tried to
show me the way. Though I loved them, I was stubborn, thinking I knew better. Instead of risking hope, I put all my trust in
trouble. And in fear.

But it was too late now. I leaned my head against the hard
railing. My hair was turning gray; my bones were aching. My
running days were over.

Besides regret, all I had was the letter. There had been no
word of my son.

I looked up at the sky. "Well, Lord." It was all that I could
say. Then I prayed one of those prayers without words, lifting
my heart up for the Lord to see, for the Great One to see the
good and the bad of my life. It was almost like I could feel Him
touching, touching all the bruised places, touching all the hurt
I had been through. My eyes closed and tears, quiet tears, came
from my eyes.

I thought about all the things I had been through. Good
things, bad things—things I'd done right and things I'd done
wrong. I thought on all the people I'd been with and all the
places I'd been. I mean really took a good look at it. The Breath
Giver does things—giving some people so many to love, so
many people to love them back. Other people, like me, don't
seem to get nothing.

I thought about Willie and the night he left, then my little Abraham Proof. My family came to mind—my mother, my father, and my brother. All that was left was Mama Emma. I had been fighting it so long on the inside of me, being sad about being alone, about hating Mama Emma, and about loving her because she was all I had left. It didn't seem fair to me. But there was nothing I could do about it.

So, I just stopped fighting. I guess that's what making peace is. Not acting like you don't see what's wrong in your life; that's just pretending. But I guess making peace is looking at it, and just trusting, just giving in to whatever it is.

It was gone be what it was gone be. I just let go.

There I was, tears running down my old face. The more I cried, the more it was like that flower water my husband Willie had bathed me in so long ago. It was like I rested my head on the Breath Giver's shoulder, like He held me on His lap. Then peace came to sit with me, peace I never thought I'd have again. I didn't have nothing, but peace sat with me anyway.

CHAPTER SIXTY-ONE

$\mathscr{I}$ HELD WILLIE SAUNDERS'S LETTER AND ROCKED, AND thought about Abraham.

"Ma'am, I think we been looking for you."

I barely opened my eyes, squinting, and looked at a whole group of people standing in front of me, all colors, kind of like a speckled pup in front of my porch. "No, I don't think you're looking for me. I don't think there's anything I can do for you." I could offer them a meal, some water, some conversation—but I didn't have much more than that. Maybe some of the peace that sat beside me.

The fellow speaking persisted. "Ma'am, is your name Armentia?"

"Well, yes." I looked them, the speckled pup, over again.

"Ma'am, do you have a star?"

I squinted at him. Thought about jumping up and running into the house for my walking stick. But I wasn't fast anymore. I'd been sitting too long.

And to tell you the truth, the water ran cold in my veins.

What trouble was this that had found me? I was an old woman, just an old woman trying to live in peace. But, if trouble had found me, I figured I might as well look it in the eye. "Well, sure enough, I do." I'd been tricked before—no doubt, I would survive it again.

The fellow speaking pointed to some of the people standing with him. "Well, we are your people, then. We are the children of your son, Abraham Proof."

"Abraham Proof?" My knees got some life in them, and I stood up and looked around for my baby. My eyes got watery, so I couldn't see. "What do you know about my baby?"

"We're what's left, ma'am."

Oh, it was just more people trying to make a fool of me. I wiped my face with the back of my hand. I looked more closely at that speckled pup. None of them appeared to be my little Abraham. "I don't have any money. You might as well be on your way."

"No, ma'am. We're not here for money."

They told me how my Abraham Proof had been in New Orleans, in Texas, and other parts of the land. He was daddy in all them places. Then they said that he had married and had two children before he went to South Carolina. They told me my Abraham had passed on, shot in that old Civil War. "But he told us all about each other, and all about you."

It took me a while standing there to think my little Abraham Proof, his legs running, his arms pumping, was a grown enough man to have children of his own. It was hard to imagine him with a gun in his hand. Worse, it was hard to imagine my baby gone. I pulled at my shirt sleeve. There wasn't anything to say. My baby gone. Everybody gone . . .

It was even harder to think that they might have found me. Tears came to my eyes again. I didn't know what to say.

Well, I almost fainted, but I was too excited to pass out.

"You sure, now? You sure you come here for me?"

"Yes, ma'am."

"You're not pulling an old woman's leg."

I sat down before I passed out. I had too much to do, hugging and kissing them home to my heart!

That speckled pup was mine! And all those speckles had found each other and come home to me.

"Daddy told us to find you. And we're supposed to find the star, and we're supposed to find the land!" a woman named Portia told me.

The fellow that was doing most of the talking, who was named Golden Bear Proof, pointed at a little child near him. "This here is my grandson, he's the littlest son of Abraham Proof. And just like him, his name is Abraham."

I was up and down on my feet so many times I lost count!

Lord, I thought I was going to bust wide open with joy. That baby stood there looking like my little Abraham, but bathed in the color of my sweet Johnnie Freeman. I bent over to take his hand. "Well, you sure are good medicine for my soul!"

"Grandma?" he looked up at me. "Can I see that star?"

When that stick stuck in my ankle all those years ago, it hurt something awful. But this littlest Abraham made me thank God for that long-ago pain. "Why, sure you can, baby." When I sat down and showed him my star, he touched it and looked up at me like he had been searching and finally found treasure true.

Me and that littlest Abraham spent a good old time, him touching and me grinning. Then all the rest—lots of them named Abraham, Golden Bear, Johnnie Freeman, the names I'd taught Abraham Proof in the stories—took turns looking at that star of mine, and soon we was all crying and laughing.

I didn't have to lift a finger; they wouldn't let me. They got to stirring pots. They didn't know how to make the old Cherokee dishes, but we feasted well nonetheless.

But just as I was full and happy to tears, a sadness came over

me. "But, children, I got to tell you—ain't no land for us here."
I told them the sorrowful story. "The land is gone in what's
now North Carolina." I told them about how I'd been taken
away to Texas during the Civil War, that I'd been freed there
and told to claim my land. "Now I'm back, but they say I'm
not Indian, I'm not Cherokee. They say I have no claim." I
didn't want to cry in front of them. "They say they don't know
me. They won't give me any land."

It was supposed to be a happy time, and no one wanted to
see an old woman's tears. But they came burning from my eyes
anyway. "I don't have any family left that will claim me. They
say I'm not one of them. They say they don't know me anymore, they don't remember me carrying water to them from
the well."

I told them about the money that I had lost.

So many years had passed; so many things had changed.
"There's land for rush now." The land had been allotted in
Indian Territory—land that was supposed to be ours free—
Indians had gotten a portion, White men had gotten the best
land, some Black men had gotten portions of what was left.
Now there was land wide open for taking. You only had to get
to it, to register, then run to stake your claim.

I told them about the land rush, the only chance I had for
a piece of land. "They letting people rush for what's left. Find
a piece of your own and stake a claim." I looked down at my
legs. "But I'm too old to run."

The littlest Abraham was still sitting near me. He reached
down and touched that star. "Don't worry, Great-Grandma."
He looked up at me. "I'll be your legs. I'll run for you."

As it turned out, on the day of the land rush, April 22,
1889, I had a whole lot of legs running for me. "I don't know
just where our piece of land is," I told them. "But it will have
a stream, or maybe a natural well." I drew pictures on the

ground with a stick. "It will have lots of trees that will look like a bother, maybe look like much of nothing. But you just put our flag stake down there. It may not be much, but we'll make it into something."

You should have seen the people lined up on that sunshiny day! There was green grass, but the sun had bleached some of it brown. Flat land, it was, so the eye could see far.

There was White folks, colored folks, Red folks, and even some speckled families like us. Hope and excitement was so thick it made the air wave. Some might have said it was heat, but I know it was the excitement of all the people there.

There were horses, rearing and bucking, and there were wooden wagons, some of them covered. Plenty of people were on foot. Rich folks were there, but some was so poor. Like us, that day was their only chance to have a home, to turn things around. Most of them, like me, were hoping that today was the day—the day when troubles would be over.

As many people as there were, no doubt there were just as many people that discouragement had kept from coming. It almost kept me away, but my little speckled pup wouldn't hear of it. "This is our day!" they said. Their hope had me standing in line with the others who had found the faith to make it that day.

Oh, it was something, people and excitement as far as the eye could see.

We had all stood in line, registered for a chance to stake our claim. Now we were in line waiting for the gun to fire and send us running!

I hobbled myself to that line, all crooked over, but I was determined that if my speckled pup was going to be there, I was going to be there with them.

When that shot fired, when it cracked the air wide open— Lord, have mercy! My heart jumped. Then it started racing. I took a step, then another, trying to keep pace!

Horses and wagons took off rolling. People on foot, on either side of my speckled pup, took off too.

You should have seen my family! My Abraham would have been so proud. They took off, their shirts and blouses flapping in the wind—hats flying off their heads. They ran just as my brother had taught me! Who would have thought a thing could pass down through the generations?

And my littlest Abraham, he took off too! It did my heart good to see it. If we didn't get any land, it was good enough to see those legs moving and those arms pumping. His arms and legs were pumping like his namesake's—my brother, his great uncle before him—and like my son Abraham Proof's.

Wouldn't it have been good if I could have run all the way with them? Maybe if we'd had a wagon, I could have made it when my old legs gave out. But I took a few steps, and then I just waved and shouted them on.

Because the land was flat, I could see them running for a good while. People around them stopped, sticking their flags in the ground, throwing their hats in the air. But my little speckled pup kept going until I couldn't see them anymore.

But I watched as long as I could. They ran like my brother Abraham, the promise on their shoulders. I watched my mother and father's promises run with them. Especially the littlest Abraham, though it seems like it should have been a load too great for him to carry.

My father believed it would happen. He didn't live to see it happen, but he believed. I stood there keeping an eye on his behalf. Nothing can stop a father's promise, it seems. Not even death. My father's gone, my brother Abraham, and my son Abraham Proof, too. But there I was looking at that littlest Abraham smiling at me and running for me! It took generations, but here his hopes had taken off running. I saw it with my own eyes.

The sun went down, and I sat there, on the ground where

we started, wrapped in a blanket. Situated there, with all the bundles of pots and pans, of clothes and food, and all the little we had, I got to thinking. I got to doubting. My family had just found me; I shouldn't have let them go, my people. They'd just found their way back home. "Lord Jesus," I prayed. "I don't have to have no land. I don't want to trade my family away for nothing. Lord, I need my people. Just send them back, Lord." I got to imagining all kinds of terrible things happening. People going crazy for land and hurting my speckled pup. "You don't have to give us nothing. We can make a home wherever we go."

Sometime, I fell asleep. I know I fell asleep because I woke up when somebody shook me. "Come on, Grandma." It was one of the girls, Portia—well, she was a woman now. "Come on, wake up. Come and see."

Portia and I, and those that were with her, gathered up our things. My answered prayers and I grabbed our bundles.

We started off. I walked as far as I could, the stars starting to show overhead. But now, like many of the old ones who walked the Trail of Tears with me, I was too old to make it on foot. "You just go on. I'll make it directly," I said.

You just never know, when circumstances are staring you in the face, how things are going to turn out.

Some of my older grandsons, grandsons I didn't even know I had not much more than a day before, lifted me up like I wasn't much of nothing. They took turns carrying me. How could I keep from crying? They were determined to get me to the land. We traveled as the sun traded places with the moon, beneath the stars. We had to stop sometimes, but by daylight, we were there.

Just like I had described to them, there were trees. There was a fire waiting for us. In front of the trees, I could see our stake. And next to the flag sat my littlest Abraham.

I stood there, my feet planted on that growing, living hope

and promise. The Great Spirit, the Good Lord, was with us, even in the land of red earth.

Now, that land didn't have a stream, but it was good land.

That land is this land you're sitting on with me, right now, today.

CHAPTER SIXTY-TWO

$\mathscr{I}$ NEVER HAD MORE WORD OF MY BROTHER ABRAHAM.
It was as though he disappeared. When I think of him, I think
of him changing and flying away. I think of him guarding our
family from up above.

I've had some sorrow in my life. You know all about my
loss, but I've had a lot of gain.

I had me a marriage and, for a little while, a blanket to wear.
In my heart, I still have all my family and, even the land that
was stolen from us. I don't have Africa, and my Cherokee still
claim they don't know who I am.

Still, I got no more secrets bottled up inside me. No more
covering for other people, no more covering for wolves. I'm a
smarter sheep—an old one, but still smarter. And I feel mighty
good about that.

And that girl, Emma, she even taught me to read.

But this is what I know to be true. Long ago, I lived in a
place with black earth, a place that holds the bones of my
fathers. It was a place of green trees and clear water.

I come from people who come from over the seas and I am also Cherokee, one of The Principal People. They may no longer know me, I may be in exile, but I know who I am. And I believe that someday they will call me home.

I walked the Trail of Tears. I lost my mother, my father, my sweet Johnnie Freeman, and The One Who Guards His Family.

I walked the thousand miles. I am still Black. I am still Cherokee. I had a son named Abraham.

I was lost to him, but in my latter days, my family—his family—found me. And, like my father promised, we got the land. I'm sitting here, right now, on my father's promise!

The ones who used to be my people, they may no longer know me, but I know who I am. Like Moses floating in a basket on the Nile, I am a hidden part of my people. I walked the Trail, over a thousand miles. I lost much—my sweet Johnnie Freeman, my husband Willie Saunders, my father, my mother, and The One Who Guards His Family.

But when I sit here on this land with my family, having been married, having learned to read—when I sit here a free woman—it makes me feel like I'm dreaming. After all I lost, my people found me! It makes me think back to the Red Bird on the Trail Where We Cried and the song he sang to me.

When the LORD turned again the captivity of Zion, we were like
them that dream.
Then was our mouth filled with laughter,
and our tongue with singing: then said they among the heathen, The
LORD hath done great things for them.
The LORD hath done great things for us; whereof we are glad.
Turn again our captivity, O LORD, as the streams in the south.
They that sow in tears shall reap in joy.
He that goeth forth and weepeth, bearing precious seed, shall doubt-
less come again with rejoicing, bringing his sheaves with him.

It took a whole lot of years, but I'm here! I am Black and I am still Cherokee; and I had a son named Abraham.

And in the latter days of my life, my people found me.

We built us some houses, a shop or two. It wasn't easy. We had to trade sometimes. We struggled sometimes. We had to fight sometimes. It was mighty hard and many times it took more than it seemed like we had to give.

But we built up. And over time, just like my father promised, we dug ourselves a well. We dug that well deep and we dug it true.

And we named that well Abraham.

A Note From the Author

••••••••••••◆••••••••••••

Two of my earliest memories involve Native Americans.

The first year of my life was spent on a Navajo Indian reservation in Kayenta, Arizona. Shortly after my birth, my family moved there. My mother and father, newly graduated from Bishop College in Marshall, Texas, were assigned to the reservation as schoolteachers.

My mother told us how my family made our way to Arizona from Texas, with little money, warming my baby bottles on our car's transmission hump. She talked about not having enough money, at first, for food, and about not having enough money for a needed operation. So, like her mother before her, she said she turned her face to the wall and prayed; and God answered.

I know the reservation was a place of peace for my mother, a place that held some of her fondest memories. I know it because all through the years—from my earliest childhood through my adulthood—she would gather my father, brothers, and me to view slides of our time in the painted desert. We saw pictures of her and my father with their friends, my brothers and I sitting with her, and of her surrounded by Navajo children—all of this juxtaposed against turquoise blue skies and red and purple mountains.

My mother taught my family about traditional Navajo foods, like pan-fried bread; she taught us words like, *ya-ta-hey!*

She taught us about customs and places like the *hogon* and locations like *Tees-nos-pas*.

When she spoke of the reservation, she spoke of it as though she was home, as though she never wanted to leave. Then she would point to the Native American children on the slides and look at us. "When the children are older, they take them from their families."

In my life, there was no greater horror than being separated from my family. I shared the Navajo children's desire to be home. Their terror was mine.

Eyebrows raised, eyes wide, her words sounded like a warning to me. "They forbid them to speak their language and they make them cut their hair. They keep them at boarding schools."

These were not nameless, faceless children to me. The Navajo children held my mother's hands, they smiled in my mother's face, and I took what happened to them personally, as though it could and was happening to me.

My mother showed us jewelry and the moccasins she had worn in the desert. We held them in our hands. It was real for me, not something from a television screen.

So my memories of the reservation, of the native people, my earliest memories—those that are my own and those that have been handed to me—are memories of beauty, belonging, mystery, and faith.

The second memory I have is in the form of a recurring dream. In the dream, I am a very small child standing on a mountain ledge that looks out over a canyon. It is only now that I know it is a canyon. As a child, I was terrified by how high I was above what looked like an enormous tear in the ground. The gash in the earth and the surrounding land and mountains were flaming red, orange, and purple rock. In the bottom of the gash, far beneath me, is a crashed airplane.

The dream, for me, was a nightmare.

As I watched, the plane's pilot crawled onto the wing,

flames licking all around him. I wanted to save him. That's what tormented me. But what could I do? In the dream, I was too young and too small. So, in the dream, I stand on the edge of the cliff fighting with myself. There are no adults around to help, or even to console or counsel me. Even if I reach him, I think, the plane will probably explode and we both will be burned.

I had this dream almost every night of my life from my earliest childhood—I know I was having it before I turned three—until I turned thirty. It has only been in the last year or two that I realized that what I saw in my dreams is the Grand Canyon.

So then, Native culture is part of my beginning. It is part of my earliest identification.

Yet, it is only recently surfacing.

There's Indian in my family. . . .

All of us said it on the playground. And though adults in my family also said it, somehow I never took it seriously. It was like an ancient song about some mythical land.

It was part of our pre–Civil Rights Movement yearning to be whole people, to be special, to be anything but Black. We could not even say the word. To call someone Black, back then, was an invitation to war. "I'm not Black." We would point to our skin. "There's Indian in my family." We would point to our softly straight "baby hair" framing the edges of our foreheads.

The greatest shame, maybe, is to be ashamed of who you are. So, I put it all away. In the enlightenment of the sixties and the seventies, I embraced the me that I knew.

There is Indian in my family. . . .

What did it mean? *I never saw these Indian people*, I thought. None of my family looked like the people portrayed on television.

My maternal grandfather, whom I adored, was supposed to be part Cherokee. He had beautiful black, curly hair; dark, smooth skin; and dark eyes ringed with blue. But how could he be Indian? He didn't wear a loincloth. There were no feathers in his hair.

My maternal grandmother, who died before I was born, was said to be mostly Irish. My grandmother Bertha was church-going, testimony-giving, and acted as church secretary. But her sister, my aunt Emma, whom I did meet, was a sporting woman and said to be mostly Cherokee. She was tough-talking and hard-living well into her eighties. But neither one of them looked like the Indians on television; they did not wear bands around their foreheads or rawhide in their hair.

There was no proof, so it was a myth to me. I wore my hair in an Afro and I was proud. Besides, no one stopped me on the street and said, "You look Indian to me." I knew my mother's

Grandmother Bertha & Grandfather R. Lovelace
with my mother on his knee

hair was fine and straight, and that she had to work to make an Afro, but none of it ever really connected to me.

On my father's side, there were the same rumors. But my grandmother didn't have a papoose strapped to her back, like in the movies. She was a principal at an East Texas school—which I now realize was segregated. She and my grandfather didn't smoke peace pipes; they went to church. My paternal grandfather had a large farm and he raised cattle. It was in his front yard that I saw racism and watched the cows come home. How could he be Indian? He raised the best watermelons around, and I never saw him with a tomahawk.

My mother was a schoolteacher. My father was a highly placed civil servant. How could they be Indian?

My heritage was in front of me, but I did not recognize it. I was looking for the wrong thing. And if I did not recognize it, it is no wonder that census takers and government workers didn't either.

I think my discovery, and the notion to write this book, began with my daughter, who was working on her thesis. She was going to call it "Indian in My Family" and it would track the movement of African American slaves on the Trail of Tears.

Of course, she had heard the stories. I'm sure I whispered them to her and her brother. "We're part Indian"—like singing an ancient lullaby.

It was a thesis for her; it was new information for me. We are history buffs, many in my family. So she and I began reading books and trading information that we found.

Maybe now I was ready to write another historical novel. My first book, *Passing by Samaria*, had required over a year's research. The research process was exciting, but exhausting and time consuming, and I shied away from it. It was not just research; while writing, I lived in the long-ago place. But the words of one of my college professors haunted me. "We have so many stories that need to be told, and you have the talent to do it." It took years before I heard her, more years before I believed her, and even more years before I had the courage to try.

So I committed to writing *Abraham's Well*. It is the story of a Black woman, a Native American woman—a Black Cherokee slave of mixed heritage—who walked the Trail of Tears. It is the story of her fight to survive and a nation's struggle to mature.

We did not study the tragedy in school. Instead, we discussed Manifest Destiny:

> Manifest Destiny is the belief that the United States had a mission to expand, spreading its form of democracy and freedom. Advocates of Manifest Destiny believed that expansion was not only good, but that it was obvious ("manifest") and inevitable ("destiny"). Originally a political catchphrase of the 19th century, Manifest Destiny eventually became a standard historical term, often used as a synonym for the territorial expansion of the United States across North America towards the Pacific Ocean.
>
> Manifest Destiny was always a general notion rather than a specific policy. The term combined a belief in expansionism with other popular ideas of the era, including American exceptionalism, Romantic nationalism, and a belief in the natural superiority of what was then called the "Anglo-Saxon race".—excerpt from *http://en.wikipedia.org/wiki/Manifest _destiny*

But, by reading authors such as historians William Katz and Patrick Minges, and former Cherokee Principal Chief Wilma Mankiller, I learned so much more.

The Trail Where We Cried, *Nunna daul Isunyi,* was a forced march of one thousand miles. Some estimate that approximately 17,000 Cherokee people—including slaves, free men of color, many of mixed heritage, and some whites who had intermarried—were forced from their homes in what are now North Carolina, South Carolina, Virginia, Alabama, Tennessee,

Kentucky, and Georgia. Simultaneously, other Native peoples—the Seminoles from Florida, the Chickasaw, the Choctaw, and the Creek—were forced from their native lands.

Many of them made the journey on foot, forced off their land by the United States government at gunpoint, to a land that was strange to them—Indian Territory, west of the Mississippi.

They were forced to move so that another group, people of another color, could have their land. It was Manifest Destiny, the political spin of the time said.

In 1830, the United States served the sovereign nations what was, in essence, an eviction notice from their lands. There were court battles and many pleas from leaders like John Ross and Nancy Ward, but little land was saved. Some Cherokee moved right away, the Old Settlers. The battle, for the Cherokee, was lost with the signing of the New Echota Treaty in Georgia in 1835. There, twenty men, well-known and respected, but not the official leaders of the Cherokee Nation, signed the treaty giving away the land and agreeing to the move to Indian Territory. Ross, the Principal Chief, and others continued the fight in the courts and in Washington hallways and offices.

The Seminoles fought on the ground for their Florida land, and rejected notions that Black members of their nation were slaves. They continued fighting into the 1840s.

But it ended for the Cherokee in 1838. President Andrew Jackson, defying the Federal Courts, signed the removal order into law.

That is when the forced removal of the Cherokee begins. That is when Armentia's march begins.

They were forced—leaving their homes, most of their belongings, and the "bones of their fathers"—and evicted to what is now Oklahoma.

It is estimated that one-fourth of them died along the way.

Those who survived were forced to start over—building homes, planting crops in soil they did not know—and to find roots and build families and communities from what was left.

Perhaps, to make the forced removal more palatable to the populous, the Native population was painted as ignorant, un-civilized, and warlike. The historical record shows something quite different. Formally educated—some of whom were college-educated statesmen and women who walked the halls of Congress, like John Ross or Stand Watie—or traditionally educated; non-Christians, Christians and even preachers; farmers—traditional or modern; mixed breed or full blood; homeowners, good people and bad guys—were all swept away. None of that mattered; it was about greed for their land.

For the sake of land, what was soon to become the domi-nant culture sacrificed trust, honor, and fellowship for land tainted by betrayal and blood. The scars of that betrayal still remain.

I also learned why, most likely, that it was only whispered that there was Indian in our families. Native American blood was all that was required to be torn from the land, to be sepa-rated from the memories of those they loved. Some, during the forced removal, stole away into the mountains. Others avoided the removal by embracing their White or Black heritage, while denying their Native American ancestry. They *passed* as White—saying they were Black Irish or Black Dutch—or passed as Black, conveniently denying their heritage because of skin color and hair texture. Only a blessed few escaped removal because of the courts, like those of the Eastern Band of Cher-okees in North Carolina.

I began writing to tell their story—in particular the story of African Americans on the Trail, those that were servants to the despised; to speak in slave narrative format—more episodic than driven by dates or locations—so that I could give voice to a story rarely told.

But as I wrote and researched—reading books, newspapers, personal accounts, and slave narratives—I found myself on the journey. Like Moses in a basket plucked from the Nile, I discovered my own people—Black, White, and Red.

While researching, I looked into some genealogy, and found my paternal grandmother, Emma Erwin. According to Census records, while her parents—my great-great-grandparents—were in Indian Territory and were likely part of the forced removal, she was in Tennessee at an Indian Christian School.

The story I was writing was not just their story; it became my own. Not only were Navajo children sent to boarding schools; so was my great-grandmother.

After more digging, I found Emma Erwin at the Clarksville Female Academy, in Clarksville, Tennessee, in 1878 where a school brochure listed her as Choctaw, though my family insists that she was Cherokee.

The 1870 Census Records show my great-great-grandmother and grandfather—Emma Erwin's father. My great-great-grandmother's name was Caty. My great-great-grandfather's name was Alford Erwin. Living with them was 89-year-old Evgoin Erwin. Both Evgoin and Alford were born in North Carolina—she in approximately 1781 and he about 1835.

The 1870 Census Records also show my great-grandfather, Newton Ewell, in Fayette, Tennessee, as a four-year-old child who lived in association with a white man named P. D. (Phillip) Ewell from Tennessee. Emma and Newton met in Tennessee at some point, and then moved to Texas where they married. My great-grandmother had two children from previous encounter(s), relationship(s) or marriage(s) with white men. All told, with my great-grandfather Newton, she bore and raised my grandfather Valcris, his brothers and sisters, Ruby, Georgia, Jewell, Audry, Otha, Thomas Jefferson, Elijah, and Ara.

My maternal grandparents' backgrounds are still mostly a

mystery. Perhaps that is as they intended it to be. They came to southern Illinois from Kentucky and southeast Missouri—the way of the Trail of Tears.

Though I have learned a great deal, I still have not processed what it all means. Perhaps it is the chasm that haunted my dreams.

My paternal grandfather Valcris, Emma's son, whom I sat with on his farm in Texas, was as much or more Native American than Black. Somehow, that disturbs me. I know about being an African-American, about the search for my lost Native African roots. I know what it is, I think, to be Newton Ewell's great-granddaughter. But I'm not certain what it means to be part of Emma Erwin's speckled pup.

I do not know that part of myself.

I know what it means to experience discrimination, to be

Marriage License:
Grandpa Newton and Emma Erwin Ewell, 1885

called ugly names as a Black person, and I know what it is to live in a newly integrated neighborhood. My family talked about civil rights, voting rights; my grandmother had a cross burned in front of a schoolhouse she built to teach illiterate adults. They talked about Native Americans—and though I empathized because of our Arizona experiences—I never thought their experiences were mine.

Perhaps I have not wanted to unweave the web of related class, loyalty, and race issues.

I do not know what it means for my children. For the longest time, my daughter thought that some of my older relatives were White, because of their complexions.

Great-Grandmother Emma Erwin Ewell

It is still a beautiful mystery to me. I am Black, I am Red, and probably White.

The Indians in my family were always right in front of me.

And I am not alone: according to the 2000 U.S. Census, more than 10 percent of the African American population (of those reporting) indicated that they were of mixed ancestry. Of that group, 16 percent indicated that they were of some combination of Black, White, and Native American heritage.

I have found them. But I still have not been welcomed home. But there is hope: in March 2006, the Cherokee Nation Judicial Appeals Tribunal (JAT), the Nation's highest court, ruled that descendants of Freedmen should be allowed to join the Cherokee Nation and vote as full citizens. There is opposition, but as of this date, the ruling still stands.

BIBLIOGRAPHY

•••••••••••••••◆•••••••••••••••

Inspired by true events and accounts, like slave narratives and articles from the *Cherokee Phoenix* newspaper, *Abraham's Well* is a work of fiction. Any resemblance to real persons is coincidental. Names of real persons—like, Evan Jones, Jesse Bushyhead, Brother Jesse, Nancy Ward, John Ross, Stand Watie, Major Ridge, John Ridge, Elias Boudinot, Emma Erwin (my great-grandmother), and Newton Ewell (my great-grandfather)—are used only to add realism to this work of fiction.

If you would like to learn more about the Cherokee Nation, the Trail of Tears, African and Native American relations, or about the individuals listed above, the bibliography below may offer you a place to start.

About Texas, Texas State Library and Archives Comission "Juneteenth." www.tsl.state.tx.us/ref/abouttx/juneteenth.html. May 29, 2006.

"The African-American Mosaic: Ex-slave Narratives." Library of Congress—Exhibitions. http://www.loc.gov/exhibits/african/afam015.html. July 5, 2005.

African-Native American History and Genealogy Web Page. http://www.african-nativeamerican.com/. 2006

"Amazing Grace in Cherokee." www.cyberhymnal.org/non/chr/agcherok.htm. May 10, 2006.

"The Attack on Fort Wagner." www.civilwarliterature.com/
3BlacksAsPrincipalChars/TippooSaib/TheAttackOn
FortWagner.htm. May 29, 2006.

"Black Indian Interviews." http://members.aol.com/angelaw
859/estelust.html. April 20, 2006.

"Black Seminole Indians." Handbook of Texas Online.
www.tsha.utexas.edu/handbook/online/articles/BB/
bmb18.html. Accessed April 20, 2006.

"Born in Slavery: Slave Narratives From the Federal Writers' Project, 1936–1938." Manuscript Division, Library of Congress.
http://memory.loc.gov/ammem/snhtml/snhome.html.
July 2005.

Brown and Ewell Papers. Tennessee State Library and Archives
www.state.tn.us/TSLA/history/manuscripts/mguide09.htm.
March 29, 2006.

Burnett, Private John G., and Captain Abraham McClellan's
Company, 2nd Regiment, 2nd Brigade, Mounted Infantry,
Cherokee Indian Removal, 1838–39. www.cherokeeby
blood.com/trailtears.htm. May 18, 2006.

"Cherokee by Blood." Black Indians and Cherokee Freedmen.
http://www.cherokeebyblood.com/blackindians.htm. 2006.

"Cherokee Indians." Handbook of Texas Online.
www.tsha.utexas.edu/handbook/online/articles/CC/
bmc51.html. April 21, 2006.

"Cherokee Outlet." The Cherokee Strip Museum. www
.cherokee-strip-museum.org/cherokeeOutlet.htm. April 29,
2006.

Cherokee Phoenix newspaper 1828–1834. www.wcu.edu/library/
CherokeePhoenix/. January 12, 2006.

Cherokee Phoenix, Wednesday, June 18, 1828, Vol. I, No. 17, page
1, col. 1b–3a. www.wcu.edu/library/CherokeePhoenix/Vol1/
no17/pg1col1b–3a.htm. May 18, 2006.

Clarksville Female Academy Catalogue and Announcement,
1878. www.tngenweb.org/montgomery/cfacademy.html.
May 22, 2006.

Department of the Interior. Office of Indian Affairs. "Index to the Applications Submitted for the Eastern Cherokee Roll of 1909 (Guion Miller Roll)." www.archives.gov/research/arc/native-americans-guion-miller.html. 1849—09/17/1947.

"Descendants of Freedmen of the Five Civilized Tribes." www.freedmen5tribes.com/index.html. April 21, 2006.

Durham, Philip, and Jones, Everett L. *The Negro Cowboys*. University of Nebraska Press, 1983.

Ehle, John. *The Trail of Tears: The Rise and Fall of the Cherokee Nation*. New York: Anchor Press, 1988.

"Estelusti—The Oklahoma Freedmen." http://members.aol.com/angelaw859/okfrdmen.html. April 29, 2006.

Fayette County Will Book A, 1836–1854, "Slave Names in Fayette County, Tennessee." www.spiny.com/naomi/people/slaves/#ewell. May 22, 2006.

"History and Culture," Cherokee North Carolina Indians. Official site of the Eastern Band of Cherokee Indians. www.cherokee-nc.com/history_main.php? December 2005.

"Important Dates in Cherokee History." www.powersource.com/nation/dates.html. April 29, 2006.

Kansas Institute for African American and Native American Family History. http://web.mit.edu/wjohnson/www/kiaanafh/KIAANAFH_PORTAL_PAGE.html. 2006.

Katz, William Loren. *Black Indians: A Hidden Heritage*. New York: Simon Schuster, 1997.

Katz, William Loren. *Black Women of the Old West*. Illinois: Atheneum, 1995.

Mankiller, Wilma. *A Chief and Her People*. New York: St. Martin's Press, 1993.

Mankiller, Wilma, moderator, with Dr. Willard Johnson, Dr. Daniel Littlefield Jr., Patrick Minges, Dr. Deborah Tucker, Dr. David Wilkins. "Exploring the Legacy and Future of Black/Indian Relations." Transcript of the 57th Annual Session of the National Council of American Indians. The

Kansas Institute for African–American and Native American Family History. http://anpa.ualr.edu/other_resources/ncai _transcript.pdf#search='mankiller%20minges'. October 2005.

Michaels, Elan. "Native American Quotations, Sayings, and Thoughts." www.angelfire.com/md/elanmichaels/naquotations.html. May 5, 2006.

Minges, Patrick. "All My Slaves, Whether Negroes, Indians, Mustees, or Molattoes. Towards a Thick Description of 'Slave Religion.' " The American Religious Experience. http://are.as.wvu.edu/minges.htm. April 22, 2006.

Minges, Patrick. "'Are You Kituwah's Son?' Cherokee Nationalism and the Civil War." Union Theological Seminary. www.us-data.org/us/minges/keetoo1.html. January 2006.

Minges, Patrick. "Beneath the Underdog: Race, Religion, and the Trail of Tears." U.S. Data Repository. U.S. GenNet Inc. www.us-data.org/us/minges/underdog.html. October 2005.

Minges, Patrick. *Black Indian Slave Narratives*. Winston-Salem, N.C.: John F. Blair, 2004.

Minges, Patrick. "The Keetoowah Society and the Avocation of Religious Nationalism in the Cherokee Nation, 1855–1867." U.S. Data Repository, U.S. GenNet, Inc. www.us-data.org/us/minges/keetoodi.html. May 1, 2006.

"Nancy Ward c. 1738–1824 Cherokee tribal leader." Women's History. Biographies. www.galegroup.com/free_resources/whm/bio/ward_n.htm. May 18, 2006.

"North American Slave Narratives." Documenting the American South. http://docsouth.unc.edu/neh/. February 2006.

North Carolina Chapter of the Trail of Tears Association. North Carolina Office of State Archaeology. http://www.arch.dcr.state.nc.us/tears/links.htm. 2006.

Paxton, Jennifer. "A Small Lexicon of Tsalagi Words." Raven's Tsalagi Resources. http://public.csusm.edu/public/guests/raven/cherokee.dir/cherlexi.html. May 18, 2006.

Pohanka, Brian C. "America's Civil War: Fort Wagner and the 54th Massachusetts Volunteer Infantry." www.historynet. com/wars_conflicts/american_civil_war/3035986.html. May 27, 2006.

Routh, E. C. "Early Missionaries to the Cherokees." Oklahoma Historical Society's Chronicles of Oklahoma. http:// digital.library.okstate.edu/Chronicles/v015/ v015p449.html. May 10, 2006.

Seybert, Tony. "Slavery and Native Americans in British North America and the United States: 1600 to 1865." Slavery in America. www.slaveryinamerica.org/history/hs_es_indians_slavery.htm. April 29, 2006.

"Trail of Tears Era." History. Official site of the Cherokee Nation. www.cherokee.org/home.aspx?section=culture&culture =history&cat=R2OKZVC/B7c=. December 2005.

Turner, Steve. "Amazing Grace: The Story Behind the Hymn." *Washington Post* discussion. http://discuss.washingtonpost .com/wp-srv/zforum/02/sp_books_turner120602.htm. May 10, 2006.

U.S. GenWeb Census Project—Texas. www.usgwcensus.org/. 1850.

Williams, Nannie H. "History of the Clarksville Female Academy." Clarksville: W. P. Titus, 1899.

Other sites

www.rosecity.net/tears/trail/blackindians.html.

www.tngennet.org/tncolor/underdog.htm.

http://english.ohmynews.com/articleview/article_view.asp? article_class=5&no=232087&rel_no=16.

http://web.mit.edu/wjohnson/www/kiaanafh/KIAANAFH _PORTAL_PAGE.html.

http://hebrewman7.tripod.com/the-choctaw-nation_B.html.

www.kuce.org/sb/resources.html.

www.weyanoke.org/hc-blackindianrelations.html.

www.blackindians.com/.
www.african-nativeamerican.com/.
http://faculty.smu.edu/twalker/1992.htm.
www.cherokeebyblood.com/blackindians.htm.
www.blackwebportal.com/wire/DA.cfm?ArticleID=443.
www.colorq.org/MeltingPot/America/BlackIndians.htm.
www.bellaonline.com/ArticlesP/art281.asp.
www.richheape.com/native-american-videos/Black_Indians
    _An_American_Story.htm.